MIRROR
IN THE
SKY

MIRROR IN THE SKY

—

ADITI

KHORANA

razor
bill

An Imprint of Penguin Random House

An Imprint of Penguin Random House
Penguin.com

ISBN: 978-1-59514-856-8

Printed in the United States of America

1 3 5 7 9 10 8 6 4 2

"Should *is a futile word. It's about what didn't happen. It belongs in a parallel universe. It belongs in another dimension of space.*"

—Margaret Atwood, *The Blind Assassin*

For my grandparents

This first one is for you

ONE

THE news broke sometime after midnight on a Friday evening—the last Friday before school started. I was already beginning to feel that mixture of melancholy and restlessness that strikes toward the end of the season, those few days of languor and light, left behind like the trashy novels at the community pool. I felt it every year before the start of the school, but even more so this year—an acute awareness of time slipping through my fingers, and the slight but persistent fear that I was wasting my hours with petty thoughts. I always dreaded the first day of school, but it was so much worse on this day than I ever remembered it. It was my junior year, and my best friend, my *only* friend, Meg Stevens, was leaving to spend a year abroad in Argentina.

A better version of me might have been happy for Meg; after all, there was nothing I could do to change the fact that

Meg herself was happy about leaving—thrilled, even. But all I could focus on was my own fate as the loner of Brierly, the length and span of an entire junior year awaiting me—a year with no friends. I wanted to be the kind of person who was hopeful, not brooding. I wanted to be more like my mother, who hid her anxieties and frustrations beneath a veneer of charisma and magical thinking. But I couldn't. I was stuck being me, and this meant I couldn't hide my worst fears from myself, or from anyone else.

I had only half been paying attention to the static hum of tense voices coming from the TV when my father's Honda pulled into the driveway that night, my cue to do what I did every Friday night when my father returned home: venture into the kitchen to collect three plates, three napkins, and three glasses of water and bring them to the living room, where we ate dinner on Fridays, and always after midnight.

My mother acted as though this was somehow very cosmopolitan of us, telling us this is how they did things in Ibiza. But southwestern Connecticut wasn't Ibiza. And the blue-and-white Corningware plates that we balanced on our knees as we sat before the TV didn't make any of us feel particularly worldly. I think it was her way of reminding us that she had once been to Ibiza, that she had sipped countless glasses of tempranillo at Café del Mar and waded in a white string bikini in the Mediterranean sea. But that was a long time ago.

"You know, whenever I was sad when I was young, I'd just remind myself: There's always cake," my mother said to me now.

"Cake isn't going to change things," I grumbled.

"Cake for breakfast," she said. "We'll do it tomorrow morning. It's one of the few great pleasures of life. Sometimes an indulgence makes everything better."

"Cake isn't going to make Meg change her mind."

My mother sighed. "I think you should take Meg's departure as an opportunity," she said authoritatively. "You should see it as a chance to explore a new world."

"Is that what you would do?"

I could see her considering my question for a moment. "No. I'd be miserable," she finally said. "What's so great about Argentina anyway?"

"A lot, apparently."

"Who goes away for their junior year of high school, for God's sake? You have a whole lifetime to get away from your real life."

"It's good for college apps. And she hates Brierly. Almost as much as I do."

My mother didn't respond to this. After all, what was there to say? Nothing could change the fact that I had never quite fit in, that I always felt like I was on the fringes at school.

"I bet she'll land, hate it, and be on a flight back within the week." My mother smiled. "Then you can tell her 'I told you so.'" This sounded like my mother, whose rules for living included magical solutions and unconventional behavior. This had always been the case, for as long as I could remember. Sometimes when she saw me studying too hard, she would sit down on the kitchen table across from me and gently close whatever book was in front of me.

"Let's go to the beach," she'd whisper. Or "Come meditate with me," or sometimes, "Let's go out for Chinese food. I'll let you have my fortune cookie," she'd plead, making a pitiful frown face. I don't think I ever once refused. My mother had a particular charm, an allure that was magnetic. She was the most interesting person I knew. I had never learned how to say no to her.

"We should do a tarot reading for you for the year. There's some opportunity in everything that's happening. I bet it's going to be a really awesome year. I can totally just tell!" She began to rifle through the dining room cabinet, where she kept an odd collection of candles and tarot cards and memorabilia, when something caught her attention. I watched her as she turned toward the TV.

"What the . . ." She walked before the screen, as though in a trance, and turned up the volume.

Over the sound of the news, I heard my father's car pull into the driveway. "Dad's here," I said. But my mother didn't respond.

My father had just closed the restaurant for the night. I remember that he lingered in the mudroom longer than usual that evening, slowly untying the laces on his shoes and removing his jacket, the slight trace of coriander that always bound itself to his clothes, stalking him wherever he went, mingling with the scent of his aftershave.

Finally, my mother noticed him. "You have to see this!" she called out from the living room sofa, shattering the anticipatory silence, as she often did. Her eyes were caught in the hypnotic glare of the screen as a crimson banner of breaking news cascaded across it, the zealous flag of manufactured alarm.

"I heard something about it on the radio," my father mumbled in his soft voice, always a few decibels below my mother's. He was holding a cardboard box of Pomodoro's pizza in his hand, a grease stain soaking the corner. "Turn on the BBC," he told my mother. "I can't watch this CNN nonsense."

My father reserved a very particular disdain for American news outlets, which was understandable, given what the news had become in his lifetime—the fourth estate had been reduced to a decayed Satis house, its once glimmering surfaces now rotting beyond boarded windows.

I was too distracted that night to be thinking about global concerns. In fewer than sixty short hours, the new school year would start. I thought about Meg again. About the day she told me she was leaving Brierly for the duration of our entire junior year, the most important year of high school. We had been sitting in the sand at Tod's Point, watching seagulls spurtively dive toward cautious mollusks, lifting them into their beaks and lobbing them on the jagged rocks by the shore. That morning, Meg had urged me to squeeze lemon into my hair to lighten it; by early evening her chai-colored locks developed streaks of gold, while my black hair turned the color of mud and the texture of straw, alarming my father when he saw it that night.

I dug my toes into the sand as Meg excitedly told me how nervous and eager she was to meet all the boys she would kiss, how much she would improve her Spanish, how good this would be for her college applications. I closed my eyes to the harsh glare of the sun and wished that I wasn't me. I was already at the bottom of a food chain of upperclassmen, but to be without Meg meant that I would be laid bare, adrift in a sea of virtual strangers I had known since the fifth grade but who had nothing to do with me, nor I with them.

To make matters worse, junior year was the year of academic reckoning that guidance counselors couldn't speak of without the use of verbal grenades like "stress," "breakdowns," and "the year that really counts," in between complaining about the air quality in the building and then returning to their dank offices filled with piles of transcripts. I didn't know how I would get through it without Meg.

"I can't believe it!" My mother clapped her hands together, causing me to jump. "Another world, can you even imagine?" She was speaking to no one in particular, and I continued to set the coffee table, placing plastic containers of parmesan and crushed red pepper next to the mason jar full of dahlias and lilies that my mother had brought in from the garden that morning. "It's amazing!" she exclaimed, shaking her head in delight.

"It hardly changes anything for us," my father told her, slipping down on the far end of the sofa. His button-down shirt, crisp and starched when he left home this afternoon, was by now crumpled, a yellow stain on his wrist.

"It changes everything!" she exclaimed. "We're not alone. I always suspected it, didn't you? But now . . ."

Her voice trailed off. On other parts of the globe, wars

were being fought, bombs were being detonated, children languished in refugee camps. But here, in this tiny strip of real estate known as Greenwich, Connecticut, best friends left for Argentina, mothers gave in to their temptations, guidance counselors continued to file away transcripts, contributing what they referred to as "cautious optimism," the lowest-grade variety.

But for once, the story wasn't about our world but another, lingering just beyond the edges of our very own solar system, an entire sphere that, till now, we had somehow managed to miss. And yet, on this day, a small turn of the hand on the cosmic kaleidoscope had revealed a different sight.

It had always been there, all this while, when we looked out into the night sky, a lone planet lingering in the "Goldilocks zone," they called it, that congenial slip of space where the improbable became probable.

What we couldn't have realized then was that the difference between knowing and not knowing about something light-years away would change us all in the year to come.

TWO

IT could have been the kind of story that came and went, eclipsed by another news cycle. But what my mother experienced as a transcendent moment of amazement at the idea of another world like ours so far, far away turned out to be only the exterior of a package labeled, stamped, and sent to us with a kind of precision and foresight we might have expected from the cosmos had we been the sort to believe in things like symmetry and order. And yet its contents still remained a mystery.

I went to buy school supplies with my father the next day. We parked in front of a newsstand on Lewis Street, the trashier rags filled with large-font declarations like "ALIEN PLANET DISCOVERED!" while the *New York Times* furnished a complex diagram of the Milky Way on its front page. My father picked up a copy of the *Times*, and I watched him as he shook open the oversize leaves of paper, smoothing out the center crease with his fingertip as we walked.

"Tara, I know you're sad about Meg leaving," he said without looking up.

I shrugged. Every year since the sixth grade, I had gone back-to-school shopping with Meg. We'd buy outfits together at Rags, pencils and notebooks at the stationery shop at the bottom of the Ave, even order our backpacks together months in advance of the first day of school. It made the experience of returning far less dreadful, maybe even fun.

But Meg was shopping for different supplies this year—Spanish-English dictionaries, voltage converters, sunscreen, and racy lingerie. When I thought about this shopping list, I felt a pang of betrayal.

We walked past the Starbucks on the corner of Havemeyer Place, and through the plate glass, I could see a cluster of Brierly kids hanging out over their iced lattes and laughing—Nick Osterman, Sarah Hoffstedt, Alexa Vanderclift, and Halle Lightfoot. I couldn't hear their laughter, but I could tell it was loud and raucous from the expressions on the faces around them, just as it always was in the student center of Brierly. They didn't seem to care. Halle, standing over a seated Nick, grabbed something from his pocket—a paperback—and held it high over her head, just before he grabbed her by the waist and pulled her onto his lap.

I carefully studied Halle, something I had often caught myself doing in class. She had an effortless ease about her, and it seemed to filter into every area of her life, whether it involved flirting with the cutest Brierly boys or knowing exactly what to say when a teacher picked on her in class. She knew how to make people laugh, but there was always insight to whatever came from her mouth. I was both awed by her and resented her for making it all look so easy, for being beautiful and brilliant.

"Do you want to go in and say hello?" my father asked, observing the eerily approximate rendering of a scene from the J.Crew summer catalogue unfold before us.

"God, Dad, no. Of course not!" I don't know why my father assumed that just because I went to school with these people, just because we were the same age, and in the same grade, we had something to say to one another.

I wondered, for a moment, what it must feel like to be them—it was unlikely that they were walking around with brick-sized pits in their stomachs, dreading the first day of school. Why would they? They would arrive at Brierly on Monday morning like telluric gods and take over the best table in the student center, where they would reign for yet another year.

At the stationery store on Greenwich Avenue, I walked past the handmade cards and carbon-colored stacks of Moleskines, each sealed with a fluorescent lime-colored scrap of authentication. My father followed me into the pen section.

"I know how difficult it can be to make new friends," he said tentatively. "It was difficult for me when I first came to the United States."

"I know, Dad." I didn't want to discuss it with him, any of it. I didn't want to tell him how hard it was, how I felt as though I would never fit in. I never had, not since we had arrived in

Connecticut in the fifth grade. For one thing, I looked different. My father was Indian, and my mother white. We had moved here so my father could open his own restaurant after years of working in the kitchen at someone else's, and also so I could attend Brierly.

"We're both making a new start," he had told me as we packed the last of our belongings into oversized cardboard cartons, our entire history as a family fitting neatly into the back of a small Penske truck. "We'll have a much better life in Connecticut. You'll be able to ride a bike to school, and we'll even have a backyard."

This was how the suburbs had always been sold to city kids, even though I couldn't care less about being able to ride a bike. And what could I have needed a backyard for? I was a bookworm even then, my nose perpetually buried in some new subject or another. This was another reason my parents wanted to move to Connecticut. I would do well in middle school and eventually be able to attend Brierly. I would have more opportunities to flourish academically in Connecticut.

But I had always liked our two-bedroom apartment on the Lower East Side. I liked my friends at the UN School. I didn't mind city living, the fact that brick and cement seemed constantly to be exercising a strategy of encirclement over every green, forcing an occupation of Central Park. I liked the fact that we shared a building with twenty-four other people. Our neighbors felt like extended family. They had all known me since I was two, and were always there to offer help or advice at a moment's notice. When I got sick, Mrs. Hirshbloom would bring me chicken soup, and when my mother broke her ankle trying to carry a TV she had found at the Goodwill up the stairs, Kelly Loffman, a recent college graduate in a Teach For America program, had stayed with me, helping me build a helicopter with my Legos while my father took my mother to the ER.

In Connecticut, we were all alone, adrift in a sea of whiteness and wealth, and it really did feel like a sea I was drowning in. I felt as though I had to paddle as hard as I could, every day, just to survive. We were different here—it was obvious from the start. My father and I looked like no one else, for one, and on a near-regular basis, tension over money hung over us, a thickly, discomfiting humidity, sticking to our skin, marking us with its heaviness. But perhaps the worst of it was that here, we had no extended family. We just had us.

"I think this should do it," I said, handing my father the red plastic basket containing highlighters and pens, loose-leaf sheets and spiral-bound notebooks.

"What can we do to make you feel better?" my father asked me after he paid for the supplies. "Do you want me to talk to Mrs. Treem?"

"Dad, ugh, no! She's such an idiot. She's just going to make things worse."

Mrs. Treem was my guidance counselor, a woman so caught up in wanting to appear to be relatable and current to the students she dispensed advice to that she came off more as a pathetic poser than as a voice of any sort of authority at school.

I turned to my father now. He had always been the more sensitive one of my parents, the one who genuinely wanted to fix things. My mother, on the other hand, was my best friend—my other best friend besides Meg. She commiserated with me and came up with grand schemes to distract me from whatever was at hand. But my father was grounded, practical, and too naive to realize that practical solutions couldn't solve the problems faced by an American high school student with no friends.

Nick and Halle were standing by the newspaper stand when we walked out of the store. She was wearing cutoffs and sandals and a tight white tank top, her golden hair whipping around her face like a blaze. I walked a little faster as we passed them and tried not to make eye contact, as though speed and silence could serve as a much-needed invisibility cloak, but then I heard Nick's slightly throaty voice.

"Oh hey . . . Tara."

I was already by the car, but I forced myself to turn around. He was resting his elbow on Halle's shoulder. Since last spring, they had been perpetually tied together in a way that made me simultaneously jealous and fascinated.

"Getting ready for school on Monday?" He smiled at us, waving sheepishly at my father, who nodded back in acknowledgment. Halle inspected the newsstand as he talked, her hand resting in his back pocket.

"Yeah. Just getting some supplies," I mumbled, looking away from my father's dusty gray Honda, trying to distance myself from a car that must have looked to Halle and Nick like garbage on wheels.

"Crazy, this stuff with that new galaxy, huh?"

"It's not a galaxy, you idiot." Halle laughed. But her eyes were fixed on him, refusing to acknowledge me.

"A planet, whatever. My parents have been glued to the TV. Did you hear the news today about the signal?"

"What signal?" I asked, genuinely curious now.

"You haven't heard yet. She hasn't heard!" He turned to Halle. "Check your phone! It's some seriously crazy stuff."

I stood there before them, tongue-tied and yet unable to look away. It was an unusually hot day, and the sidewalk was like a cement baking stone, but the heat somehow complemented them, making them sparkle even more then usual. It was hard not to notice the gleam of sweat on Nick's upper lip, the dewy glow of Halle's décolletage.

"Yeah. Well, I guess I'll see you both on Monday."

"Yeah. Junior year. See you there." He smiled that electric smile that for some reason always made me think of an Anne Sexton quote I had read in freshman-year English, "being kissed on the back of the knee is a moth at the windowscreen." I quickly got into the car and couldn't even bring myself to roll down the window until we were well on our way down Post Road.

"They seem nice," my father said, turning on the radio.

"They're fine," I said, rummaging through the plastic bag of school supplies to stop my hands from shaking.

I hadn't spoken to Nick since the eighth grade, when we

were assigned to do a mock presidential debate for our social studies class. It had been almost three years since he had seemed to notice me, since we had dressed up as Barack and Michelle Obama and recited speeches together. (I had always wondered if I had been assigned this role because I was the only person of color in the entire class.)

Since that last contact, I went to school, swim practice, yearbook club. I talked to Meg on the phone, and I watched the lives of those whom I considered charmed unfold from a safe distance. In particular, I watched Nick. I observed him day after day, joking around with Jimmy Kaminsky and Hunter Caraway in the student center, listened eagerly to the speeches he gave during student council elections, smiled as he dazzled our teachers, and despaired at the way he endlessly flirted with Halle. I knew that his eyes were hazel, with yellow flecks. That when he was concentrating on something, he bit his lip and drummed his fingers on any available surface. That he liked soft pretzels with yellow mustard and practical jokes and soccer. I knew all this not because he had told me, but because I had studied him as though I were getting a Ph.D. in Nick Osterman studies. What I didn't know till that day was that he actually remembered my name.

The sound blaring through my father's lo-fi car speakers brought me back to the moment. On NPR, Oliver Spiegel was interviewing a NASA scientist.

"For our listeners tuning in now, explain to us what the Arecibo message is."

"Certainly. The Arecibo message was a radio broadcast

that we sent into space a good forty years ago. We aimed it at the globular star cluster M13. We calculated that it would take twenty-five thousand light-years to reach its destination, but it would seem that the message was intercepted by the inhabitants of our newly discovered planet. B612 is what astronomers have named it, Terra Nova is what most laypeople are calling it, and within twenty-four hours of discovering it, we're seemingly getting a communication signal from there."

"And how can we be sure that it was intercepted?"

"Because of the response transmission we received this morning."

"And explain to us what the response was."

"Well, interestingly, it's a radio signal that's almost identical to the Arecibo message."

"The exact same signal?"

"Well, no. And this is the important thing to note. It's very close, but with a couple of tiny variations. So tiny that they wouldn't even be discernible if we weren't paying close attention, but different enough. It's almost as though it's been replicated for our benefit, but slightly modified in order to let us know that yes, we received your message, and here is our response to it."

"And we're certain that Terra Nova is where that response signal is coming from?"

"Once we were able to pinpoint the exact location of Terra Nova—which we recently learned is similar in size and scope to Earth, we aimed the Allen Telescope Array at the SETI Institute—that stands for the Search for Extraterrestrial

Intelligence—toward the planet. As you may or may not know, we've been monitoring radio signals in the universe for some time now, but since the discovery of Terra Nova, we knew exactly where to look for a possible transmission. So yes, the radio signal is coming to us from Terra Nova."

"What does this radio transmission tell us?"

"It tells us there is a strong possibility that intelligent life exists on that planet. They managed to intercept the Arecibo signal—we're not quite sure when or how—but this is perhaps their way of letting us know they're here. It could be their way of saying hello. B612 is still too far away for us to travel to— at least for now, given our limited technology—but continued communication with them will allow us to learn more about the planet and its inhabitants, and that's incredibly exciting."

"Terra Nova—the newly discovered Earth-like planet that we've received a radio transmission from. Back with more after this break."

We pulled into our driveway just as the broadcast cut to a promo for the weekend lineup. We lived in a tiny yellow Cape Cod–style house across the street from Riverside Station. A lone tree draped the front porch in a curtain of pepper berries. While many of my classmates lived on sprawling estates with driveways that unspooled like black grosgrain ribbons, my daily journey from the main street to our front door was a mere few steps.

"It's pretty cool, isn't it?" I asked my father, feeling a grin spreading over my face for the first time in days.

He didn't answer. Instead, he gently removed the key from the ignition and turned his head to inspect the edges of our lawn, embroidered with my mother's pink azalea. The expression on his face scared me. He looked around without a glint of recognition in his eyes, as though it was the first time he had ever encountered this particular lawn, this very driveway, as though the home before him wasn't his own.

He turned to look at the bay window of our living room, and slowly, the recognition of where we were returned to his eyes. "Your mother's probably sitting in front of the TV watching all of this right now," he commented wryly. I followed his gaze, noticing that the television was indeed on and that my mother was sitting on the sofa before it, her knees drawn up to her chest.

Just then, my phone rang, Meg's name glowing on the screen.

"Meg! When should I come over? I have to see you off, girl!"

"Yeah . . . listen, I know we had plans to meet today, but it's gotten really crazy with packing and stuff . . ." Her tone was flat, and at the sound of it, my heart sank.

"Really? I can drop by for, like, ten minutes. I just want to say goodbye . . ."

"I don't think that's gonna work. It's just waaay too crazy right now. I'm not even done with all my shopping, and I'm headed to the airport tonight. So . . . just wanted to say bye."

"Oh. Okay," I said. I could hear the defensiveness in my tone, and we were both quiet for a minute before Meg broke the silence.

"I probably won't call you right away when I get there. I'll be busy with my host family and orientation and all that."

"Just send me a text to let me know you got in safe," I told her. Then quietly I added, "I'll miss you," and I felt the sting of fresh tears in my eyes as I got out of the car, pausing in the drive as my father continued to the door.

I could hear Meg take a deep breath before she went on. "Listen, I don't want you to be upset or anything, but things are going to be different with us from now on," she said. There was a casual flightiness in her voice that made me flinch.

"Different how?" I asked.

"A lot can happen in a year, Tara. And I think I might come back from Argentina a different person. I just want you to get used to that idea. We might not be the way we were when I return."

"Are you serious? What the hell is that supposed to mean?"

"I mean . . . I'm going to be on my own, in a foreign city. And you're going to be . . . here. I just don't want you to be hurt, you know . . . if we grow apart."

"So you're ditching me?"

"Don't take it the wrong way, okay?"

"And what way am I supposed to take it, Meg?"

Meg sighed loudly before she continued in a patronizing voice, rushing me off the phone. "I don't want to fight, okay? And anyway, I don't have time for drama right now. I've gotta go. Maybe I'll send you a postcard," she said before she hung up the phone.

I swallowed the lump in my throat. It was pathetic enough

admitting to myself that Meg's departure made me a nobody, but *growing apart*? *Maybe* she would send me a postcard? How could Meg, who had been my best friend since the moment I had arrived in Greenwich, be so heartless? I wanted to cry, but I didn't want to be that person—a junior, crying to myself the day before school started.

I ran inside, wanting nothing more than to drown myself in whatever the networks were saying about Terra Nova. In that moment, it was the kind of news that sparkled like a piece of broken glass in the sand, catching the momentary light of the sun, distracting me with its infinitesimal brilliance.

THREE

"DID you hear?" My mother looked up at me with alarm in her bright hazel eyes as I entered the house. The soothing chime of the BBC's opening intro played in the background. "They're trying to tell us something. Or at least that's what these reporters are saying . . . but . . . I'm not so sure . . ." She shook her head. "Come sit with me." She smiled, patting the cushion next to her.

For a moment, she glanced at me with concern in her eyes, but she quickly turned her head toward the voices on TV, as though in a trance. She looked like a child with her oversized oatmeal heather sweater pulled over her shins. My mother was always cold, even in the middle of summer. It could have been because she was preternaturally thin, with no body fat to keep her warm. Of all the mothers at Brierly, she looked as though childbearing and rearing had barely taken a toll on her, either physically or emotionally. On some days, I wasn't sure if it really had. But she was also the youngest mom I knew. She was just barely twenty-four when she had me.

"Shouldn't you be at work?" I asked her, curling up beside her, pressing my feet under hers.

She turned to me for a minute and tucked a strand of my hair behind my ear. I thought she was going to ask me if I was okay, but instead she simply responded, "I called in sick." Then she turned back to the TV.

"You don't look sick to me," I said, but what I was really doing, if I had to be honest with myself, was trying to engage her. I wanted to tell her about Meg, about what had just happened, and it was as though she was completely oblivious to anything that didn't have to do with the discovery of this new planet.

"I'm not. I had Christy sub for me. I can't possibly teach toddlers ballet with all this going on!" I looked to my father, who raised his eyebrows at me.

"Jennifer, it has nothing to do with you," he said quietly, tentatively.

"If you only listened closely, you would realize that it has everything to do with us!" There was an uncharacteristic edge to her voice that said, *Stop bothering me. Stop asking me questions. Just stop.*

My mother taught ballet six days a week. She worked mostly at the local community center and the Y, but occasionally she taught private lessons, complaining the entire time about her students' lack of talent.

"It's a real discipline, you know?" she told me once.

"Practicing ten hours a day, cross-training, eating nothing but almonds and grapefruit and coffee . . . most people, they just don't have what it takes. I mean . . . *I* did, but then, you know . . ." And then her voice trailed off. Something told me not to ask any questions, as though even the smallest sigh or gesture in that moment was like taunting a rattlesnake.

I looked at my mother now, grateful that I had inherited her slim dancer's build. Brierly was hard enough as it was—I couldn't imagine going through four years of it like Moira Edwards, the "big girl" in our class who spent all her lunches in the library, reading. I felt a sharp stab of panic when I thought of Moira—would I spend all my lunches in the library too now that Meg was gone?

"Doesn't it just completely blow your mind?" my mother pressed. Her eyes didn't leave the screen.

"It's pretty crazy," I said, but in that moment, all I could think about was Meg, about the things that she said to me. I couldn't understand the tone of her voice, her casual callousness. It was as though she had transformed into a different person overnight.

I got up and ventured to the kitchen, opening the fridge to peruse shelves of produce. I found a Tupperware container of leftovers from the restaurant. It was filled with spinach pakoras, soggy but still appealing, and I despondently took a bite before I rejoined my mother on the sofa, the container still in my hand.

"Do you want me to heat those?" my father asked. I shook my head.

"There are some carrots and hummus in the fridge too, in case either of you want a healthy snack," my father said.

"Did you buy my granola bars?" my mother called out.

"Yes." My father laughed. "As usual, I bought all your favorite snacks and stocked the pantry," he said.

My mother smiled at him before she turned to me. "He loves it, you know? His favorite thing in the world is running around doing errands."

I smiled back. She was like that sometimes—mercurial. Her moods could change on a whim, and just like that, her irritation had somehow alchemized to delight.

"Well, if I didn't, who would?" he teased. My mother giggled in response, but I was caught in the vortex of the news, and its medicinal effect was hard to ignore.

"What do you think they're like? I wonder if they're just like us," I said.

"Do you want to know what I think?" my mother asked, even though we all knew that the question was rhetorical. "I think maybe they didn't even *mean* to send that message to us. We certainly didn't mean to send a message to them forty years ago. Maybe *we* accidentally intercepted something that was never intended for us to begin with. We act as though we're at the center of everything, but we're not."

This felt like a surprisingly insightful admission on the state of humanity from my mother, who was often so focused on her own reactions to things that she barely took note of what was going on around her.

"Why are you so moved by this nonsense anyway,

Jennifer?" My father always pronounced my mother's name Jen-ee-fer. I think, for a time when they first met, she found it charming, but I noticed that lately she frowned every time he said it that way.

"I don't know why you're not, Sudeep." Even though their discussion was making me tense, I realized it was true. My father had been quiet since the announcement yesterday, which was surprising. His very reason for coming to this country, after all, was to study physics. He had arrived in New York seventeen years ago on a balmy summer day not dissimilar to this one, in order to complete his postdoctoral work at Columbia. But when he learned my mother was pregnant, he dropped out of school and started working in the kitchen of a restaurant in Jackson Heights, the same restaurant he would work at for a decade, until we moved to Connecticut so that he could open a place of his own. My father was practical—he believed in the things he could see, or in ideas that could be proven empirically, and he made sure to express this sentiment to my mother and me on a regular basis.

"We still don't know all the science behind it yet. This," my father said, pointing a spatula at the TV, "is mostly hype."

But my mother shook her head adamantly. "I don't care about the science," she said. "I care about what it *means*. I'm telling you, I feel like this whole thing has *changed* me, you know?" she said, but by now, my father was rummaging through the fridge.

"I'm realizing that it's not about us at all. It's not about our tiny little world and our tiny little stories. This is so much bigger than us, you know? It's like . . . it should make us less selfish. It should make us realize that the universe doesn't revolve around us."

"And if it does, that's a wonderful thing," said my father, heating up a pan and pouring some leftover lamb korma and rice into it. "But let's be honest, Jennifer . . ." he said, looking at her. "What real, practical consequence does any of this really have on any of our lives?"

The question hung in the air, thicker than glue. I once heard that space-time was like a dense roll of sticky fabric—a vast, gelatinous quilt that held everything within it, all the planets and stars and asteroids tucked into its surface. The moment my father asked that question, it felt as though it became a permanent part of that quilt, floating indefinitely into the air around us.

FOUR

MY father knocked on my door at six thirty on Monday morning, and I woke with the faint memory of yesterday's encounter with Halle and Nick lingering in my mind, some sparkling mobile of a thought . . . I tried to summon the remnants of the dream, but it was already gone.

"Ready for your first day of school?" he asked. I groaned and rolled over to face the wall. Just the question made my stomach turn. *No*, I wanted to tell him. *I'll never be ready for my first day of school.* I thought of Meg attending her first day of school in Argentina, where everyone would find her new and fascinating and cool, and I wanted to scream.

After my father left, I pulled off the covers and began to dress, slipping on a pair of dark skinny jeans, a black tank top, and a turquoise cardigan. I had saved my allowance for months to buy the cardigan—it was cashmere, purchased at a boutique in Old Greenwich. I threaded a pair of silver earrings through my ears and inspected myself in the mirror that hung over my bureau as I brushed my hair. *Not bad*, I thought. The "highlights" that Meg had prescribed looked better by now, and my hair had grown long over the summer, falling well past my shoulders.

I was about average height, with olive skin and light brown eyes, and a delicate bone structure inherited from my mother. I looked like no one else in Greenwich. I stood out in ways I didn't want to and yet still managed to fall below the surface in ways I found equally disconcerting. If only I could be more like Halle—confident in her difference, yet still able to comfortably fit in. How did she manage to do that? I had observed her for so many years and I still didn't know the answer.

In precalculus, we had studied Venn diagrams, and whenever I looked at her, I thought about the particular alchemy that occurs within the center of those three circles of popularity, beauty, and awareness of self, not to be confused with self-awareness. What gave her a resolute and unusual power was the fact that she knew just how powerful she was, and the demonstration of this required only the lightest touch—a fleeting smile, a wink, a casually lovely gesture that, when directed at her prey, left him or her stunned by its beauty.

I got ready and made my way to the kitchen. "Not again, Dad," I mumbled as I sat down at the counter to face my father. He was holding a jar of honey in his hand. A plate of waffles, beaded with blueberries, topped with a pat of melting butter, sat before me.

"It's a tradition, Tara. That's how traditions work." Every year, on the first day of school, my father would open a bottle of honey and feed me a teaspoon of it, though in the past couple of years, it had been more of a force-feeding. His mother had done the same for him, and her mother for her. Supposedly the sweetness of the honey was imparted to the act of learning, making it sweet.

"It's stupid. It doesn't even mean anything. It doesn't make a difference."

"It will this time," he said, holding the spoon in my face till I had no choice but to swallow it. "And you've done well in school all these years, haven't you?"

I shrugged. I was a good student, but sometimes I felt as though both of my parents' dreams were pinned on me, that I was pierced again and again by their expectations. And still I remained mute, hopeful that I could somehow repay them for their sacrifices, resentful that I felt that I needed to.

"Where's Mom?" I asked.

"She's still in bed. She stayed up late watching the news."

I reached for the jar of honey and poured a glistening spoonful over my waffles.

"And it's . . . you know, the anniversary of the day."

"Oh," I looked up at him. "I totally forgot."

"It's too bad it falls on the first day of school this year. Be nice to her when you get home. She might be down."

When my mother was seven years old, her parents—my grandparents—died in a car accident. She was the only person in the car who survived. They were taking a road trip to

Orlando to visit Disney World, but instead of riding in teacups and visiting the Haunted Mansion, she woke up in a hospital in Georgia. She spent the next ten years shuttling from the home of one relative to the next, till she was old enough to move to New York on her own.

Every year on the anniversary of the accident, my mother was morose. And every year, she would invent a new ritual to honor her parents. Once she left candles burning all over the house. The living room carried an overwhelming stench of stale vanilla for days. Another year she brought home a family of stray cats, which my father promptly made her take to the local animal rescue society. Then there was the year she held a séance in our kitchen and cried herself to sleep because her parents had failed to make an appearance. I still remembered the way she had sobbed, probably the same way she had sobbed when she first learned that her parents were gone. This was something that worried me about my mother—that she was capable of breaking her own heart again and again. I wondered what she would be doing today when I returned home from school.

"Did they say anything new on the news?" I asked my father, changing the subject. I could tell from the dark purple circles under his eyes that he had stayed up late watching too. He glanced at the ancient Sony TV that perched on the kitchen counter. Clad in plywood and the size of a microwave, it was a vestige of the early '90s, a relic from well before I was born.

"We should get going. You should be thinking about school, not all this NASA stuff." I *was* thinking about school, actually, if you count thinking about Meg abandoning me as thinking about school. My thoughts quickly turned to Nick, almost as though my brain knew to go into survival mode in that moment, filling me with an immaterial abundance of hope to bolster my dwindling morale. I recognized this mental self-trickery right away. I wasn't about to fall into the trap of false security on the first day of school. I had to be vigilant, even with my deepest, unspoken hopes. Then I found myself giving in. I did want to talk to Nick again. I wondered if I would get another chance this year.

"This is educational, Dad. And besides, I thought you wanted to work for NASA when you were a kid." I didn't mean for it to come out like an accusation, but my father ignored it and reached for the car keys instead.

"The most important thing for you is to be focusing on school right now. You can't remove your eyes from the prize." My father always botched idioms. He often told me that I was yelling up the wrong tree or that I had bitten off more than I could eat. "This is the big year. If you do well this year, I think you can get into Browns."

"It's Brown, Dad," I told him, putting down my fork and sliding my satchel over my shoulder. "They didn't say anything else on the news last night?"

"Same thing, basically . . . just more details about how they discovered B612. They're saying that we couldn't see this Terra Nova planet before because the light of its sun was too bright, but then they detected a transit—that's when a planet eclipses its sun—and they measured the size of the planet and its movement around its sun, and that's how they realized it was similar to ours."

"Movement? You mean the revolution around the sun?" I asked, following my father out the door and onto the driveway. "So their year is the same length as ours?" I asked, wondering if that meant that they had a school year, summer vacation, winter break, but my father never gave me an answer and insisted that we drive to school without the radio on, leaving me to simmer in my own thoughts.

FIVE

MY heart raced as I hurried down the glass corridor to the student center. What I was rushing for, I didn't know. It was more that I wanted to get this moment over with—the moment I had been dreading all summer.

Even though Brierly was more than a hundred years old, sometime in the '70s, some wealthy alumnus had donated a ton of money to the school under one condition: that they tear down the old-world brick and ivy and let the donor's son— an architect whose previous commissions consisted largely of prisons—redesign the school. His prior design experience was evident in the new campus: all concrete, the halls dimly lit. The few windows facing the green didn't open, just looked out over the campus like desperately large eyes.

I pushed through the glass doors into the student center,

and I was greeted by a blast of cold air, followed by the click of the doors closing behind me, as though to vacuum-seal me in.

I looked around, my heart racing as I inspected the hall. The student center was an acre-large cavernous space with forty-foot-high ceilings, enclosed by four enormous slabs of concrete. Two large cement stairways swirled down onto either side of the room, like clumsy mechanical drills attaching the floor to the ceiling.

Brierly was broken into a range of social castes, and each one had a designated section in the student center—you couldn't just sit anywhere. The popular kids in their preppy-chic uniforms sat by the café stall, while the thespians occupied the south side of the building, the only section of the student center unsurprisingly filled with constant and profuse theatrics. The jocks sat close to the exit and spent their days tossing wads of paper at each other, while everyone else sat in the worst spot, under the Bella House stairs. This is where Meg and I would have sat, had Meg been here with me.

Terror washed over me as I realized everyone came in pairs or groups, some in threesomes. They were smart enough to know that there was power in numbers, and so they spun around each other like valence electrons forming covalent bonds.

I held tight to the strap of my satchel as though it was the only thing in the world I had to hold on to, the rough leather digging into my sweating palms. How would I fit into this complex ecosystem now? I looked around for a familiar face, realizing that they were all familiar in a vague and slightly unsettling way.

"Now *that* is a dress!" Tricia Larsen eyed Melanie Carter's outfit in the thespian section. Melanie, known for her eccentric costumes, was dressed in a polka-dot green '50s housewife dress and matching hairband. Melanie had been in my freshman biology class. She had always been nice to me. I could venture over there, couldn't I? But my feet felt rooted to the floor.

"It's gonna be an awesome year, dude!" Hunter Caraway laughed and bumped fists with Jimmy Kaminsky, who looked cool as always in his jeans, a distressed T-shirt, and vintage Wayfarers. They were standing in the popular section, where Sarah and Halle and Alexa and Nick always sat—a land that was altogether foreign to me. There was no way I could walk over there.

"Tara, I'm so glad to see you! Excited about a new school year?" I looked up. It was Mrs. Treem, stepping right into my path. "How do you feel about Meg not being here?" she asked, her voice conspiratorial. I opened my mouth to answer, and then Treem put a hand on my shoulder and leaned in, a little too close. "I know she's your best friend—I've never seen you two apart! But I think it might be good for you to spread your wings a little." She smiled.

"Yeah, no. I'm fine," I lied. I wasn't going to talk to Treem about my "feelings." She was the kind of person who was desperate to dispense advice—and not particularly useful or substantive stuff at that.

"I want you to see this as a good sort of challenge. We love Brierly students to be dealing with challenges. But not, you know, the really tough kind." She made a face as though she were contemplating the "really tough kind" of challenges. I wanted to suggest to her that being brown in an all-white high school was its own variety of challenge, but instead, I just smiled a tense smile.

"Make new friends," she said. "That's what I suggest. Friendships are the best thing about high school. I'm still friends with the girls I went to Miss Porter's with. Did you know that?"

Why would I know that? I wondered. "Well, have a great first day!" she said, her eyes already scanning the room to find someone new to accost.

After Treem left, I looked around for anyone to talk to. Making new friends was, like many of Treem's directives, an unrealistic bet for me right at this moment. Right now, I just had to focus on *not* looking like a loser.

My heart quickened as I was engulfed by the echo and hum of voices bouncing around this demented sound chamber. It slowly dawned on me that I was all alone. There was no one here who would ask me how my summer was, compliment my earrings, assure me it was going to be an awesome year. I lingered for a moment by the edge of the lunch tables, trying to decide what I should do next, where I should go. I could head to the library or perhaps slowly make my way to the science wing for my AP physics class. Just the thought of it made me want to cry.

But something within me—I don't even know what it was—told me to just stand there and wait. Maybe there was something to be said for stillness, after all. We had all been sitting still, and that radio signal had come to us. It reminded me of a Kafka quote my mother had stuck on the refrigerator years ago: "You do not need to leave your room. Remain sitting at your table and listen. Do not even listen, simply wait, be quiet, still and solitary. The world will freely offer itself to you to be unmasked, it has no choice, it will roll in ecstasy at your feet." *But wait for what?* I wondered, walking the tightrope of a tense interior conversation with myself.

"Oh hey, Tara." I turned to see Nick. He was coming over to me by himself, his rust-colored JanSport backpack slung casually over his shoulder. He looked like a magazine ad in his tailored navy blue shirt, a weathered hat, and jeans. "Did you hear the latest news report? Crazy stuff, huh?"

I looked at him, my mouth slightly ajar. He had that same loose grin on his face, the one that always made me tongue-tied. I couldn't believe he was talking to me.

"Do you have Grover for physics?" he asked, nudging my wrist with his own. I looked at his hands. He had long fingers, tan and tapered at the fingernails, and a silken down of light brown hair on his arms. "Oh, cool. We're in the same class," he said. He was standing over my shoulder looking at the schedule in my hand, so close that I could smell his cologne, see the stubble on his chin, feel the heat of his body radiating off him. He was an entire head taller than me, and his hair curled up from under the edges of his hat. If I turned just so, I could press my face into his neck. "I can't wait to hear what he has to say about this whole thing, can you?" he asked me just as the bell rang, causing me to jump slightly.

"I guess I'll see you there. Halle asked me to wait for her. She's always late." He smiled again, a warmth in his hazel eyes.

I took off slowly, still looking back at him, realizing that once again, I had behaved like an idiot mute around Nick. But as I crossed the student center, I was feeling the same kind of amazement my mother must have felt upon her discovery of Terra Nova, an injection of astonishment flooding through my veins like a potent and dazzling ink.

Nick and Halle walked into physics class together, ten minutes late, giggling loudly. Grover looked up at them briefly but neither acknowledged them or admonished them for being late to their first class on the first day of school. He simply continued to talk about the year's curriculum.

"It's a very special time to be studying physics. Can anyone tell me why?"

Halle had barely made it to one of the only empty seats on the far end of the classroom, but she raised her hand.

"Yes, you . . . Miss . . . ?"

"Lightfoot. Halle."

"Miss Lightfoot, enlighten us."

"The discovery of a new planet within a solar system resembling ours suggests the existence of a multiverse." Grover didn't look up from his syllabus, but from the way he raised an eyebrow, I could tell he was impressed.

"And can anyone tell me the definition of a multiverse?"

Everyone was quiet. Halle raised her hand again.

"Miss Lightfoot?"

"I can't speak to it from a physics perspective, since I haven't taken this class yet . . ." At this, a few people laughed, but Halle continued, looking as confident as ever. "But from a philosophical perspective, the multiverse is a set of infinite possible universes that fill . . . pretty much the entirety of space."

"That's a good answer, Miss Lightfoot, but the multiverse theory actually has little to do with the discovery of a new planet or new solar system like ours. From a *physics* perspective, the multiverse theory posits that when the universe grew exponentially, in the first fractions of a second after the Big Bang, some parts of space-time expanded at a quicker rate than others, and the result of this rapid expansion was the creation of bubbles of space-time. These bubbles later developed into other universes."

In the back of the room, someone yawned.

"But we'll get into more of that later in the year. And thank you for your insights, Miss Lightfoot."

But Halle couldn't be deterred. She cleared her throat and pushed a strand of her long blond hair behind her ear. She was sitting sideways on her chair and leaned forward slightly, her hands on her knees, determination in her eyes.

"But I actually *do* think it has something to do with the

multiverse, Mr. Grover. It's a planet, similar to ours, and it's beamed a signal to us, so close to our own that one has to wonder . . . how similar are these people to us? Are they human? Or, I guess, human-like? We can discuss theories forever, ad infinitum, but on the eve of a discovery like this one, I want physics to be *relevant* to me in terms of what's going on in the world. Not just some random class that I took my junior year to put down on my transcript and forget about once I'm done."

"I agree," Hunter Caraway called out from the back of the class. He was the one who had audibly yawned earlier.

"Yeah, I do too." Nick followed suit, looking at Halle with wide, adoring eyes. The expression on his face made me flinch.

Within seconds, the entire classroom was nodding and voicing their agreement with Halle. Grover actually smiled. "All right, I think we're going to have quite a year, then," he said.

Only Halle could have done that. It was a mandate to Grover, and of course Halle had issued it. She had essentially put him on notice. *Bring your best game, buddy,* she had told him as though he were an equal, not a superior. *Don't just saunter in here with last year's handouts and xeroxed quizzes and pretend to do your job.* Instead of Grover motivating us, she had somehow managed to motivate him, to challenge him without him even realizing it, and it wasn't the first time I had seen her do this. It was the first class of the first day of school, and Halle had established her extraordinariness for anyone who wasn't already aware of it.

I had questions about Terra Nova too, beyond the obvious one of whether it was inhabited by life. Why was the signal we received similar to ours but not exactly the same? Why did they modify it for our benefit? Or *did* they modify it for our benefit?

But on this day, I simply watched Halle out of the corner of my eye as she spoke, realizing that I would never have had the self-assuredness to raise questions like the ones that occupied my brain. Or to call out a teacher on not doing his job properly. I wondered what it must be like to move through life with that kind of confidence.

I don't know what we discussed the rest of the class because I was too busy watching Nick's attempts to play footsie with Halle, to make her laugh. But Halle remained serious. She was even dressed semi-seriously in a men's button-down oxford (maybe it even belonged to Nick), unbuttoned to the spot between her breasts, and a trove of chain necklaces.

I looked out the window to the track field outside. It was freshly mowed and presumptuously green, those tiny fledgling blades of grass unaware that they would be relentlessly trampled on by Pumas for the rest of the season.

SIX

BY the time I got out of AP calculus it was lunch hour, and the air in the student center carried the stale stench of adolescent sweat and French-bread pizza. Juniors were allowed to leave campus, but I didn't have a car, leaving me stranded in Brierly purgatory.

I thought about going outside and walking the grounds but knew I would run into the stoners who always lingered on the edge of campus on the far end of the track, smoking cigarettes and looking deliberately bored, and I didn't want to run into my old friend from the sixth grade, Laurie Hoffman. I hadn't spoken to Laurie since her parents divorced in the seventh grade and she had dyed her hair blue and pierced her nose.

"You would look good with a pierced nose," she told me the day she invited me over to her house to see it.

"What, because I'm Indian?" I asked her. I didn't like

the defensive tone in my voice, but I often felt I was walking through a field of landmines in Greenwich. People—teachers, other students, parents—constantly made offhand comments that didn't mean much to them, but I read something else in their words. A hidden language that told me I was different. Or maybe I was so aware of my own difference that I was just looking to be offended by other people's words. Anyway, I don't think that was the reason we stopped speaking, but we had, shortly after that conversation. During this lapse, several other piercings had followed. These days Laurie skipped classes frequently, and when we passed each other in the corridors of Brierly, she looked through me, as though we had never been friends at all.

I'd like to think I took stock of my options before I made the decision to head to the library, but I was fooling no one. Kafka himself would have told me to stop waiting. He was a pragmatist, after all. And yet, as I walked the length of the glass corridor, I realized that spending lunch at the library had been my biggest fear, the ultimate concession to the fact that I had no friends anymore.

I wondered what Meg was doing right now—probably eating a medialuna and sipping coffee in some glamorous café in Buenos Aires, talking in broken Spanish to Argentinian boys who found her charming.

I stopped for a moment to look outside, my eyes scanning the perfectly azure sky. Nothing looked different, and yet it was. The summer was over, I was an upperclassman, Meg was gone. Around the globe, a million different events were unfolding at once. People were falling in love, wars were being fought, children were born. And on that other Earth? What was happening there? I frowned at the thought that I would have a year of lunches in the library to ponder that question, not unlike an incarcerated criminal thrown into solitary confinement.

The long wail of a fire alarm interrupted my thoughts, the flash of red and white lights bringing a smile to my face. I covered my ears as bodies funneled through the corridor like a bag of marbles split open.

"Such a stupid waste of time, these drills," I heard someone say.

"It's not a drill!" Mrs. Leonard, the AP calc teacher, interjected. "This is not a planned event!"

"Okay, hysteria," I muttered. I made my way outside and was greeted by a rush of humid air. Within seconds, I was pushed by the swell of the crowd toward the sidewalk near the main gates.

"It has to do with that planet. It's like a solar flare or something, I bet." I heard a familiar voice behind me. It was Alexa Vanderclift, one of Halle's best friends, the one I had seen her with at Starbucks over the weekend.

"Solar flares affect GPS systems, you idiot. They don't cause fire drills," Veronica Hartwicke declared. "And besides, there's a major difference between the sun and some random planet that isn't even in our solar system. Anyway, where'd Nick go? I thought he was going to have lunch with us?"

I turned to look at them, my ears perking up at the sound of Nick's name.

"I told him to just go without us. I wanted to have lunch with my girls," Halle said.

"He seriously adores you," Alexa insisted. "I mean, the way he looks at you!" She shook her head.

Halle pursed her lips into a tight smile. "He's definitely insistent on spending a lot of time together. Like A LOT," she said, rolling her eyes and making a goofy face.

"Whatever, Halls, just break up with him if you don't want to be with him anymore." Veronica lit a cigarette and blew a ring of smoke into the air. Veronica and Halle were best friends, but I had always sensed a rivalry between them, and Veronica was the only person in school who wasn't afraid to disagree with Halle in public.

"Break up with Nick? But why? He's so great. And you have no idea how much it sucks to be single," Alexa said.

I raised my head slightly so I could hear them better, bumping my arm into the edge of someone's iPhone.

They were about six feet away, sitting calmly on a stone wall, eating their lunches, oblivious to the crowds around them. Even in the midst of a fire drill, they had found the VIP seats and claimed them. Halle was picking sushi out of a plastic container with her fingers, her legs swinging back and forth, while Veronica artfully swirled noodles on a pair of chopsticks. She was tall and angular, prettier than Halle, but there was something about the severity of her face, her no-nonsense attitude, that made her intimidating. She was wearing a pair of electric-blue heels with red soles. She had always been the most fashionable of the bunch.

Alexa, who used to take dance lessons with my mother in middle school, was rumored to have an eating disorder. She sipped on a plastic bottle of green juice, one of the many she often carted around. She kept adjusting her loose-fitting yellow halter top, tugging at it with her long, skeletal arms. None of them even made an attempt to hide the fact that they were openly eating on the grounds, literally right next to a sign that said: NO FOOD OR DRINK ON THE GROUNDS. Hiding was for people like Moira. If you were a certain type of person, you could break the rules in public and no one would stop you.

I tried again to remember the dream I had about Halle and Nick the night before, but trying to remember a dream is like trying to thread a needle. It requires that same exquisite concentration that can only be developed if the granularities of daily life don't keep getting in the way.

"What are you guys doing after school?" Alexa asked Halle and Veronica.

"Bitsy and Walter are going to some charity event in the city. You guys should come over," Halle said, a strange eagerness in her voice.

"Can't. My parents always want to have dinner together on first day of school," Veronica responded.

"Sure you don't want a romantic evening with me?" Halle teased, linking her arm through Veronica's.

"That's Nick's job. Not mine," Veronica coolly responded, unlinking her arm.

Halle looked down at her tray of sushi. "Bitsy was like, 'I can't miss this.' It's for the Brooklyn Botanical Garden. Or maybe the Greenwich Yacht Club? I can't remember. Anyway, she's the committee chair, she can't *not* go." Bitsy was Halle's mother. She was a petite blonde who always wore sunglasses indoors and had cheekbones that looked like they were sharp as knives. I saw her at school events occasionally, and she always flashed my mother and me fake veneer smiles from a distance.

"Come over for dinner, Halls. My mom was asking about you," Veronica said.

Halle shook her head. "I wouldn't want to intrude on a Hartwicke family tradition."

"What are you going to do?" Alexa asked. "I *hate* being alone."

"We're well aware of it," Veronica snorted.

"I'm going to tell Nick I have a ton of work to do, pour myself a finger of whiskey, and start looking over college applications."

"You're a *junior*, Halls."

"Doesn't mean I can't get a head start. I should start looking over that Stanford application."

I watched Alexa roll her eyes at Veronica, but Veronica didn't look back at her. She jumped off the edge of the wall, her eyes scanning the crowds. She was looking for a waste bin, holding the empty noodle container with the tips of her thumb and forefinger. I looked around. I was standing next to the garbage can. I turned away, trying to disappear, but it was too late; she was already right next to me.

"Oh hey, Tara," she said, eyeing me coolly as she tossed her container away. "How was your summer?"

I shrugged. "Uneventful. Yours?"

"I was in London. It was fabulous; stayed around Brick Lane. Great Indian food. Does your dad still run that restaurant, by the way?"

I looked away, embarrassed that my father's restaurant, the only Indian restaurant in town, was considered a defining characteristic of my identity. Then again, I had become used to this. Teachers were generally the worst, asking me questions about Gandhi and Diwali and where to buy Indian bangles and scarves.

I looked at Veronica now, and I could hear a hint of resignation in my voice as I answered. "Yeah, he still runs the place."

"I've been craving that stuff. Maybe I'll ask my parents if we can eat there tonight." She smiled, but it was an uncomfortable smile, as though she wasn't sure whether she had said the wrong thing.

I smiled my own counterfeit smile back. She had never been *un*friendly to me, which was strange because Veronica snubbed her peers like some people reached for salt.

"I was just about to . . . take off," I told her, realizing the stupidity of my comment the moment it came out of my mouth. Where was there to go? We were all clustered across the grounds till it was okay to go back inside again.

"Okay, see you later," she replied, and I turned and pushed through the crowds, my whole face red. I felt like such a nobody around them, I thought as I squeezed through a tunnel of backpacks and bodies till I emerged on Hillside Road, the tree-lined street that led to our school. If you followed Hillside all the way up north, it led to backcountry Greenwich, where Halle and Alexa lived. But if you took the road south, it spouted out into the busy intersection of the Post Road, the road I traveled every day to get to school.

I started walking toward the Post Road. I wasn't sure where I was going, I was too busy berating myself for my stupidity around Veronica. *Just . . . forget it*, I told myself. *She probably already has.*

It was a pretty day, and the only good thing about Connecticut was how blue the sky was those last few days of summer. Oak trees bowed and swayed in the wind like sea hydra, and every surface was covered in a carpet of rich green—moss climbing up rocks and stone walls, ivy running rampant over people's homes, tripping unwelcome feet on the sidewalk. It was such a contrast to the deadened cement of the new campus.

At the end of the road, a black Labrador puppy dashed past me and then came back, sniffing at my ankles. A puppy without its owner was definitely an unusual sight in Greenwich, where all dogs were kept tightly on leash. He leapt up to my waist, wanting to play.

"Hey, buddy." I smiled, petting him. "Where'd you come from?" The dog ran a circle around my ankles. He had a tag on his collar, and he looked groomed, but when I asked him to "sit," he just pawed at my knees. He was adorable.

"Looks like you're lost, huh? Who do you belong to?" He

sniffed at my hands and put a paw on my knee as I reached for his collar, but just as my fingers grazed the tiny metal tag, he pulled away and ran off, down the sidewalk and toward the busy intersection.

"No, no, no!" I yelled, running after him. It was as if I had lost the memory of all other words in my vocabulary. I ran as fast as I could, a tree root tripping me on the pavement. I fell hard, scraping my knee, but scrambled to get up and make it to the intersection before the dog did.

I could see him just ahead of me, his graceful, brisk run, the way he stopped for a moment to look around, almost as though he half-expected someone to call out his name, take him back home. But he was in unfamiliar territory, trying to find something that might anchor him.

I ran faster, and as he saw me approaching, he seemed to think we were playing a game of tag and turned and ran up ahead of me.

"STOP!" I yelled. "Seriously, I can't run that fast!" I was already overwhelmed with regret that I didn't grab him when I had the chance.

He was running so fast that he was just a blur of black zipping across the street and around the bend. And then I heard it. The shrill screech of tires, a horn, a thud, and a gasp—my own. I ran even faster now, my feet pounding the pavement, my heart racing.

My brain didn't make the connection right away. At first, I thought it was a black blanket accidentally strewn in the middle of the road. But then the blanket moved and made a

sound, causing me to cry out. I ran to the middle of the intersection. Cars honked. The light turned yellow, then red. It was
instinct—the way people describe saving their infants by lifting boulders. I threw off my satchel and reached for the dog,
cradling its head in my lap, listening to its wheezing breath, my
heart racing so fast I could barely think.

His fur was damp and hot, and when I lifted my hand,
it was covered with blood. I tore off my cardigan, wrapping
it around the dog's body, but within seconds it was soaked
through. Everything was happening too fast. I needed time to
slow down so I could think, so I could figure out what to do. I
looked at the dog's collar. "Mario," it said.

"Mario. It's okay. You're going to be fine," I cried into his
eyes. He whimpered, trying to move his paw, but it was trem-
bling as though he had no control of it. I reached for it, holding
it tight in my fist.

"I know you're scared," I whispered to him. "It's going to
be okay. We're going to take care of you." I had never before
felt such a desperate instinct to go back in time, to undo what
had already been done. A few seconds, a loose grip on a collar,
the light turning green instead of yellow—if only I had thought
quicker, moved faster . . . *Stop it, Tara*, I told myself. *Focus on
now.* Mario whimpered in my lap, squirming in pain.

"Oh my God, that's Halle's dog!" I heard a panicked voice.
It was Nick's. He had left his car—a green Jeep—in the middle of the road, and he was crouching next to me now. "I saw
who did it. I think it was Sarah Hoffstedt. She was in that red
Porsche, just sped off, I can't believe it!" His voice was strained,

and his face was florid. He placed a hand on my back. "Are you okay?"

"We need to get help!" I cried.

"I don't think he's . . ."

"He's breathing! We need to call a vet, or 911, someone, something!" I said. Tears were beginning to stream down my face. Already, my cardigan matched the color of Nick's rust-colored bag.

"Okay. I'm calling right now."

I looked at Mario's eyes. They were glassy.

"Let's get you out of this intersection," I said to him, but when I tried to move him, he yelped in pain.

"You're going to be okay," I said, trying to comfort him, but my words came out garbled, my tone high. I couldn't bring myself to let go of Mario, like he was some sort of extension of me.

I could hear Nick on the phone behind me, his voice frantic.

"Hello? Please! We need help!

"I'm at the intersection of Hillside and the Post Road.

"No! No, it's not a person, it's a dog! Just a dog!"

Nick sat down beside me on the road, cars circling around us.

Eventually, the ASPCA came in a white van. A young vet, clean-shaven, looking not too much older than us, jumped out and nervously took notes on a clipboard.

"Is it your pet, sir?"

"No, he's my girlfriend's dog! Can't you do something?"

The vet crouched down next to me. By now, Mario's

breathing was shallow. His eyes kept closing, and I felt the need to gently shake him awake.

"It's okay. I'm here, don't go," I said, but his body was becoming more and more still. "*Please, please* don't go," I begged.

The vet placed an oxygen mask around Mario's face, pressing down repeatedly on his chest. There was a jarring violence to it, and it filled me with terror.

"What are you doing? You're hurting him!" I screamed.

"I'm sorry, but I have to."

It went on for what felt like an eternity. "I'm going to try the paddles now. You have to move aside," he said.

I shook my head like I couldn't comprehend what he was saying.

"Come on, Tara," Nick said gently, pulling me away from Mario. The moment he did, my knees buckled underneath my legs and I fell to the ground again, my eyes still on Mario.

I watched his body twitch and jolt with the current of the electric paddles, one time, then two, then five.

Mario remained still. The vet pulled a syringe from his bag. "I'm sorry, but he's in pain," he said. "I don't think we can bring him back. We have to do this."

"No!" I cried. "Stop!" But it was too late. I watched as he injected the poison into Mario's body. I pulled him back into my lap and stroked his head, letting my tears fall. I don't know how long I was sitting like that in the middle of the intersection.

"I'm sorry, ma'am. We have to take him away now, get in

touch with the owners and . . . take care of the body." I heard the vet's apologetic voice. I looked up. I had forgotten he was there. Tentatively, I loosened my grip on Mario's paw.

Nick put an arm around me. "It's okay," he said, over and over again, but I still couldn't stop crying. He sat with me for a few minutes before he pulled away. "Listen, I have to call her," he said. He got up, slowly walking toward his car. I watched him, the muscles in his back tensing.

"Halle . . ." His voice broke. I could see that his hand on his phone was shaking. "I have bad news . . ."

I closed my eyes and pulled my knees up to my chest, burying my face in the rough fabric of my jeans.

I didn't want to go back to school, and Nick offered to drive me home. I sat in the passenger seat of his Jeep, my head against the windowpane. Nick tried to talk to me, but I couldn't even speak. I had never before thought of how hazardous it was, just being alive.

"Hey." Nick reached for my hand again before I got out of his car. "You were there for him. That's what matters. Halle was broken up over it . . . But she was *so* grateful that you were there."

SEVEN

"EVEN though Terra Nova is still trillions of miles away—about four-point-two light-years, to be exact—we have reason to believe that it is inhabited by intelligent life. Of course, it's still too early to do more than speculate."

"But . . . are they like us, meaning, like humans? Are they . . . human-like?"

"Of course they are!" my mother exclaimed. She was in front of the TV when I returned home, and this time she didn't even look up. I could tell she hadn't showered because she was still in her pajamas.

Adam Bryson had a different answer. "We don't know if they're like us. But there has been a new development. Early this morning, NASA intercepted a new message—this one appears to be something like a bitmap. We're in the process of decoding it right at this moment. For our viewers, this is what it looks like," Bryson declared as a pixilated image cascaded across the screen.

"Hi, sweetie. Did they let you out early?" my mother asked. But she didn't wait for an answer. "I had to call in sick today. Have you seen this image? They don't know what it means yet, but they're trying to decode it. Crazy, huh? Wait, listen to this part . . ."

I was shell-shocked, standing by the door, covered in blood. My mother didn't even notice. I slowly turned to the TV just as Lauren Matson began to speak.

"But if Terra Nova is trillions of miles away, then how could we have received a response to our transmission in such a short amount of time?"

"One theory is that what we thought of as a *response* to our signal is not a response at all. Perhaps it was simply a transmission sent by the inhabitants of Terra Nova, independent of our own. It's possible that, like us, Terra Nova sent out a radio signal with no expectation that it would reach us—perhaps they were aiming it at an entirely different star cluster. It could be that when they sent it, they had no knowledge of us. It's *also* possible that they never received our transmission."

"So let me get this straight—you're saying that there's *no* relationship between the two signals beyond their similarity?"

"All I'm saying is . . . it's a possibility."

"Well then, I guess the big question is . . . why is it so similar to our own?"

Adam Bryson raised an eyebrow. "Coincidence?"

"That's the best answer you got?"

"That's the only answer I got, Lauren."

"Isn't that exactly what I said?" declared my mother with vindication in her voice. I didn't respond. I felt as though my mother and I were miles apart, rather than just ten feet from each other. I wanted to curl up next to her, tell her what had happened, and yet, more than that, I wanted her to *know* what had just happened, to turn to me and throw her arms around me and ask me if I was okay. But she didn't. I watched her for a moment, her eyes fixed on the TV, her hair unwashed. She felt like a different person all of a sudden, but it wasn't just the obsession with the news and her slothful behavior.

"It *is* exactly what I said."

Her certainty felt like an odd novelty, because my mother was rarely confident of anything at all. In the produce aisle of the supermarket, she often stood for several minutes, a beet in one hand, fennel in another, uncertain of the global consequences of purchasing one over the other. She was the one who had explained to me, in a slightly panicked voice, that a butterfly flapping its wings in South America could affect the weather patterns in Manhattan.

To my mother, every tiny event, every tiny decision had an impact somewhere down the road, and on most days she believed that impact was an impending nuclear bomb waiting to exterminate everything and everyone she knew rather than something welcome . . . or even nothing at all. This was the kind of thing you would never know about her if you saw her on the street, if you took dance classes with her. But I knew this about her because I lived with her day in and day out. She was the person I knew best in the entire world. But Terra Nova was changing something in her, something that couldn't really be seen by the human eye, such an imperceptible difference that it may as well have been the flapping of a butterfly wing.

"I'm going upstairs," I said, hoping that she would turn and look at me.

"Don't you want to watch with me? You know what I think this means? It means they're just like us. Maybe they *are* us."

"They can't be us. *We're* us," I said. I could hear the frustrated edge in my voice, but she didn't pick up on it.

"Has anyone ever explained Schrödinger's cat to you?" she called after me.

I shook my head, but my mother didn't see me. "Ask your dad about it. I can't explain it."

No one could really explain any of it—an alien planet, a dead dog, Meg leaving home, my mother acting weird. It was as though over the past twenty-four hours, my entire life had become a story that broke constantly and iteratively, like waves crashing into the sand again and again and again, the questions outpacing any answers that were likely to survive.

I climbed up the stairs to take a shower. I felt a momentary wave of anger that my clothes were blood-soaked and she hadn't even noticed. Then I realized: It was the anniversary of my grandparents' death, and she didn't even seem to remember.

EIGHT

IT was still early evening when I woke up, the first glimmer of twilight revealing itself in pink and purple streaks of light across the sky. Despite the events of the afternoon, the sky insisted on proudly unfurling its beauty at us, a matador taunting us with his lack of interest in the particulars of any individual life.

When I came down the stairs, my mother was still there, planted before the bright blue screen. But this time, she turned and looked at me, her eyes wide with alarm. I was relieved. She looked like my mother again.

"Listen, Linda called me. Why didn't you tell me what happened?" she asked, looking me up and down. "It sounds just awful! Are you all right, babe? You should have said something the moment you came in the door! You're supposed to tell me these kinds of things."

Linda was Nick's mother. She was on the PTA and had short gray hair cut in a bob and always wore Hermès scarves. She was the kind of mother who seemed to know what to do in an emergency.

"She called Mrs. Treem and told her what happened. The phone's been ringing constantly the past half hour—Linda, then Treem, then the vet called—they had your contact info and wanted to get some information from you."

"Great, now Treem's going to want to talk about it. God, I hate her."

"I know. She's so false! You can just hear it in her voice."

"She drips falseness."

"You should switch guidance counselors . . ."

"You don't even know the whole of it. She makes such annoying comments and she's like this consummate alarmist, and now she's going to want to have, like, a long discussion dissecting the 'incident' and my 'feelings' about it tomorrow. But it's not going to help anyone, because she's kind of an idiot."

"You should just lay it all out. Tell her to leave you alone. You don't need her help," my mother said as I retrieved a jar of peanut butter from the cabinet and began to eat it straight with a spoon.

"I can't do that."

"You totally can."

"I told her once that the cement walls on the new campus make me melancholy, and she asked me what I meant by that. And then I realized that she didn't know what the word 'melancholy' actually meant."

My mother laughed. "That's not true!"

"No, seriously, it is. Ever since then, I totally feel like I can't trust her. And she has an actual say in my future! And then another time, freshman year, she complimented my English," I said, suddenly remembering that awkward conversation.

"Why would your English be bad?" my mother asked.

I pointed to my face.

"Because you're . . ."

"Yeah. She basically looked at me and pegged me for an ESL student."

"You never told me about that! I would have set her straight."

I shrugged. "I just worry that's what the whole world is like outside of Brierly. Just a few idiots who've somehow been assigned the role of gatekeepers."

My mother shook her head. "It's not like that," she said. I slumped down on the couch next to her, and she stroked my hair. "Well, sometimes it is . . . I know it's been tough for you. God, what a crap first day of school! Anyway, you don't have to do your homework today. Mrs. Treem's orders."

"Awesome." I rolled my eyes, as though that was any sort of consolation prize for watching a dog die in your arms.

"Look at this," she said, turning her attention back to the TV. "People are really responding to this stuff."

She pointed to the footage of masses of people gathering in the woods, in the mountains and deserts, performing odd rituals at sunset and sunrise, chanting melodic chants, standing in the streets, holding signs that said: WE ARE NOT ALONE, and THEY ARE WATCHING US, and WHAT DO THEY KNOW? The ambiguity of this last question seemed intentional. What did it matter what they knew when we barely knew or understood anything ourselves?

"There are all these . . . groups forming. All over the world, like newfound religions. They think this new planet is our 'celestial twin.'"

"It's kind of premature for that, isn't it?" The formation of something, anything new that allowed one to look outward, upward, and still beyond had always been a refuge for the lost. I always wondered about people who voluntarily joined groups with some sort of enthusiasm or willingness. Don't get me wrong—I was on yearbook and swim team and Amnesty International, but only so I'd have those things on my transcript. I didn't actually feel like I was part of anything. No matter what, I felt separate from everything at school, like I was there to observe people rather than to actually interact with them.

But my mother felt differently. "It *is* comforting, the idea that we're not alone," she mused. "I guess I just find it all meaningful. Your dad thinks it's a big joke or something."

I looked at my mother. She was eating a granola bar. The discarded wrappers of her granola-bar meal plan littered the coffee table.

"Mom, I think you're getting kind of obsessed," I said to her.

"It's just so . . . mesmerizing!" she exclaimed. "I know, I know. I promise I'll go back to work, but I just needed this. It feels like an infusion of vitamins or something."

"What does that mean?" I asked.

But she didn't answer, and I could tell she wasn't listening to me anymore. Her eyes returned to the screen, and her hand reached for the remote to switch to another news network.

I got up. "I think I'm going to go visit Dad," I told her. She didn't protest, so I took my bike out from the garage, and by seven thirty I was crossing the threshold of my father's restaurant, the clang of bells overhead, a vertical thread of seven chilis and a lime hanging in the doorway to ward off the evil eye. A small waitstaff tended to a bustling dining room, steel plates of puri and naan and chana masala and chicken tikka floating by in deft hands.

I was greeted by the smoky smell of the incense by the door, which always made me sneeze. This functioned as a greeting, and Amit, the head server, gave me a nod.

"Is my dad in the kitchen?" I asked him.

"He's in the pantry, taking inventory."

"*Now?* During the evening rush?"

Amit shrugged. "Maybe he thinks we have it all handled."

This was the longest conversation I had ever had with Amit. He was a sophomore at Trinity College, working a few nights a week at the restaurant for the extra money. Our interactions were minimal, mostly just "hi" and "bye" and "Do you need any help?"

The one time I saw him outside of work, coming out of a bar on Greenwich Avenue with a group of friends, it shocked me that he had a life outside the restaurant. He was dressed in torn jeans and a T-shirt instead of his uniform of black slacks and a black button-down shirt. His hair was rumpled, and he was holding hands with a tall brunette with an obnoxious laugh. We made eye contact for a brief second, but I ducked into a pet store, hiding behind a wall of aquariums to avoid an awkward interaction, and by the time I emerged, he was gone. Neither of us brought it up afterward.

"You should go say hi to him."

"How come it's so busy today?"

Amit shrugged. "Maybe the last book club selection was *Orientalism*." I took this as a cue to find my father, threading my way through the narrow corridor past the restrooms and the kitchen.

Occasionally I helped out at the restaurant. I liked the organized chaos of the place. Tickets coming in, mounds of ginger, onion, garlic, and tomatoes waiting to be thrown into sizzling pans, rolls of dough tossed into the tandoor transforming into chewy rounds of naan, blackened and crispy at the edges. It was this metamorphosis that delighted me—there was something satisfying about it, starting with something and ending with something else entirely.

Sometimes, on early summer mornings, I would watch my father steep tamarind with jaggery, chili, and ginger to make chutney, observing it bubble and thicken on the stove. Or I would inspect the glass jars of pickles that lined the windowsill of the kitchen—orbs of preserved lemon suspended in sugar syrup, slivers of raw mango salted and blended with mustard and cumin seeds.

My father had made those pickles. He loved the precision

of cooking, believed in "correct" measurements and cleaning up workstations as you go. These things seemed to bring him a sense of satisfaction.

"Dad?" I called out as I entered the storage room. "How come you're in here?"

He had his back to me and was stacking large industrial-sized cans of whole tomatoes.

"It's gotten so disorganized," he said, frustration in his voice. "Everything's a big mess! I keep telling Amit that we need a system, a process. You can't just dump things everywhere. Everything has a place, and if you don't put things in their proper place when they come in . . . this is where you end up." He gestured to the large burlap sacks of multicolored lentils around him, to the bulging nets filled with red onions and ginger and ghostly white garlic. The pantry didn't look any more or less disorderly than usual to me. For a moment, I thought he was referring to the restaurant itself—how he had ended up within it.

He turned to me then, his voice softer now. "Shouldn't you be at home doing your homework?"

"I just felt like . . . I don't know, visiting you." It was true. I thought about telling him about Mario, but I still wasn't ready to talk about it.

"Can you tell me about Schrödinger's cat?" I asked him.

He paused for a minute, a large plastic container of turmeric suspended in his hand.

"What made you bring that up?"

"I don't know. Mom said I should ask you about it."

My father turned to face me, placing the container on the floor. He sat down on top of a sealed sack of basmati rice. His eyes were distant. "I haven't thought about Schrödinger's cat in years. I told your mother about it on our first date. It's . . . a thought experiment . . . the idea that two contradictory possibilities can exist simultaneously."

"What do you mean?"

"Well, think about a cat. Let's say you take this cat and you put it in a box with unstable poisonous gas in it. The gas has a fifty percent chance of poisoning the cat and killing it, and a fifty percent chance of doing nothing. It's a closed box, sealed. So we don't know whether the cat is dead or alive until we actually open the box and look at it. But the thing is, if you do the experiment enough times, the cat lives half the time, and dies half the time."

"Okay . . ."

"So according to quantum mechanics, before we look in the box, the cat is simultaneously dead and alive." He looked at me to make sure I understood.

I nodded. "Go on."

"The cat's reality is tied to the experiment—it either sees the radioactive poison released and it dies, or it doesn't see it released and it stays alive. But our observation of this experiment forces the outcome of it to collapse toward one reality or the other, so we're part of the experiment too now—if the cat dies, then we see it dead, but if the cat lives, we see it alive . . ."

"Yeah?"

"So if we apply this thought experiment to us, one has to

wonder: Is there someone watching us, trying to observe the outcome of our reality? We live in a world of choices too. Does life for us move in one direction or the other? Or do both possibilities exist?"

"How can they both exist?"

"In parallel within a larger multiverse. Possibly alongside many other possibilities."

"So . . . do they all exist? All those possibilities?"

My father shrugged. "No one knows. It's the biggest question in quantum physics."

I wanted to keep discussing Schrödinger's cat, but my father got up abruptly and rubbed his eyes. "I think I'm going to leave early today. I'll have someone else close up. Let me check the register, and I'll meet you out front in fifteen minutes. We can throw your bike in the back of the car."

"Okay," I told him, following him out of the storage room. I watched him duck into the kitchen as I tried to piece together everything he had just told me. I was so distracted that I didn't even notice the tall figure standing in front of me.

"Oh my God, Tara! I was hoping I'd run into you!" I looked up to see Veronica's lean frame pressed against the pink wall of the corridor, a concerned look in her eyes.

"Veronica . . . what are you doing here?"

"Just waiting for the restroom." It took me a moment to register that she had mentioned coming to the restaurant earlier that day. It felt like ages since we had that conversation.

She turned to face me, blocking the narrow hallway, a

conspiratorial look on her face. "I heard about what happened! Nick called me."

At first, I couldn't understand what she was talking about. My brain felt like a broken calculator, unable to add up the information before me. But the mention of Nick surprised me. I realized that he had talked to her about this afternoon, about the dog, about me.

I slowly nodded, unsure of what to say. "It was . . . yeah, it was awful." I hoped that this was the end of the conversation, that I could just walk away, but she went on.

"Halle's pretty fucked up over it. She loved that puppy. Her housekeeper was, like, driving all over Greenwich looking for it. They didn't think it could get off the estate and make it to the main road. And Sarah . . . oh my God, I don't think she has any idea what's coming. Nick said it was definitely a red Porsche—he saw it, and Sarah's the only one in our class with a fucking red Porsche. *And* she has a free period before lunch, so she was definitely off campus."

"I . . . I guess. I don't really know."

"Didn't you see it? You should report her to Mrs. Treem."

"No. I didn't actually see the accident. And telling on Sarah isn't going to bring that poor dog back to life." Tears began to pierce my eyes as I thought of it.

"Are you okay, Tara?" She looked around uncomfortably for a minute.

I closed my eyes tight, shaking my head, certain that I didn't want to start crying in front of Veronica. First Meg leaving, then the dog. If the past forty-eight hours were any indication of what this school year was going to be like, I was really in for it. And yet there was nothing I could do. I couldn't move away, or stop going to school, or get out of any of it. I was stuck.

"That was really nice of you to stay with him," she said quietly. "Most people, they wouldn't have done that. They would have just kept walking."

I opened my eyes, surprised at this revelation. "Most people are horrible."

"No doubt."

"I can't stop thinking about it. He was this cute little Lab . . . just a puppy. He was running—you know, the way puppies run. All enthusiasm, not even looking. And then that stupid car came out of nowhere and . . . He had no idea that the day would end like that, that his life would end like . . ."

"But you were there with him, Tara. He was lucky to have you sit with him those last few minutes of his life."

"Why do people keep saying that? He was all alone."

"That's not what Nick said. He said that you sat there in the middle of the street for close to an hour. That when the ASPCA came, they told you to leave, but you wouldn't till they had euthanized the poor thing."

"It was heartbreaking . . . the way his big eyes kept looking at me like they were asking me to help him, begging me to take away the pain. He could barely breathe. He just . . . he wanted to die," I told her. "I've never . . . that's never happened to me. I don't have any pets; I've never watched someone or something die." I closed my eyes, trying to pull it together. I couldn't believe it was Veronica, of all people, whom I was revealing everything to. I was rarely this open with people. Not even with Meg.

I thought she'd jet out of the hallway as quickly as possible, make a run for it while she still could. Smile that false smile of hers and tell me her family was waiting, but instead, she continued to linger in the hallway with me, her head leaning against the wall.

"Look, all I'm saying is, you were there, not like that horrible Sarah, who just zipped off in her Porsche. And I think Nick was glad that you were. You were so thoughtful. You're a sensitive one, I can tell."

I had barely spoken ten words to Veronica in the five years I had known her. She thought I was sensitive? And yet when I looked at her now lingering in the hallway, I had to wonder if in another world, in another dimension, we might be friends.

"Seriously traumatic first day of school. Listen, come by and say hi to my parents. They heard what happened. I think they'd want to see you. And . . . there's a party at Halle's on Saturday. You should come," she said before she walked away.

When my father came out of the kitchen, he wanted to know why I looked like I had been crying. "Is it about Schrödinger's cat?" he asked. I shook my head. I was still sad, but some of the sadness had left me, and I felt oddly grateful to Veronica. But after I said hello to her parents and her younger brother, after Amit nodded goodbye to my dad, promising he'd close up, after we had loaded my bike into the back of the car and merged onto the Post Road, I had to wonder about a fire drill, a tiny dog, Nick Osterman in his Jeep, Veronica in my father's restaurant . . . was this what my mother meant when she talked about the fluttering of wings, the migratory patterns of small creatures? A series of events—large and small—that seemed to be creating a new path for me, too fast for me to understand how or why.

NINE

IT reminded me of the "spot the difference" game we used to play as kids, the one in the back of *Highlights* magazine. Two images side by side, and you circled the things that were missing, or a different color, or added in. Except none of those games sent a trail of goose bumps up my arms.

It was after midnight. I was already in my pajamas, about to go to bed, when the alert popped up on my phone. It was Meg. My heart sank when I saw her name, but I was also curious what she might have to say to me. I opened up Instagram and saw the message:

Megz23 mentioned you in a comment: **@TKrish**, isn't this insane?! It's all anyone's talking about in Buenos Aires. Hysteria here over Terra Nova!

Meg was always sending me messages over Instagram, and I wondered for a second if this was her way of apologizing for the way she had acted before she left.

I clicked on the image. At first, it didn't make sense. It was two images, small and side-by-side. They looked identical. One of them was blurry, but not so blurry that you couldn't make out what it was. A street market of some sort. Most of the faces were obscured, but you could clearly see a woman's face in the crowds. She was looking toward the camera, smiling, wearing a big blue raincoat. All around her, street vendors sold fruit and toys. Signs and billboards written up in an undecipherable language.

On the right, the same image, but as I looked closer, I realized that it wasn't the same. It was slightly different. The signs were in a different language. The woman was wearing a red coat instead of a blue one. A vendor sold apples instead of what looked like pears.

I looked at NASA's comment.

On September 1, 2015, NASA decoded the bitmap image received from B612. The image appears to be that of a street market on Terra Nova. We posted this image on our feed right away. On September 2, NASA was contacted by a follower from Tokyo, Japan, alerting us to an Instagram photo taken a year ago of the Ameyoko Market between Okachimachi and Ueno Stations. As you can see, the images are

near-identical. The picture on the left, the image
we received from Terra Nova, shows a woman at a
street market. The composition, the colors, even the
location look surprisingly similar to the image from
Tokyo, with a couple of small variations. In the image
on the left, from Terra Nova, the woman wears a blue
coat. Behind her a vendor sells pears. We have not
been able to decipher the language on the billboards
and signs, but linguists are currently investigating.
The image on the right, from Earth, shows a woman
wearing a red coat. The vendor behind her is selling
different fruit, but the similarities have raised a
number of questions.

I looked at the image on the left, the decoded bitmap from
Terra Nova, and then back at the image on the right, from
Tokyo, Japan. From Earth.

In freshman-year biology, we watched a video of an amoeba
splitting into two—pinching in half, its nucleus dividing till
there were two identical organisms where there had once been
only one. From this day onward, that was how I would feel—
physically, I was still the same, but in some part of me, I had
become divided. Just the thought that maybe there was another
Tara somewhere in the universe made me half of a whole now,
not just one. How could this not change everything about my
world?

I dropped my phone to the floor, my hands shaking.

TEN

AT school the next day, everyone was talking about it.

"Oh my God, and they're, like, trying to track down that lady in the picture."

"I heard she's already come forward but they're, like, interrogating her or something?"

"That's, like, so stupid. Why would NASA interrogate her?"

"Not NASA, like, the Japanese government."

"Nuh uh. The Japanese government can't hold her hostage. She hasn't done anything wrong."

"Not like a hostage, you idiot. They're just questioning her." This was Veronica, getting impatient with Alexa again.

"They have, like, Instagram, dude," Jimmy Kaminsky announced to everyone.

"What, the Japanese?"

"No, the aliens, you idiot."

"Don't call me an idiot, you moron. And there's no way to confirm that. It's just an image."

It was just an image, but it had left me tossing and turning in my bed, scouring the Internet on my phone for information all night. But there was nothing new to report. Even the experts were perplexed. Who would have ever thought that my mother, of all people, had been right? *Maybe they are us*, she had said, her eyes wide, a conspiratorial tone in her voice. But she was right. I felt certain, somehow, that there was another me up there—the only other person in the universe who knew what it was like to be me. I wished I could talk to her. I wondered if *her* mother was acting strangely too.

When I left for school that morning, my mother was still perched in front of the TV, her eyes rimmed red.

"Mom, you're going to work today, right?"

She waved her hand at me. "I can't call in sick forever."

But I was dubious. And rightfully so, because just then, she turned to me, a grin on her face.

"Unless you want to stay home with me today . . ." she said. "We could order in and watch this stuff together. It'd be so much fun!"

On any other day, I probably would have joined her, or felt grateful that she had asked, but I shook my head, and she looked back at me with disappointment in her eyes. For a moment, I felt as though I was the disapproving parent and she was the child, which was odd, because we'd never been like that. My mother rarely expressed disapproval of me, and I felt uncomfortable with the judgments floating through my head in that moment. But I couldn't stay home with her today. There was something depressing about sitting in front of the TV with my mother all day. And besides, for the first time in years, I was excited to go to school, eager to hear what people were saying. Plus, I wanted to see if Nick and Veronica would speak to me again.

I crossed the student center slowly that morning, making sure that I walked right by Veronica, Halle, and Nick's table. "Oh hey, Tara, come here," Veronica called out to me now. I had been eavesdropping on their conversation, and I uncomfortably wondered if it had been obvious.

"Hey, girl, feeling better?" she asked me, giving me a slightly tentative hug. "Halle stayed home today, but she wants me to let you know she's super grateful to you. Oh, and . . . I totally forgot to send you the invite to the party, with all this Terra Nova news going on!" she said, pulling out her phone. "Where is it? Hey, Nick? Will you forward Tara Halle's invitation?"

I knew it for certain then—that Veronica's invitation to Halle's party wasn't an empty one, a sympathetic gesture that could easily be undone once she came to her senses, like untying a shoelace to remove a restrictive shoe. I felt a wave of excitement when I realized this, followed by momentary panic. Everything had somehow sped up in a way that I couldn't make sense of. I thought about Mario, running too fast around the bend. The joy in his eyes, his blind enthusiasm. Was I the one running too fast now? I was standing at their table, surrounded by Hunter and Jimmy and Janicza Fulton and Ariel

Soloway. I looked around the room then, realizing that I had never before seen it from this vantage point.

"Oh yeah," Nick said, whipping his phone out of his pocket. I was the human equivalent of a pinball machine, finally landing on the unexpected and thrilling conclusion: I was actually invited to Halle's party. Veronica had invited me. Nick was forwarding me the e-mail.

"Dude, the last time Halle threw a party, I ended up drunk, naked, and spread-eagle on a diving board!" Hunter exclaimed.

"Hunter, when are you *not* naked and spread-eagle on a diving board?" Ariel asked.

"You'll come, right, Tara?" Jimmy asked me. He put his hand on my arm, his thumb stroking my wrist in a way that surprised me.

I hesitated for a moment. "Yeah. I guess so," I said.

"Awesome," he said, a grin on his face. "Gives me something to look forward to."

"I'm bringing lemon bars," Janicza announced. "I think they're good party food."

"Yeah, at, like, a 1950s Tupperware party." Ariel laughed.

"Laugh all you want, but you're going to be the first person gorging on those after a couple of drinks. Remember the first time we all got drunk at Halle's?" she asked.

"Oh my God. And, like, Sarah was wearing those pajamas with the hearts on them and she, like, puked all over herself?" Ariel laughed.

"Halle's so done with her," Veronica announced.

"What do you mean, done?" Alexa asked.

"Well, you guys heard about the accident and poor Tara, right?" Ariel, Alexa, and Janicza turned to look at me.

"Did she really hit Halle's dog?" Janicza asked.

I opened my mouth to respond, but Veronica spoke for me. "She's been disinvited from the party this weekend."

"What do you mean, disinvited?" Alexa asked. "How can you just disinvite someone?"

"Halle doesn't ever want to see her again. I have been asked to deliver the message. She doesn't even want to speak to her."

Alexa raised her eyebrows at Janicza, who shrugged but didn't say anything.

I was in AP English when my phone buzzed. Meg never texted or e-mailed me during class. In fact, no one texted or e-mailed me during class, and so I was surprised when I saw the text from Veronica.

OMG. You have to see this, it said. There they were, in my hand, on my phone—the e-mail about Halle's party, and a series of texts between Veronica and Sarah—like a primer on the social dynamics of the most popular group of people at school.

To: Alexa Vanderclift <avanderclift@gmail.com>, Sara Hoffstedt <Shoffstedt@gmail.com>, Janicza Fulton <JF98@gmail.com>, Hunter Caraway <Hunter1111@ gmail.com>, Ariel Soloway <arieljsoloway@gmail.

com>, Nick Osterman <Nicholas.Osterman@gmail.
com>, Jimmy Kaminsky <JJKam23@gmail.com>,
Veronica Hartwicke <Veronica.Hartwicke@gmail.com>

*On Sun, August 31, 2015, at 9:25 PM, Halle Lightfoot
<hallelightfoot@gmail.com> wrote:*

My loves,

In celebration of my parents' anniversary (and their
annual trip to the Vineyard), our promotion to upperclass
life, and the discovery of Terra Nova, I invite you to join
me for an Aquarian Age fete at the Farm! Hooray!

Time: 10:00 PM this Saturday

Place: 33 Upper Cross Road, Conyers Farm 06831

Bring: yourselves, your lovers, and something from your
parental bars

Forward this: to anyone you deem worthy

Drive: slow and with your brights. Deer on the loose.

Let's show those aliens how we do it on Earth!

Much love,

Halls

I couldn't help myself. I read and reread that e-mail hundreds of times that day—in between class, in the bathroom,

once I got home. Again and again, feeling the same rush of voyeuristic intimacy wash over me with every read.

And then there were the forwarded texts between Veronica and Sarah.

Umm, can you believe this? She is such a monster! And seriously, the denial makes everything so much worse!

Just want to let you know, don't bother coming to Halle's on Saturday night.

Ummmm . . . why would I not come?

Because no one wants you there, you are an animal killer, and Halle hates you.

I don't know what you're talking about, Veronica.

We all know what you did. Nick told us. Come and I'll make your life a living hell.

What the hell, Veronica? You're being such a crazy bitch.

We're all through with you. Don't bother coming, or hanging out at our table, or reaching out to anyone. DO NOT try to talk to Halle. She's through with you. Seriously, Sarah. What you did was the final straw. Unconscionable.

What did I do?

You know what you did. You killed that dog. Halle
is heartbroken. Poor Tara is traumatized. And Nick
too. I care about my friends, and you only care about
yourself. Bye.

What dog? Seriously, V. I don't know what you're
talking about!!! And I don't know why you're always
being Halle's henchman. Can't you see that she's
ALWAYS using you?

Sarah. Stop. Seriously. Stop it right now. People are
appalled at your behavior. You've changed.

Is this because of that thing that

But here the screenshot cut off. I was fairly certain I wouldn't
see Sarah at Halle's party. I had seen the way Veronica snubbed
people in the past. It was surgical, clean, the mess contained,
if only because no one wanted a face-off with Veronica. She
could be volatile, cold, or outright cruel, but once someone was
cut from the group, they were gone for good. I had seen it happen to Jesse Ballantine last year, and he ended up transferring
schools second semester, effectively erased from the halls of
Brierly.

Everyone was acting in bizarre and strange ways. My mother
was glued to the TV instead of dancing and worrying. Nick and
Veronica were being nice to me. And I—me—Tara Krishnan—I

was invited to a party at Halle's house? It went against every notion of order and logic that overnight, Sarah Hoffstedt, one of the most popular girls at Brierly, had suddenly become an outcast, and I was invited to Halle's party. Against my better judgment, I sought affirmation from Halle herself.

The next day, I saw Halle warming up on the quad on my way to swim practice. She had been on the track team since freshman year, and she had that easy sprint you saw on Nike commercials. Her form was perfect and unlabored; even her face was serene as she circled the track. She was the kind of runner who made you want to take up running. Like everything else she did, she made it look effortless.

I approached her slowly, trying to think of what I would say to her. She was doing a quadricep stretch, her heel tucked under her backside, her lithe shoulders thrown back. The sun was catching the gleam of her shoulders just so, a smattering of freckles across the bridge of her nose. She was at once stately and special, yet still just a regular sixteen-year-old girl on the trajectory of her life. For a moment, her world was as open as a clamshell washed on the shoreline.

"Hey, Halle?" I didn't mean for it to come out like a question, my uncertain voice meeting her powerful stance.

"Oh hey, Tara. What's up?" She smiled, looking up at me and gently placing her foot back on the ground.

"I'm sorry about your dog."

"Yeah, well. I'm sorry too," she said.

I waited for a moment before I awkwardly got to the point

of the conversation. "Listen, Veronica told me about the party at your house."

"Yeah, are you coming?" she asked. So she did know. Or if she didn't, she was being polite.

"I was planning on it. Ten o'clock, right?"

"Yeah." She paused for a moment as she lifted her other leg behind her. "Are you driving?" she asked, her brow furrowed.

"I was just going to have my dad drive me."

She quickly released her foot. "No, that won't do. Your dad's going to want to meet my parents, or he's going to hear all the noise and freak out. Don't you have a car?"

I stiffened. We only had one car, and my father would need it to drive to the restaurant after dropping me off. I opened my mouth, trying to think of how I could explain this to a girl who had a garage full of gleaming vintage cars in her home, a garage built specifically to house them, but thankfully, I didn't have to.

"Just have Nick drive you," she said, placing her hands on the ground as she leaned down in a lunge.

"Nick?" I asked. I could practically hear the stupidity in my tone. "So should I just ask him?" I looked at her, nervously tugging at the strap of my gym bag.

"I'll let him know. He'll pick you up at nine thirtyish."

It was only when I reached the pool that I realized Halle hadn't batted an eyelid about offering up Nick as a chauffeur to the party. But then, why would she? I was hardly a threat to her. Nick was smitten with her.

I wondered what it must feel like to be adored like that. Of course, I knew how Halle felt: bored beyond imagination. Bored enough to send Nick on an errand picking me up from my house on a Saturday night, her kitchen scraps the very thing I felt starved for. Something about this made me feel ashamed, even as I couldn't believe that Nick Osterman was my ride to Halle's party.

ELEVEN

"EXCITED about your party tonight?" my mother asked, a grin on her face. She was standing in the kitchen, wearing a yellow dress and making a fruit salad. The mere sight of her showered and dressed and not in front of the TV shocked me. She had even gone to the local Asian store to buy starfruit and lychee and guava, my father's favorite fruits. I had mentioned the party to her in passing, uncertain that she was even listening. But she looked different today than she had in more than a week—relaxed and happy and genuinely enthusiastic for me. She pushed a strand of her long honey-colored hair out of her eyes with her forearm, and her blue-gray eyes twinkled in a way that made her look as though she were the one attending a high school party.

"Yeah . . . how come you're not all in front of the TV right now?"

"I got tired of watching, I guess. Anyway, I was going to walk to the farmers' market to get some eggs. Your father's still asleep. Want to come?"

"I'm in my pajamas," I said, but the thing was, today *I* actually wanted to sit in front of the TV and watch the latest news. I wanted to know anything I could about that other Tara. Of course, CNN wasn't going to report on this per se, but I could extrapolate, I could take any crumbs that were thrown at me. I wanted nothing more than to play with this puzzle that had been tossed in my lap—in all our laps.

But my mother had other ideas. "Get dressed. It'll be fun," she insisted. "We haven't had a chance to catch up in so long." I looked at my mother, her wide eyes watching me with a kind of curiosity I hadn't seen in days, beyond her curiosity about Terra Nova. And it was the first time this week that she was dressed in something other than sweats. I grudgingly agreed to go with her.

A handful of protestors blocked the entrance to the market. There weren't that many, but they looked menacing, holding signs declaring: GOD CREATED ONLY ONE EARTH FOR MAN, and DON'T BELIEVE NASA'S LIES, and IT'S A GOVERNMENT CONSPIRACY.

"Outside the farmers' market? Really?" my mother asked as she reached for my hand. "What a nuisance!" she whispered to me. "Excuse me," she said loudly as she pushed through the cluster.

One of them stepped in front of us. "Excuse *me*, miss. Do you believe that Jesus Christ is our savior?"

I tried to sidestep him, but he kept talking. "There's only one God, and he created only one Earth." His voice was young, and when I turned to look closely at him, I realized he was probably in his twenties, but his skin was leathery and weathered, and he had a long beard and stringy hair tied back in a ponytail. He was wearing all black.

"I'd just like to buy some groceries," my mother told him.

"Don't believe what NASA tells you, little girl," he said, getting in my face.

"I'm not a little girl." I scowled.

I followed my mother into the bustling market, my heart racing. My mother shook her head.

"Idiots," she said. "They don't get it." She shrugged. She looked unfazed, but my hands were shaking. Confrontations, especially unexpected ones, always threw me off guard. "I feel sorry for them," she said.

"Why?" I asked.

She shrugged. "We're all looking for answers, something to hold on to. I get that. But trying to convince someone what you believe? That's just fruitless."

I found myself silently agreeing with her. I considered telling her what I thought of Terra Nova—how I couldn't stop thinking about an alternate version of me—but I was certain that my mother would widen her eyes and agree with everything I felt, and this would somehow diminish the validity of my belief. My mother was the least scientific person I knew, and my father, the opposite. Validation from my mother on my ideas seemed to mean that there was something flimsy about them. But my father would force me to investigate my thoughts from every angle, to articulate them in the clearest way, to measure and inspect them until there was no magic left. Sort of the way he made me chop onions or potatoes at the restaurant.

"That's not a quarter-inch dice," he would tell me. "That's more like a half inch."

"This is the proper way to chop okra."

"You're putting in too much salt. This is what half a tea-spoon looks like."

Then he would laugh. "All right," he would say. "I suppose you're just going to do it your way." But that was the thing. I didn't really know what my way was. It was somewhere between my mother's way and my father's way, and I still hadn't found it.

We wove through the market. Flower vendors sold orange and magenta sunbursts of dahlias, whimsical poufs of hydrangea, sculptural pink and purple lilies; merchants meted out golden samples of honey on tiny wooden spoons; and pyramids of shiny apples and pears, the first of the season, sat before us.

"I absolutely love flowers," my mother said, pausing to smell them. "They're such a luxury," she said as she selected a bouquet of hydrangea. "You know, when I first moved to New York, I had no money to buy anything, really. But it was this insanely glamorous city, and I wanted to be a part of it. There was this one day, right at the beginning . . . I walked into this fur shop to try on furs, just for the fun of it, and the owner, this ninety-year-old guy—Hamish was his name—he knew I didn't have money, and he didn't want to embarrass me, so he said I could borrow a fur if I went out dancing with him."

"Eeew."

"No." She laughed. "It wasn't like that. He was old; he had just lost his wife. He loved to dance . . . ballroom dancing. And he could tell I was a dancer . . . Anyway, one day he just gave me this fur to keep. My lucky fur, I called it . . . I had so many adventures wearing it out on the town. I still have it. I was wearing it when I met your dad." Her eyes scanned the market now. She seemed restless again.

"Tell me again . . . how you met." I had heard it a million times before, but I loved hearing this story.

She paused, tasting a sample of Fujis. "It was at a party on West End Avenue. I snuck in. A duplex that belonged to some famous Columbia professor. It was gorgeous. There was music, and I started teaching people the samba, the calypso. I was chatting everyone up, having fun. Those grad students really needed to lighten up. Anyway, no one seemed to catch on to the fact that I completely didn't belong there, or if they did, they didn't say anything. Your dad was just standing in a corner, this shy grad student, and I went up to him and asked him when he was planning on asking me out to dinner. He was so cute, such a handsome guy. He seemed so . . . proper. He got all tongue-tied. But I was . . . certain." She sighed. "I was like, *I'm going to end up with this guy, whether he wants to be with me or not.* I was beyond smitten," she said, fishing some dollar bills out of her purse. "We talked for hours. He was so intense, so grown-up. He seemed like a real adult to me, even though he was only a few years older than me. Not the type of guy I usually went for, but . . . I was so carefree then. Had nothing to lose. Literally nothing. Just a few dollars in my pocket and a borrowed fur coat," she said wistfully. "Anyway, tell me what's going on at school." She quickly changed the subject.

There was something restless in my mother's voice as she relayed the story she had told me so many times. I wondered for a moment if my parents were beginning to fray at the edges, caught in the relentless middle of their time together. They were hemmed in by a past that had begun brilliant and shiny, and a future of . . . what? It was hard to say. Something about the hint of this was upsetting, and I had to turn away and take a deep breath before I answered.

"Ummm . . . I like physics. We're learning about this thing called 'seeding,'" I told her.

"What's that?"

"It's like . . . as the solar system moves through the Milky Way, it hits these dust clouds filled with comets. The comets are, like, remnants of other planets, and they're filled with microbes."

"Mmm hmmm."

"So when comets hit the Earth and make contact with water, the frozen microbes come back to life."

"Just like that?"

"Yeah, apparently. Anyway, so the comets actually 'seed' the planet, plus, they launch remnants of our planet into space, and so other planets get our microbes. It's like this continuous

cycle. And now scientists are trying to figure out how the seeding process might relate to Terra Nova. I mean, are there exact
DNA copies of us up there? Or slightly different? And the big
question is, did they derive from the same source? And what is
that source to begin with?"

"You're so brilliant. Just like your dad." She sighed. "I
wasn't the best student. Maybe I could have been . . . I don't
know," she said, and her voice trailed off for a minute before
she added, "I know high school has been tough for you, but I
really think that's going to change with being invited to this
party and everything. I like Meg, but it's good you're meeting new friends." My mother knew how much I hated Brierly,
but we rarely talked about it. My time with my mother was
always fun. We didn't linger on the bad stuff. "I guess everyone goes through tough spells," she added. "That's actually
what I wanted to talk to you about," she said, settling on four
Pink Lady apples, handing the vendor a couple of dollar bills.
"I haven't talked to your father about it yet, but I thought
I should share it with you first," she said, giving me a look
like she was about to tell me a secret. I loved it whenever she
shared secrets with me. It made me feel privileged, special.
She packed the apples into a net bag she pulled out of her
purse.

"So . . . I've decided to go away for a little while."

I stopped, watching her as she carefully counted her
change. "What do you mean, 'go away'?"

"It's just a few months, and it's California, babe. Not a big deal. I think it's time for me to have an adventure." She didn't look up as she placed the change in her purse.

A jolt ran through my body, a shock that left me shaking, and I felt an impulse to start crying, right then and there, surrounded by strangers. "A few *months*? In California? An *adventure*?" I asked, swallowing hard. *My mother is leaving me.*

"All of this news, it's inspired me. I keep thinking about those people on Terra Nova—they're alternate versions of us, right? But with slight differences. That picture changed everything for me, Tara. I can't stop thinking about it. I can't shake the thought that maybe my parents are still alive up there. Maybe on Terra Nova, they never died. It's possible, right?"

I stared at my mother, my mouth agape. "And that's why you're leaving home? That doesn't even make sense!"

"I just want to understand. It's this group of people in California, and they . . . they want to make contact with Terra Nova."

"Contact how?"

"I don't know . . . psychically?"

I could feel my heart beginning to race. "Have you lost your mind, Mom?" I said.

"Keep your voice down," my mother said. She looked baffled, as though she expected me to be happy for her.

"I can't keep my voice down. This is ridiculous!"

"You don't understand what it is to lose a parent so young. To be on your own practically your whole life, and to have no one to belong to."

"But I'm losing a parent now!" I was losing more than a parent. I was losing the only friend I had left.

"I just need to talk to them one last time, and if there's a chance of that . . ."

"Why can't you psychically communicate with your dead parents here in Connecticut?"

She flinched at this. "Because . . ." she said, her eyes tearing up, "I don't know how. I need you to understand this, Tara, and maybe someday, when you're older, you will. I've just been surviving. Ever since they died, that's all I've done. Sometimes I wonder who I could have been if they had been there. Maybe I can still be that person. I feel alive for the first time in so long. I feel inspired. Maybe it's not too late for me to change . . . for things to change."

"What would you even want to change?" I gasped.

"When you were born, your dad and I had to put aside certain things we wanted to do . . . Of course it was worth it—we have you! But I wanted to dance, and your father—he had plans to become a physicist. But none of that happened, and so . . . here we are. I'm not saying we can go back, or that we should retrace our steps. Just that . . . I wonder if we can do more, be more. Your father—he's not willing to change, but I am. I have to. It's a temporary break away from being here, but it needs to happen. I just need you to—"

But I couldn't listen anymore. I was already on the other side of the market, my mother calling after me. The tears flooded my eyes, clouding my view as I ran through the gate. Just a few minutes ago, it felt like the world was opening, offering me endless new opportunities. But just when you thought things were changing for the better, they took a nosedive.

"Little girl, be careful," the stringy-haired protestor called out after me.

"Oh, go fuck yourself!" I screamed at him. He gaped at me before he started laughing.

I didn't care about the honking of horns, the precise route of joggers. Cyclists swerved to avoid me, this blinded, wounded child running as fast as she could, to a home that had become too small, so small that it needed to be broken in order for its inhabitants to escape.

TWELVE

I stayed in my room the rest of the day, listening to my parents arguing in the kitchen. Whenever people mentioned moving to California on TV, it always seemed like a ridiculous solution to imagined problems, and my mother's desire to go there only affirmed this narrative.

But by the time the afternoon light was filtering through my shades in long vertical lines, lambent slices of burnished gold, the outrage I had felt earlier that morning was replaced by despair. How could she do this to us? I knew my father didn't love his job running the restaurant, and I had certainly never fit in at Brierly, but my mother had been a part of our limping team, and now she wanted out. Now she had decided that there was a better world out there for her, a better life, and she was simply going to leave us behind in order to embrace it.

"Why now? Why *California*?" my father yelled at her.

"Because if I don't do it now, I never will!" she yelled back.

"So you're just going to run away, Jennifer? What about Tara? What about us? How can you be so selfish?"

"I can't explain it to you," she whimpered. "But if I can just see my parents again . . ."

"They're gone, Jennifer! You're here. You have us! At least value what you have! You're acting like an awful mother, an awful wife!"

It was betrayal of the highest order, and I was glad that my father was angry, yelling at her that she was an awful mother and an awful wife.

At 9:45 I got a text from Nick. **Heading your way. Should be there in 10**, it said. **I'll meet you outside**, I quickly texted back, before I threw on a pair of skinny jeans and a black halter top. My parents were so busy fighting that they didn't even notice me slipping out the door. I emerged on the driveway just as the headlights of Nick's Jeep lit up the branches of the eucalyptus tree across the street, transforming them to outstretched arms.

My heart began to race. For a minute, all the grief and outrage I felt for my mother dissipated, and when he turned into the driveway, I greeted him with the kind of enormous smile that can only emerge after a tension-filled day, an object thrust from a highly pressurized capsule.

"I hope you like the Kinks," he said as I jumped into the passenger seat, the stereo blasting old British pop.

"Never heard of them," I told him. He looked cute in a

white polo shirt, jeans, and flip-flops. His hair was slightly wet, as though he had just emerged from the shower.

"What?! Tara Krishnan's never heard of the Kinks? I thought you were all cultured and shit." He smiled that familiar, loose smile and looked right at me, making me blush.

"Whatever gave you that impression?" I laughed, buckling my seat belt.

"Didn't you grow up in the city?"

"I've been living here since the fifth grade."

"You always seem like you've got all this smart stuff swirling around your head. Like you're way beyond the rest of us. Halle says you're aloof."

"I'm not aloof," I said, hearing the defensiveness in my voice. Is that what they all thought? Is that why I had never been invited to anything, ever? "And besides, you're smart too," I said, to soften my response.

"Not like you, though."

Nick was being modest. He was one of the top students in our grade and president of the student council; but it was true, Halle and I had the highest grades in our class, not to mention the most extensive smattering of extracurriculars at Brierly. It was Mrs. Treem who had inadvertently revealed this to me in a meeting in her office, leaning forward in her chair in anticipation of a rare opportunity to seem helpful.

"I just want you to know that you have the second-highest GPA in your class. If you're able to maintain it, stick with swim team and yearbook and Amnesty International, and do well on the SATs, I'm confident you'll be able to get into a good college."

"Who has the highest GPA?" I had asked her, remembering Mrs. Treem's irritating tendency to bury the lede.

"Well, you know I can't reveal that sort of information, Tara." Mrs. Treem smiled her most falsely sympathetic smile, but I already knew the answer, and I felt it again, that shameful pang, that wave of defeat. Halle Lightfoot: 1, Tara Krishnan: 0. Except that it was more like Halle Lightfoot: 500,000, Tara Krishnan: 0. There was no competition. Or at the very least, Halle Lightfoot was certainly not in any sort of competition with me. She was too busy getting straight As, running track, editing the school newspaper, all while she walked the length of the student center as though she were Empress of Brierly, giving Hunter Caraway's loose curls a quick tug, or grabbing Jimmy Kaminsky's hat in a singular sweeping motion as she made her way past him, not even bothering to look back as she placed his hat on her own head, laughing away with Veronica and Alexa behind her. She made it look as though she were floating through crystalline waters, while I felt as though I was constantly trudging through quicksand. She was buoyant, a majestic ship sailing across a sea that was hers and hers alone, while the others were mere barnacles, clinging to her sides.

"Hey . . . who's that girl you always hung out with, your friend on the junior year abroad program?"

"Meg?"

"Yeah, is that her name? The one who laughs at her own jokes . . ." Nick grinned now, and I wondered if he was mocking me by my association with Meg. She *did* laugh at her own jokes a fair amount. I had always thought I was the only one who noticed. It was as though she had become more and more used to our exile from everyone around us over time.

"You guys were attached at the hip."

I shifted in my seat uncomfortably. "It wasn't like that."

"Yeah, I always wondered about the two of you. Odd pairing. Like the weird one and the pretty one."

It took me a second to realize that "the pretty one" was my assignation, and I looked away to hide the thrill I felt. I glanced out the window, catching the reflection of my eyes widening in disbelief.

"I'm glad you're coming to the party. Halle has a few of these a year, always when her parents are out of town, which is a lot."

"How long have you two been together?"

"Almost a year."

"I didn't realize it had been that long."

"Yeah, well, Halle wanted to keep it quiet the first six months, so we didn't really let people know till last spring."

"What are you guys going to do when you graduate?" I asked, the question tumbling out of my mouth, surprising us both, as though it were a bird rather than a question.

"We've got some time to figure things out," he said without taking his eyes off the road.

"Sorry to be nosy," I said, trying to recover.

"It's all right," he said, turning to look at me. "Don't worry about us, we'll be okay." He smiled before turning his high beams on. I didn't tell him that what had occupied my thoughts that day wasn't whether Nick and Halle would stay together but whether my parents would. There was no one I could talk to about that . . . maybe Meg, once upon a time, but obviously not anymore. Was Meg really weird? I guess she was, a little bit. But I had always found her exuberant and funny, albeit mostly when she was talking about other people's lives. And we had somehow gravitated toward one another not because we had much in common but because our similar outsider status had sealed our friendship. But beyond the call before she left, and the Instagram message about Terra Nova, I hadn't heard from Meg. And after that phone call, I didn't feel so bad about not standing up for her. She wasn't there for me either. Based on what she had said to me that day, the day of her departure, it didn't seem like she wanted to be there for me anyway.

We turned onto Halle's street, a long unlit road in backcountry Greenwich flanked by wraithlike trees springing up from the fog below.

"It's just here, down this road. I don't understand people who live here. It's sort of . . ."

"Creepy?"

"Yeah. But then, Connecticut. Who actually wants to *be* here?"

"I didn't know you felt that way."

"It's fine, I guess, but it's not the real world. I can't wait to move to the city. Once I get outta here, I'm never coming back. What about you? Where would you live if you could live anywhere in the world?"

We turned into a long driveway unspooling before us for

what felt like miles. We were almost there, and yet I wanted to stay in this car and talk to him all night.

"I don't know . . . Paris, maybe. Or Rome."

"Yup, cosmopolitan Tara. Not like us country bumpkins."

I laughed. "You're hardly a country bumpkin."

"I bet you're going to go do really cool things when you grow up," he said.

"I don't know . . ." I was getting self-conscious and felt the need to turn the conversation on him. "What do you want to do when you grow up?"

"All this Terra Nova stuff . . . it kind of makes me want to be a scientist."

"My dad wanted to be a scientist," I blurted out.

"What kind?"

"He wanted to be a physicist . . ." I said quietly. Just saying it aloud, something I had never done in front of a stranger, felt like a betrayal. It was an admission that my father had failed in some way. He had failed to achieve his dream, and so what sort of example could he set for me? Maybe my mother was right—she was leaving and going to California because my father had given up on his dream—he *had* failed. And because she wanted to talk to her dead parents. But mostly, probably, I thought she wanted to get away from us.

"He must be really into all this Terra Nova stuff."

I was quiet for a moment. I thought about that other Tara. Was she sitting in Nick's car right now too? Was she amazed at the fact that she had been invited to a party at Halle Lightfoot's house? The bigger question was, how was she different from me? Was she smarter, more comfortable in her skin? Did she know to throw back a flirty retort when Nick Osterman called her pretty?

And what about that other version of my father? Was he a physicist on Terra Nova? Did he decide to stick it out in graduate school, even if it was hard and he didn't know how he would support his family? On Terra Nova, was the other version of my mother running away to California?

I pondered these things until Halle's house came into view, making me inadvertently gasp. It was a white three-story plantation-style colonial extending out in various wings. Tall columns reached up to touch the roofline, and the windows of the house were all lit. Hundred-year-old oak trees dotted the rolling greens that spanned every direction, and the hedges were meticulously trimmed into inorganic shapes.

Nick pulled into the gravel drive, parking his car alongside a black Range Rover.

"Looks like Veronica's already here," he said, turning off the ignition. I simply sat for a moment, looking at the awe-inspiring structure before me.

"It's just Halle and her parents, right? She's an only child, right?"

"Yeah, and their two dogs—Christine Lagarde and, well, Mario. Mario Draghi was the one who . . ."

Despite the memory of what had happened earlier that week, I couldn't help but cut him off. "They named their dogs after the director of the IMF and the president of the European Central Bank?"

"See, I didn't even know who those people were when she told me."

"I have a weird crush on Mario Draghi," I admitted, embarrassed as it came out of my mouth. "I mean, the man, not the . . . dog."

"I'll bet you do." Nick laughed. "I always figured you were sort of weird and kinky like that." He got out of the car and came by my side, first opening the door and then taking my arm to lead me down a gravel path, a gesture that both surprised and flattered me.

"He's in a better place now. I mean . . . the dog. Not the man."

"I think the man's in Rome. So he's definitely in a better place than us."

"Maybe you'll get a chance to meet him when you move there," he said, grinning at me. "Come on. They're in the back by the pool."

I looked at him a moment, realizing how much he enjoyed being a flirt. The thing was, I liked it too.

"What does her family do with all this . . . space?"

Nick shook his head. "It's pretty ridiculous. There's a bowling alley and a movie theater in the basement. With a popcorn machine and everything. You should see Alexa's place, it's just down the road . . . It's got this huge wine cellar and a spa. My dad's a lawyer, and we live pretty well, but this is some serious cash money." He laughed, shaking his head. "Hedge fund managers and rappers are the only people in the world who live like this."

"And leaders of drug cartels."

"And Bill Gates."

"Brad Pitt."

"Lady Gaga."

"The Waltons."

"Oh yeah, the Walmart people, right?"

"Yeah."

"Weirdos. My dad says they're the most unethical members of the one percent the world will ever know."

"The robber barons were worse. Isn't your dad a corporate lawyer?"

"Yeah, but he does a lot of pro bono social justice work. And my mom's on the board of a halfway house with Veronica's mom. They went to college together. Classic guilty liberals," he said as we turned a corner revealing the back of the house, a cluster of forty or fifty people lounging around a pool lit by threads of hanging lights, the sound of youthful voices echoing through a venerable wood, loud music playing from an invisible sound system, probably embedded in the grounds, in the old oaks. It definitely made me wonder about the kinds of people who lived in places like this—different kinds of pioneers engaged in a different show of conquest.

"So what do you want to do when you grow up?" Nick asked. We stood apart from the scene, surveying it for a moment before we ourselves would break through and become a part of the painting before us.

"Me?"

"Yeah, you. I feel like you could do anything you want."

I took a deep breath, my eyes fixed on Halle sitting on a jute chaise by the edge of the pool in a green sarong and a black bikini top. She was talking to Jimmy, who was sitting beside her in a T-shirt and Bermuda shorts, laughing loudly.

"I just want to . . . get out of here, Nick," I said.

"I know what you mean."

"No. I don't think you do," I said, shaking my head. And in that moment, in that place, it felt amazing to finally admit to Nick Osterman the burden of the truth that I carried with me every day at Brierly. "I hate this place so much. I don't belong here."

"Pretend," he responded with an authority that made me turn to him.

"Pretend what?"

"That you do. I promise you, no one will ever know the difference." Then he turned to me, holding out his hand. "Let's make a pact. We'll meet up when we're twenty-five. We'll both have amazing lives by then, as far away from here as possible."

I had another one of those moments then—the shimmer of disbelief, like wondering if you're in a dream.

"You're going to be in the city. That's not far away."

"Just wait," he said, raising an eyebrow at me. "You're going to be . . . fantastic," he said. I watched him, realizing the thing that he didn't quite understand. Even hope was a luxury, a privilege I had never before given myself the chance to experience. But all I could think in that moment was how right my hand felt in his.

"You guys finally made it! What took you so long?" Halle

announced. She was tiptoeing barefoot across the endless marble patio. Her feet looked tiny and delicate against the white alabaster.

Nick let go of my hand. "Lots of deer crossings."

"Yeah, whatever." Halle reached for Nick with a territorial arm, kissing him on the mouth. I looked away, trying to discern the location of the sound system, but my eyes returned to Halle and Nick. Slowly, she pulled away, reaching into the hemline of her bikini, producing a delicately rolled joint.

"Have a smoke with me?" she asked, looking at me.

I had never smoked before, and the thought of doing it for the first time in front of these people, in front of Halle, frightened me. "I probably shouldn't."

Halle smiled at me. "It's okay if you've never done it before. I mean, there's a first time for everything." Maybe Nick picked up on the condescension in her tone, or maybe he didn't.

"Of course she's smoked before," he said, taking the joint from Halle's hand and pulling a lighter out of his pocket. He lit it, taking a drag, the smoke curling in the air, slowly making its way around the limber branches of those oak trees that looked alive. He handed me the joint and gave me a meaningful look. I hesitated for a moment before I took it from his hand and took a tentative puff, coughing and gagging as I handed it back to him. He smiled at me as though we had a secret language— one that even Halle wasn't in on.

Nick put an arm around her. "Where's V?"

"Manning the bar. Let's go find her and bring her this scotch. Come on," Halle said, reaching for my hand, a gesture that caught me entirely off guard. I had seen her do this occasionally with Alexa or Veronica. Even with Sarah Hoffstedt. It made me feel, for a moment, as though I was one of them.

We walked by Ariel and Janicza, sitting with their feet in the pool, laughing as they downed champagne straight out of a bottle that they were passing back and forth between them. Jimmy Kaminsky was playing a messy game of beer pong with Hunter Caraway on the outdoor dining table, which was lined with platters of fruit and cheese and crackers, all breaking and spilling and exploding every time a Ping-Pong ball hit a plate. It was the kind of violence against beauty that would have offended my mother.

"Hey, Tara." Jimmy stopped and reached for me, giving me a hug that lasted too long to feel comfortable. "Come play with us," he said.

"Later," Nick answered for me. "We'll be right out, dude."

We walked past Alexa, who was napping in a large pod-shaped chair. She looked as though she was already drunk. There were a bunch of other people too, drinking, talking, taking dips in the pool.

"Veronica makes the best cocktails," Halle told me. "She's always bartender at my parties."

"She likes to make herself useful." Nick smiled. "Wait till you see the bar."

He looked at me as though he was genuinely happy to have me here. I wondered for a moment what Sarah Hoffstedt was doing tonight. It made me think about how the GPS system in my father's car would loudly declare "rerouting" whenever we were lost in an unfamiliar neighborhood. Both Sarah's path and my own now seemed subject to this sort of complex pivot, only I still wasn't sure where this turn would take me.

We entered through the back of the house and made our way through a maze of high-ceilinged corridors adorned with art that I knew I had seen in art books. Each room we passed through was filled with tasteful modern furniture and tribal-looking kilim rugs.

We stopped at an open kitchen that was the size of my entire house. A row of windows overlooked a side yard and a greenhouse, and a long wooden table that could probably seat twenty people sat squarely in the center of the room. Halle opened the door to a fridge that was three times the size of the fridge in our kitchen and pulled out a handful of cheeses wrapped in wax paper and a bowl of cherries.

"I'm going to make another plate. Why don't you guys go grab some drinks?"

Nick nodded and gestured for me to follow him, and I did, through a teakwood-paneled dining hall with a stained glass window.

"It's a Chagall," he whispered to me when he saw me staring at it. "A real one."

Just beyond the dining room was a rustic-looking bar. Veronica stood behind it. She was wearing a pair of glasses, and her hair was blown out.

"Nicholas Osterman. You're *finally* here. Hey, Tara. What can I get for you guys?"

"A vodka tonic for me, and a glass of water for Alexa," Nick told her.

"He's so thoughtful, isn't he?" she asked, winking at me. "What about you? There's beer on tap, like, eight different kinds, and I just unearthed this bottle from the cellar. Think her parents will miss it?"

Nick squinted at the label. "Domaine Leroy Grand Cru . . . probably not."

"Yeah, there were, like, ten of them. Have a glass with me?" she asked.

"Are you sure it's okay?"

"Do these people look like they'd miss this one bottle? Please." Veronica smiled sweetly, pulling forth a wine opener. "Thanks for sharing with me. I don't want it wasted on idiots like Hunter or Jimmy."

"Hunter's not so bad." It was Halle. She was standing with an elbow on Nick's shoulder, a perfectly curated plate of cheese and crackers and cherries in her hand, her sarong tied low around the dune of her hips. "I don't know why you don't give him a chance, Veronica." Her lips twisted into a taunting smile. "He absolutely loooooves you."

Veronica gave Halle a sideways glance, a look that clearly suggested she didn't want to discuss it.

"I'll let you have some girl time. I'm going to take this water to Alexa," Nick said, tucking a strand of Halle's hair behind her ear.

"Oh yeah, she's way drunk. Poor thing, barely ate anything all day," Halle said.

Veronica shot Nick a look, but he merely nodded. "I'll see you all outside," he said. He gave Halle a kiss before he took off.

"Did you bring your bathing suit? You're a swimmer, right?" Halle asked me.

"Yeah, but I don't have my suit."

"I can lend you one. God knows I just use mine to lounge near the pool. I hate the water."

"Here we go, the Saint Barts story again," Veronica quipped.

"I know you've heard it a million times, but Tara hasn't." Halle smiled a patient smile at Veronica.

"Go ahead," Veronica said, rolling her eyes.

Halle turned to me, ignoring Veronica. "I almost drowned when I was four years old, got caught in a riptide. Totally horrible. I'll never forget it, just the sound of the ocean in your ears. I thought I was going to die. I have nightmares even now. It's practically the only thing I'm scared of—water."

I wasn't sure what to say, so I took a big sip of wine. It tasted earthy and a little sour.

Halle took my cue and did the same. "God, this really is a good bottle. Where'd you find it, Veronica?" she asked.

"Way in the back, with the best stuff."

Halle turned to me again. "But you're like some sort of superstar swimmer, aren't you, Tara?"

I laughed. "I'm on the swim team, but no superstar."

"You're just being modest. It's sweet. Anyway, the pool is pretty much wasted on me. We have the indoor one and the outdoor one. You should come by and swim sometime." She smiled before she turned to Veronica. "I tell Veronica to use it all the time, but she's not interested."

I looked at Halle, noticing for the first time that her eyes were bloodshot and her pupils dilated. She was drunk or high or both. Maybe that was why she was being so friendly.

"What are you most afraid of?" she asked me then, taking me by surprise.

I opened my mouth, but I wasn't sure of what to say. And besides, divulging my fears to Halle, of all people, was something I wasn't ready to do.

"Maybe you need a drink before you tell us," she said. "Speaking of . . . you know what I think would be so fun?"

"What would be so fun, Halle?" Veronica asked, cleaning up the detritus on the surface of the bar.

"To get the two of you drunk!"

Veronica shook her head. "I don't have any interest in being a big drunken mess." Her eyes were still on the bar, a towel in her hand, and she was scrubbing the side of a cutting board with such ferocity it made me uncomfortable.

Halle turned to me, smiling. "Tara, do you want to get drunk with me?"

There was something awkward about the moment, a tension between Veronica and Halle, and I felt like I was in the middle of something I didn't understand.

"I mean, I get it if you haven't gotten wasted before. I don't want to pressure you or anything." And even though her smile was friendly, there was a hint of a dare in her voice. She was right, I had never had a sip of alcohol before that night, and the idea of getting drunk scared me a little. Halle's eyes were on me, challenging me. If I didn't drink with her, I was a square, an outsider, and if I did, I was going to be leaping into unfamiliar territory in front of all these people I didn't know. But then I thought about the day I had endured, the fight between my parents, my mother announcing that she was leaving. I thought about the first day of school, holding Mario in my arms, watching him die.

I picked up the bottle of Grand Cru and poured about a quarter of it into my glass, causing both Veronica and Halle to laugh uncontrollably.

Sometimes I'm still able to remember bits and pieces of that night, like a hazy dream. At some point, Halle went to her room to fetch a turntable and set it up by the edge of the pool, playing records—the Pixies and Radiohead and Fool's Gold and Tame Impala. Jimmy Kaminsky wrapped his arm around my waist and tried to kiss my neck. I laughed and pushed him away.

"You look really pretty today, Tara."

"Thanks," I said, but I was too busy observing everyone to pay much attention to him. I watched Nick care for Alexa, stopping to talk to Veronica every few minutes with a look of concern in his eyes. They had an odd sort of sibling-type bond I had never noticed before. I noticed him jetting in and out of the house, making sure everyone had drinks in their hands, chatting up the girls and giving the boys high fives. I headed inside when I saw him and Halle kissing by the hot tub.

But there are two moments I remember best about that night, almost like those pivotal scenes you recall from a movie you watched some time back—those moments imprinted on your memory.

I stepped into a bathroom that was bigger than my parents' bedroom. There was a tiled fountain and tub that could fit at least six people, and two sinks and two gleaming white toilets, each in their own closets. An entire wall of the bathroom consisted of a bookshelf filled with books. Maybe it was that joint that I smoked, but just looking at that enormous bookshelf in the bathroom, I burst out laughing.

Veronica must have heard me, because she knocked on the door and joined me. We sat on the marble floor, perusing the selection of tomes. Among them, we found first editions of *Tom Sawyer*, *To Kill a Mockingbird*, and *A Tale of Two Cities*.

"It's, like . . . first editions of our entire freshman-year English curriculum!" she said.

"And it's, like . . . two feet from the toilet."

"I never even noticed these books. Come to think of it, I don't even know if I've ever used this bathroom. There are, like, sixteen in this house."

"Sixteen bathrooms?" I shrieked. Veronica nodded, and we both started laughing again. And then we were both on the floor, cracking up so hard we couldn't stop. When we finally did, it was Veronica who spoke, weariness in her voice.

"I get so sick of her sometimes."

"Who, Halle?"

"Who else?" Veronica rolled her eyes at me.

"I thought you guys were best friends." My feelings about Halle had somehow shifted in one night. Her openness had disarmed me, but I still found myself resenting her, especially when I saw the way Nick was around her. The distribution of luck seemed entirely off in this world. Here was Halle— beautiful, smart, wealthy, charming, *and* she had a great boyfriend who adored her.

My father was always telling me that envy is a terrible thing, as though you could actually do something about it when you felt it. But you couldn't. It was like your DNA, so much a part of you that there was little you could do to alter it. And yet, I wondered if the other Tara on Terra Nova was jealous of Halle. *Probably not*, I decided. *She was probably gracious, above base feelings like envy and fear.*

"Best friends . . . I guess. Whatever that means," Veronica said to me now. "It's a major pain when you've been friends with the same people your whole life. I've known Halle since we were in nursery school. She knows all my triggers, all my weaknesses, and she throws them out at me every chance she gets, just for the fun of it. All that stuff with Hunter . . ." Here she stopped and shook her head. "People become such . . . caricatures of themselves. Halle and her constant maneuvering. Alexa and her goddamned 'food allergies.'" Veronica made air quotes, her hands in the air above our heads. "Hunter's a total moron with half a brain, in case you never noticed . . . And Nick . . . I guess he's not so bad. We used to swim together naked in the kiddie pool when we were in preschool."

"I didn't realize you've known Nick for that long."

"Oh, I have. He's such a . . . boy. I don't know what you see in him."

"Me? I don't think you . . ."

"Oh, I think I do. I see the way you look at him with hearts in your eyes. You've been doing it for years. And the thing is, he likes you too, he'll just never realize it because he's so blinded by his stupid conception of Halle. And the thing is . . . she's already totally over him."

My heart raced at the mention of Nick liking me too. I thought about how he had called me pretty in the car. "Does Halle . . ."

"Know that you're obsessed with her boyfriend? No. And besides, she doesn't care; she's way too self-involved to actually care about anyone."

I was quiet for a long time before Veronica got up and looked back at me, pulling her hair into a high ponytail and fastening it with the tie she had around her wrist. "I won't tell anyone, Tara. I promise."

It was like getting those e-mails; I felt again as though I was somehow now privy to things that I had never before seen or suspected. There were cracks in the veneer, fallouts and unspoken irritations. They were transitioning too, that entire group of friends, as friends sometimes are, like a mosaic being broken and remade. What I didn't know then was how much I would be a part of it or how much would break. I was still too caught up in the dizzying astonishment of the fact that I was becoming one of them.

My last memory of that night is the one I hope to hold on to always, especially since it's the kind of thing that happens only when you're at the right place at the right time, and you catch a glimpse of something that makes you believe in endless possibilities. Or maybe it's a moment that's precious to me because it's gone. We'll never come together like that ever again. Or maybe we were just really high, I don't know.

"Do you guys really think there are alternate versions of us up there?" Nick asked, looking up into that beautifully clear sky you can only see in places like backcountry Greenwich, the stars glittering like a fistful of diamonds flung into the air.

Everyone had left except for Nick, Veronica, Alexa, Halle, and me. We lay in the grass, surrounded by the detritus of the party, passing around yet another joint. Whiskey and wine warmed my stomach, and I was too inexperienced to know what happens the next morning when you mix that much whiskey with that much wine.

"Yeah, obviously. That's what that NASA bitmap thing was all about," Veronica said.

"No. I mean, like, millions of versions. Not just on Terra Nova, but on other planets too," Nick said.

"This is going to sound really weird, but sometimes I think *we're* not really *here*," I said to him.

He laughed aloud. "What do you mean?"

"We're just . . . avatars of another mind that exists someplace out there. All of that"—I pointed to the sky—"what we call the cosmos, it's just circuitry—like we're looking at some huge . . . motherboard lighting up and firing, and we call it stars and planets and sky. *We're* really up *there*. We just think we're here." I didn't even know that I believed this till I said it.

"My mind is blown," said Nick, laughing.

"What are you guys talking about?" Alexa asked, perplexed. She had finally woken up at the end of the party, only to join us in recline on the lawn.

"Tara thinks we're avatars," Veronica told her.

"You know what I think?" Halle murmured. "I think there are, like, numerous versions of us, numerous avatars on countless planets, all controlled by a singular mind that wants to live out a multitude of experiences."

"That's very Buddhist," Alexa commented.

"Is it?" Halle said.

"No. I have no idea. I don't actually know anything about Buddhism," Alexa said, and we all cracked up.

"I like that idea, though. That there are endless versions of us and none of us even knows about each other. That's sort of beautiful," I said, lifting my head to look at her, and she nodded back at me, as though she was offering me a gift. I smiled in amazement. I was lying in the grass at Halle's house with Nick and Halle and Alexa and Veronica. For a moment, it felt like we were a family.

"It's . . . *cruel*—the idea that we're in the dark about ourselves, about our alternate selves," Veronica said. "Why would the entire universe be constructed that way? Unless there is some sort of God and he just wants to fuck with us."

"But what if that *is* the truth of it? Endless versions of us living endless versions of this life?" Nick asked.

"Maybe they're better versions of us," Halle said.

"Better how?" I asked.

"Peaceful, compassionate, entirely void of feelings like rage, jealousy. Capable of appreciating what they have."

I thought then about my own petty jealousies, my own resentments. Could Nick see them, the swell of those emotional cancers that had already begun to sprout within me? But when I looked at him, he was gazing upward at the sky, lost in another world, in that world.

"I wonder if there's a version of me out there who feels like she . . ." And I paused for a minute, because it didn't matter. I had found it, in that moment, without realizing it.

"Feels like she what?" Nick asked. His shoulder was pressed against mine.

"Nothing," I told him. I reached for his hand and held it, without thought. But I still remember what I was going to say on that crisp and clear night, lying with Nick and Veronica on either side of me, a breeze rustling the leaves on trees, Nick's hoodie around my shoulders.

I wonder if there's a version of me out there who feels like she belongs.

THIRTEEN

MY father often recounted a memory of growing up in India in the '80s. There were only two television stations back then— Doordarshan 1 and Doordarshan 2, and every family had just one TV. In the evenings, after dinner, everyone would gather around that one TV and watch the evening news.

"If you were out late and returning home during that hour, you could hear it coming from every living room, see the flicker of the TV screen in the window of every home. The same program, the same image, the same voices," he told me.

I had never traveled to my father's ancestral home, and I knew that the Delhi of his childhood no longer existed. And yet, I found my father's nostalgia contagious. It was a strange feeling, that longing for an experience you never had, for something that was never yours but might as well have been because it belonged to someone you love.

When Nick dropped me home in the wee hours of Sunday morning, I recognized that feeling again. At first, I thought it had to do with the beauty of that autumn morning, the dew on freshly cut grass, the slight crispness in the air, but then I looked carefully out the window of Nick's Jeep and saw it. Initially, it surprised me that every home on our block had a light on in the living room, at dawn, no less, but when I looked closer, I understood—in each living room, a TV, on each TV, the same program, the same image, the same voices. Different varietals of family, driven by the persistence of a story they couldn't escape.

"You should come in," I told Nick. And by the time I realized what he might think of my tiny, shabby house, I couldn't take it back. Outside of the bubble of Halle's party, something had happened, and we were both curious to learn what it was.

Any apprehension I might have felt on the ride back—about returning to the emotional debris of my mother's decision still scattered across the floor, about my parents chastising me for staying out the entire night for the first time in my life— dissipated the moment I walked through that door. My parents turned briefly to acknowledge Nick and me, but they quickly turned back to the TV, the gravity of another planet too great to ignore.

We sat beside them, all of us watching in silence.

"Can you explain to us again what scientists discovered late last night in the US, morning in the UK?"

"Certainly," said the British scientist, nodding, nervously running his fingers through his hair, "but I'd like to precede my explanation with a brief discussion of MERLIN, which stands for the Multi-Element Radio Linked Interferometer Network, which is an array of radio telescopes spread out across England. It's about seven radio telescopes that have been monitoring radio signals from space for some time now."

"Can you tell us a little about what MERLIN does?"

"MERLIN measures radio frequencies from radio-loud galaxies and quasars, and we also do something known as spectral line observations, which are essentially tools we use to identify the molecular construct of stars and planets."

"Now, have we ever, in the past, discovered radio signals from other planets?"

"Well, till now, we've been looking at different parts of our galaxy, but, as you know, the galaxy is vast, and we haven't been confident if we're even looking for life in the right place."

"But the discovery of Terra Nova changed that."

"Yes, it did. Since we've been able to identify the location of B612, our radio telescopes have been detecting a handful of signals from the planet—first the message similar to the Arecibo signal, then the bitmap image that we decoded . . ."

"The image of the market."

"Yes, that's right. And now we've received another signal . . . and we've been . . . hearing it continuously for the past eight hours. It not only confirms our belief that there is intelligent life on Terra Nova, but, like the bitmap image, also suggests that Terra Nova is perhaps some sort of mirror Earth—or rather, an alternate Earth."

"For our viewers tuning in now, let's replay some of the first sounds from Terra Nova."

I looked at Nick, and he turned to look back at me. His mouth was slightly ajar, his eyes bloodshot. He looked adorable and disheveled and exhausted, like a child. I couldn't believe he was sitting in my living room. I wondered, for a moment, if my parents could tell that we had been drinking all night, but this thought lingered only for a second, an iridescent soap bubble, before it was dissipated by the sound from the television screen. There was static for some time, and then a voice, slightly high-pitched and eager. It was a young man . . . speaking English.

"The Columbian Broadcasting System and its affiliated stations present Orson Wellington and the Mercurin Theater on the air in *The War between the Worlds* by H. M. Wells."

A line of goose bumps trailed up my arm, and my mother reached for my hand. And then there was the sound of orchestral music. It was dramatic music, the kind from old movies. It sounded . . . like us, certainly not like something from an alien planet.

"It's Orson Welles's *War of the Worlds*. But it's their version, not ours," my mother whispered. "They've been playing it all night, the entire broadcast and then snippets of it. It's exactly like ours."

"Well, not exactly . . ." my father said, but I waved at him to be silent so I could listen. The music stopped, and then there was that voice again, "Ladies and gentlemen: the director of the Mercurin Theater and star of these broadcasts, Orson Wellington."

And then there was a different voice, a deep one, projecting gravity. "We know now that in the early years of the twentiest centuria, this world was being watched close by intelligences greater than man's and yet as mortal as his own. We know now that as human beings busied themselves about their various concerns, they were studied and scrutinized, perhaps almost as narrowly as a man with a fractoscope might scrutinize the transient creatures that swarm and multiply in a drop of water."

The static cut out, and the reporter, looking ashen, spoke again. "A remarkable moment in history. I've been listening to this recording . . . all night, and perhaps we've all sunk into a bit of a delirium, but . . ." He laughed for a moment, looking crazed as he rubbed his eyes. "What exactly are we supposed to make of this? How do we know it's not some . . . hoax?" An animated banner ran under his face. AN EDWARD COPELAND EXCLUSIVE, it said.

"It's an authentic signal, and it's coming from B612. NASA has confirmed it as well. It's most definitely not a hoax. You can clearly hear the distinctions between their broadcast and the one recorded by our very own Orson Welles in 1938. Their accents are different—linguists are currently studying their speech patterns. The music is slightly different; names of people and things are different—the Columbian Broadcasting Network instead of Columbia, the Mercurin Theater, *The*

War between *the Worlds*, H. M. Wells instead of H. G, Orson Wellington instead of Welles. These are small differences."

"And the content . . ."

". . . is slightly different. In their version of *War of the Worlds*, the aliens don't use heat rays to kill humans, they use psychic rays to influence their thought patterns. The aliens are eventually *defeated* by the natives rather than falling victim to pathogenic germs. These people—we're not quite certain what to call them as yet, but they seem to be . . . very much like us, so much so that they're capable of storytelling. They have their own theaters, their own broadcasting systems, their own fears of what's out there . . ."

"That is just . . ." The reporter shook his head, speechless.

"Inconceivable?"

"No . . . it's just . . . if they have their own versions of H. G. Wells and Orson Welles . . . does that mean that there are more coincidences beyond that?"

"The bitmap message we received was the first indication that their world is very similar to ours, but we're still investigating that, and it's too soon to know . . ."

"Yes, but . . . what are we supposed to . . . what do we make of this?" The reporter looked stricken, taking a moment to remove his glasses to wipe tears from his eyes. "We can't travel there . . . at least not for a long time. We won't meet them, at least not in my lifetime. What if it's true that there's another *me* up there? Another *you*? I'm sorry if I'm being emotional, but . . . what do we do with this information we're getting? How do we process it? What do we make of it?"

"Save the tears," mumbled my father.

"Sudeep, he's . . . emotional."

"He's a journalist. He can cry when he gets home."

"Like all the rest of us . . ." My mother muttered, and my father flashed her a look. I avoided Nick's eyes. I didn't know what he thought of my family, bickering like this, or my home, for that matter—small and shabby and practically two feet from the train station. How did Nick see my life? An entire existence that was so different from his own.

"I should get going." He looked at me. "I'm Nick, by the way." He held his hand out to my father, and my father turned to look at him.

"You're the boy from outside the Starbucks."

"Oh yeah, you remember. Nice to meet you, Mr. Krishnan." He smiled.

"I would ask you why you're dropping my daughter off at dawn, but . . ."

"But Tara's a responsible girl and we're all exhausted and let's at least get a couple of hours of sleep before we talk about all this," said my mother, getting up. "I'm glad you're home, honey." She smiled at me, as though the earlier events of the day had been forgotten. I looked through her, but she continued to act as though everything was normal. "Drive safely on your way back, Nick," she told him.

I walked Nick to the door. The sun was just beginning to rise over the horizon, painting everything around us a shade of amber. I noticed Nick's eyelashes for the first time, and a cheesy thought struck me: They were the same color as the sunlight.

"I'll see you in school tomorrow," he said, giving me a hug before I watched him get into his Jeep and drive off. All of a sudden, the insecurity I had felt just a moment before was replaced by amazement.

Nick Osterman was just in my living room, I mused to myself. *I was in his car. We talked about what we wanted to do when we grow up. He made a pact with me that we'd meet up when we're twenty-five.*

By the time I returned to the living room, my parents were gone. They must have decided to finally give in to sleep, exhausted from a day that seemingly had no end, a whorl of events that left us with little to hold on to.

I was spent too, and yet exhilarated, both from the party and from the latest discovery. I had often thought about people who lived through strange and compelling times—World War II, the Great Depression, the civil rights movement. These were periods that shaped people in some indelible way. I wondered how this moment would define us. I had never before believed that there was anything special about the era I was growing up in.

I arranged myself on the sofa, a cushion under my head, a throw over my legs, the remote in my hand. In that threshold between dream and wakefulness, I listened to the rebroadcast of another Orson Welles, on another planet, far away. I dreamt of another Tara, in the arms of another Nick.

FOURTEEN

IT was different after that. For the next three weeks, the stock market plummeted, rebounded, then plummeted again. This financial roller coaster would continue its course for the next year. People took to the streets, demanding that the government cut military spending and devote more resources toward scientific research. At school, teachers continued to tie discussions about Terra Nova into the curriculum. The student center buzzed with excitement over any news. People forwarded around all kinds of hoaxy e-mails.

Then there were smaller, subtler changes—the butterfly-wing kind that my mother talked about. The air seemed to fizz with glorious static—the electricity of the Possible. It was as though the Impossible had closed up shop, shuttered its storefront, and gone into hiding.

I never ate lunch in the library again. There was always

a seat for me at the best table in the student center. Veronica
would seek me out during free period, and we'd drive in her
Range Rover to the café on the corner of Hamilton Avenue to
grab a latte or a kale-avocado smoothie. At the end of the day,
we'd all look for each other in the student center before we
separated for sports practice. Nick would give me a high five.
Halle would walk with me to the athletic department. Alexa
would buy a cookie from the concession cart before it closed
for the day, breaking it in four pieces, giving one piece to me,
another to Halle, another to Veronica. In physics, when we had
to team up in threes for an egg-drop competition, Nick and
Halle both called out for me at the same time.

"Hey, Tara, come here."

"Come on, teammate, we're gonna win this thing."

When I walked down the glass corridor, people I didn't even
know—underclassmen, even teachers (who, let's be honest, are
never immune to the sway of popularity)—said hi to me. They
actually knew my name.

"Hey, Tara."

"What's up, Tara?"

"Love that skirt, Tara!"

At lunch, we'd push two tables together in order to seat
some sixteen of us, the girls in their wool skirts in hues of
camel, fuchsia, and slate, their skinny leather belts and their
cashmere scarves, talking about their vacations in San Miguel
de Allende and Lisbon, the boys in their torn jeans and dingy
caps and polo shirts making jokes at each other's expense.

When we broke into raucous laughter, every pair of eyes in

the room turned to look at us, wondering what we were laughing about, and I couldn't help but think, *I used to be out there, but now I'm in here.* And now I knew what the endless amusement was about. Most days were the same—Ariel Soloway and Janicza Fulton making raunchy jokes, Hunter and Veronica bickering as Jimmy fed the flame of their daily fracas, Veronica making outrageous statements. And Halle, of course. It was impossible to ignore her reign over all of it, as though much of this entertainment was for her benefit.

Everyone wanted to make Halle laugh. Everyone wanted her friendship, her respect. A word of disapproval from her might ruin the entire day. Ariel and Janicza made fun of everyone else, but never Halle. Even Hunter and Veronica's fights had a performance quality about them, and it was Halle who often played moderator, the Gwen Ifill of our group.

Out in the world, cults were forming on a daily basis—this I knew firsthand, and it was impossible to think of it without thinking about my mother, who had received her "induction packet" in the mail. I had seen it on the kitchen counter, a shiny catalogue that looked jarringly like the college information packets I was beginning to receive on a regular basis.

But at Brierly, the cult of Halle reigned supreme, and her greatest worshipper was Nick. Halle was at the center of Nick's orbit. Sometimes I thought of her as that big sun of Terra Nova's, so bright that it obscured everything else in its proximity. But Nick practically glowed in her presence.

~

One day in late September, we were sitting in the student center when Sarah Hoffstedt, now a consummate pariah, sheepishly walked up to me.

"Hey, Tara, can I talk to you?"

I barely saw her around anymore and was surprised at the fear in her eyes. I was chewing on a BLT, and a piece of lettuce lodged itself in my throat, making me cough.

"Why would she want to talk to you, Sarah?" Veronica responded on my behalf as Nick thumped my back.

"It's none of your damn business, Veronica." Sarah glared at her, but I could see that the corners of her mouth were twitching nervously.

"Well, whatever you need to say, say it in front of all of us." Veronica crossed her arms over her chest, leaning back in her chair. Something about her broad shoulders, her very angularity, made her seem physically powerful when she adopted this pose. Nick and Alexa exchanged glances. Halle continued eating her yogurt. She was giggling with Hunter about something. Jimmy whispered something to Janicza, making her laugh so hard she almost spit out her milk.

"What's up, Sarah?" Nick smiled that winning smile that always seemed to defuse any tension. He was often, I realized, mitigating any disharmony with his charm. It was the role he frequently played between Halle and Veronica when they were annoyed with one another, a near-daily occurrence.

Sarah glanced around the table, all of us looking back at her in anticipation. Janicza and Jimmy were still giggling.

Ariel didn't even meet Sarah's eyes. They had once been best friends.

"I didn't do it. You must have seen it, Tara. I saw the dog, and I swerved around it. I didn't hit it. I don't know who did, but it wasn't me."

"Do you have any eyewitnesses?" Veronica retorted.

"I'm talking to Tara." She looked at me, her eyes pleading. "Tara, please. You were there. Didn't you see? I didn't do it. I'm sorry, Halle, that your dog died"—she turned to Halle now— "but I didn't do it."

I looked at Veronica, wondering what I should say. I had never really liked Sarah. She drove around in a red Porsche and laughed far too loudly. We had been on swim team together since the seventh grade, but she had never once spoken to me directly. In fact, a few times, I had seen her pointing at me and whispering and giggling with Ariel. But in this moment, she looked just as vulnerable as that dog she had hit.

"Nick saw it, Sarah. You can say whatever you want, but we have an eyewitness account." Veronica turned to Nick.

Alexa's eyes met mine for a moment before she turned to look at Nick. She was chewing on her bottom lip.

"Yeah." Nick nodded, looking right at Sarah.

"It's not true."

"But it is. And you're not convincing any of us, okay? Time for you to leave now." Veronica reached for the can of diet Coke before her, but before she could grab it, Sarah whacked it off the table, causing it to crash on the floor with a loud clatter, fizzy liquid spilling at our feet. We all jumped at the violence of it. But Sarah had decided to make me a target, pointing a long finger in my face, her face contorted.

"You think you're one of them now, but you're not. They'll drop you just the way they dropped me," she said. There was silence for a moment, and it was Halle who broke it, her voice stern.

"I didn't want to do this, Sarah, but you've really brought it on yourself. Why don't you tell Tara what you used to say about her in middle school before you continue to offer such persuasive counsel?"

Everyone was quiet, and my heart began to race. What *did* Sarah Hoffstedt say about me in middle school? I looked at Halle, wondering why she would put me in such an uncomfortable position, but her eyes were still on Sarah.

"That was a long time ago, Halle. Leave it alone."

"Tell her."

"No."

"Halle, whatever, it was a long time ago. It's not important," Nick said.

But Halle ignored Nick. "Own up, Sarah. You said some really upsetting things about one of my *friends*." She placed an emphasis on that word, but something about this confrontation didn't make me feel like I was Halle's friend. It didn't feel like it had anything to do with me, actually. I felt like I was getting dragged into something messy and gross between Halle and Sarah.

Now it was Halle crossing her arms across her chest, the judge before whom Sarah would have to plead her case. But Sarah just stood there, a scowl on her face.

"Fine. Then I'll tell her." Halle looked at me as the others sat silent and still around her. "She used to say that you're a hairy-legged ape."

I could feel the heat rising to my face, while the rest of my body went cold. I was too horrified to make eye contact with anyone at the table, but they were all quiet, waiting for a reaction from me.

It was true—I had hairy legs. I was Indian, after all, and on the stupid swim team we weren't allowed to shave our legs till the day of a meet. For years, I hid in a corner of the locker room while changing, hoping that the blond-haired girls with an indistinguishable coat of down on their legs wouldn't notice, but of course they did. We all had to get in the pool together every day. The entire season, I wore long pants to school, even when it was ninety degrees outside. I had almost considered not trying out for swim team my freshman year just for this reason, but Coach Lyndskey had convinced me that they needed strong swimmers. I never told her the reason for my hesitation, but I suspected she knew. Clearly, everyone else did. Or if they hadn't before, they certainly did now.

I sat there, stunned, realizing that I wasn't like Halle or Veronica or Nick. I wasn't immune to humiliation. And it was Halle, of all people, who had put me in this position. She was supposed to be my friend. Why was she doing this?

I was different—that part hadn't changed. And at that very moment, I felt acutely as though I didn't belong. But then I remembered Nick's words. *Pretend*, he had said to me that night at Halle's party. Pretend you belong. Pretend there's nothing wrong with you. Pretend that it's not about you at all. After all, they were all still sitting at this table, with *me*, weren't they? And not with Sarah Hoffstedt. And so what if they did know? So fucking what?

I turned to Sarah. "I might be hairy, but you're a racist bitch, Sarah. No one cares about you. I can shave my legs, but there's nothing you can do about the fact that everyone can see right through you. They can see what a terrible person you are." I saw the tears in Sarah's eyes, but I kept going. "What does it feel like to have no friends? To have nobody care about you? It must be really, really sad." I frowned, pushing out my lower lip. I heard Ariel snicker, and Sarah turned to look at her, the tears streaming down her face now. She opened her mouth to say something, but then decided against it. Slowly, she turned and skulked away.

The silence around us was deafening. No one moved or spoke, and then Janicza and Ariel began to whistle and clap, and then the entire table joined them, hooting and laughing.

"And don't you dare say anything about one of my friends ever again!" Veronica yelled after her.

I didn't laugh. Underneath the table, my hands were shaking, and only Alexa saw. She reached for one of them and looked at me. We exchanged glances, her eyes asking me, *"Where the* hell *did that come from?*" I didn't have an answer. It was a side of myself I hadn't seen before. I had never in my life been so cruel to anyone.

I turned to look at Halle, who was smiling at me, a look of contentment in her eyes. She nodded at me. Was it a nod of approval? Had I passed whatever test she had subjected me to? I didn't know, but I couldn't help but wonder if she had enjoyed this—putting me in an awkward situation, watching me extricate myself. Maybe Sarah was right. Maybe they *would* drop me one day, just the way they had dropped her. I wasn't one of them. I had let my guard down for a moment, gotten comfortable, allowed myself to believe that everything was different now.

FIFTEEN

I was reaching for my calculus textbook when I saw the note in my bag. I quickly pulled it into my lap and unfolded it. The handwriting was my mother's.

"I know we haven't been getting along lately," it said. "I miss you and want to talk to you more about this. I've booked my ticket for late October. I want to really enjoy the next few weeks together, if that's possible. Just know that wherever I am, whatever I decide to do, I still love you, okay?" She signed it "Mom" with hearts around the name. My heart sank. I crumpled the note and tossed it back into my bag. It had been a whole month since my mother announced she was leaving, and I was still hoping that it would all go away, that I would come home one day and she would tell me she had changed her mind and we'd laugh about what a silly idea the whole thing was to begin with.

I had been spending most of my time outside the house,

heading to Veronica's after swim practice so we could do our homework together. The Hartwickes lived walking distance from our house, but on a much nicer street, a block away from the Riverside Yacht Club. Their home was an old Victorian with a wraparound porch and fireplaces in practically every room. Most nights, I ate dinner with her family. Mr. and Mrs. Hartwicke liked me, and Veronica's little brother, Tim, always insisted on sitting next to me at the dining table. "He's got a little bit of a crush on you," Mrs. Hartwicke told me.

That night, I arrived home late after dinner at the Hartwickes' and quietly slipped in through the back door, hoping I wouldn't run into anyone. I could hear my parents in the kitchen, arguing again. I stopped in the hallway to listen.

"What about Tara?" my father was pleading. "What do you think this is going to do to her? She's sixteen years old. This is going to have an impact on her for the rest of her life. It'll change her, don't you understand that, Jennifer?"

"Tara's a big girl. She can handle it. It's just a few months, Sudeep! I was on my own my whole life."

"And look what it's done to you!"

"I'm trying to *fix* what's wrong with me, Sudeep. I'm trying to *heal*."

"By joining a cult?"

"It's *not* a cult!"

"It's for six months, Jennifer! That's practically the entire school year. You're missing out on one of the most important years of her life! Forget about me, think of your daughter!"

"I need to think about *me*, Sudeep. There's no way I can be a good mother to her if I don't take care of myself."

"All you've ever done is think about you! You're not a good mother to begin with!" my father yelled.

"Maybe you can give up your dreams, but I can't! I want to show Tara that she can do whatever she wants! That she can have the life she chooses, and that she doesn't have to settle."

"So all of this, this has been settling for you? The past seventeen and a half years, it's all settling?"

"We're not happy, Sudeep! Can't you see it? None of us are happy."

"But we were once. Don't you remember?" my father asked. I could hear the hurt in his voice.

"That was a long time ago," my mother said softly.

I walked to my room and locked the door, my heart racing. Was it true that none of us were happy? I had never heard my mother actually articulate this point before, and it scared me. Saying it made it real. *We are an unhappy family.*

Just that week, we had started reading *Anna Karenina* in AP English, and I thought about the opening line: "All happy families are alike; each unhappy family is unhappy in its own way." What kind of unhappy family were we? Could we ever be happy again?

I made a decision. Not something that would solve our problems or make us happy. That part I wasn't capable of. But blame was something I could do.

Alone, in the dark of my room, my outrage grew, in the

way that dark and lonely spaces incubate all intense feelings. But I didn't realize that night just how lonely I was, even as I put on my earphones and blasted the Pixies, looking out my window to see if I could identify that one particular star—the sun of another Earth far, far away. I wondered what that other me was doing right at this moment. I wished I could speak to her, wished I could tell her everything. She was the only one out there who would understand any of this. The only person in the entire universe who could understand me.

That was the night I decided to stop speaking to my mother.

SIXTEEN

On Tuesday, October 27, 2015, at 12:14 PM, Megan
Stevens <meganstevens@gmail.com> wrote:

Hey, Tara—

Sorry it's been so long. Argentina is fantastic! The
food, the sights, the boys!!! It's beautiful out here,
seriously you need to come visit. It took me a while to
settle in, everything here is so different. I'm living in a
neighborhood called Palermo Soho. My host family is
great. My host father, Ernesto, cooks steak every night
for dinner, and my host mother, Clara, insists that I drink
wine with her every evening! The apartment I live in
is kind of small, but I have my own room, and there's
a balcony overlooking the street below. Ernesto and
Clara are artists. They don't have kids of their own and

they say they don't plan on having any, but they love American teenagers. They say they host kids from all over the world to "open minds," but I think they also do it to supplement some sort of trust fund they live off of.

This Terra Nova stuff is pretty crazy, huh? There's practically no other news here. That woman from the photo is giving an interview tomorrow, did you hear? I wish I were home so I could watch it with you.

Anyway, how are you? How is junior year going? Is Treem still completely insane?!? I get e-mails from her all the time, telling me to be safe, sending me articles about Argentina. I think she's one of those people who's never been anywhere outside of Connecticut. She sends me e-mails like I'm living in a war zone. What an idiot.

I really miss you. I miss my family too. I guess I'm homesick. Spanish is really hard to follow, and the girls here are kind of bitchy. It's been hard to actually meet people and make friends. I guess it's the same everywhere.

I wanted you to know I'm coming back for second semester! Yay! I hadn't planned on it, but now that I think about it, a whole year away is a lot, and besides, after senior year, I'll be going away again. I've also gained, like, ten pounds from eating a ton of dulce de leche and empanadas. They serve them from carts outside my school, and they're AMAZING. But can't get into my bikini anymore, so I'm going to have to go on a steak diet or something!!!

Anyway, write back! And seriously, think about coming. Chau!

Megs

I thought about responding, but I couldn't. I felt a sinking feeling in the pit of my stomach at the realization that I didn't want Meg to return next semester. So much had happened in the past couple of weeks—a planet had appeared in the sky, a radio signal had been detected. Nick Osterman had given me a ride to a party. My mother had announced that she was going to California for six months; my father had despaired. There was school and life, swim practice and hanging out at Veronica's house.

It always started small. A couple of cancer cells, the collapse of a bee hive. Nothing—not war or disappointment or hate or love—really happens in a snap, the way people sometimes think it does. It happens more slowly than that, over days and months and sometimes years, a thread undone here, a small tear there, until one day, the effects of time are so obvious that no one can ignore them.

Meg had missed all of it, everything important, everything petty, the entire universe of my new life. I hoped, for her sake, that she changed her mind and stayed in Argentina through the year, because I wouldn't know what to say to her if I saw her now. She didn't fit into my new life, she wasn't a part of it, and everything was always moving forward; after all, the Earth rotated in the same direction every day, but there was no going back.

Another thought crossed my mind, and I knew it to be a rationalization for what I was about to do: I knew why Meg had waited an entire two months before e-mailing me. She had gone to Argentina carrying the hope that a year in Buenos Aires would transform her into someone who wouldn't need to send me e-mails anymore. I thought about how coolly she had told me about spending the year abroad, about the offhand tone in her voice when she said that things would be different between us from now on. She thought something better awaited her, or rather, that she would become better by being away from me. But that hadn't happened, and so I closed my laptop, telling myself that I could always respond later, telling myself that we were no different. Telling myself that if it were Meg in my place, she would have done the same.

"Want to go to Pizza Post for dinner? Go shower. I'll wait for you."

Halle tilted her head to the side, her face transforming into a pouty plea. I was dumbfounded to find her waiting for me after swim practice in the locker room. I hung out with her every day in a group, but I had never spent time with her alone.

"Okay." I nodded at her before heading to the showers.

"I'm so glad someone finally has the same schedule as me . . . you know . . . aside from Nick. Veronica doesn't do sports— like school sports. She's an equestrian, and Alexa . . . well, you know Alexa." This was almost always how Alexa's eating disorder was referred to, but everyone in the group knew about it. We were sitting in a booth at Pizza Post, our hair wet, our gym bags nestled beside us like small, loyal creatures.

The TV was on—a news report about one of the organizations that had formed in the aftermath of Terra Nova. This one was in Nevada.

"Ugh, such weirdos," Halle said as she looked at a group of people in white shirts and black slacks being interviewed. "They even have uniforms."

"If Washington continues to thumb their noses at us, we need to defend ourselves from their blatant abuses," one of them said. "We're demanding a ratification of the Constitution. The people of New Terra Novia have a right to their own lands and their own sovereignty. We have a right to secede from the Union."

"God, and we used to think Texas was full of secession-minded crazies," Halle said. "These people . . . they're such total morons. I mean, what do you think it would take to just pack up your bags and join one of these cults?" Then she lowered her voice as though she was thinking about something. "I mean, how damaged would you have to be abandon your family?" she asked.

I thought about the note my mother had left in my bag and pretended I was still listening to the news report. Before I stopped talking to my mother, she told me about the organization she was joining. It was called Church of the New Earth and had been formed just after the discovery of Terra Nova.

"It's just a community of seekers—young and old. They're

from all over the country, all over the world, really. And they all have questions about Terra Nova. They're all trying to resolve something in their lives. I feel so lucky to be living in this time of spiritual awakening," she said, just before I left the room.

Later that day, I did an Internet search on the organization. The people photographed for the website looked unusually cheerful and tan and appeared to spend their hours painting and hiking through the Santa Monica Mountains. I hadn't decided yet whether it was a cult or not. All I knew was that the fact they weren't in uniforms had given me a sense of relief, but now I was beginning to wonder if I was deluding myself about who or what they really were.

"Hey, I was wondering . . . what are you reading right now?" Halle changed the subject.

"In class, you mean? *Anna Karenina.*"

"No, I mean, that thing you do." Halle giggled.

"What thing?" I asked.

"You're always sitting in class reading a novel under your desk, on your lap—I've seen you doing it for years. How do you even know what's going on when teachers call on you? You always have an answer." I had no idea that anyone else knew I did this. I had tried to be discreet, but Halle had noticed. Still, she was wrong on one count.

"Not always. Sometimes I have no idea what the class discussion is about."

"You're not missing out. But I've always wondered . . . why do you think you do that? Read all through class?"

I shrugged. "I just like to read, I guess."

Halle squinted at me. "No, that's not it," she said. And she was right. It wasn't. Books were like a shield. They protected me, kept me safely invisible. When I had a book in my hand, people left me alone. It was as though I could observe them at my own discretion, at a distance, but they couldn't see me. But I didn't say this to her.

"I mean, it's not like it's affected my grades or anything . . ."

She laughed now. "Yeah, that part I know. Treem keeps rubbing it in my face. The fact that you have the highest GPA in our class."

"Me? She told me *you* had the highest GPA in our class."

"Yeah, well, Treem's a moron." Halle smiled.

"That's putting it lightly . . . I'm reading *Cat's Cradle*," I told her.

"Isn't that on the AP English syllabus for later this semester?"

"Yeah, but sometimes I feel like class discussions ruin books for me. So I read them myself first."

Halle grinned at me. "You're amazing, Krishnan," she said. "And I love *Cat's Cradle*. My parents are like a karass. No, wait . . . a duprass. They're attached at the hip—they're, like, in Venice right now. What are your parents like?"

I hesitated, unsure of what I could say. "I don't know . . . They're just . . . parents, I guess," I said, shifting uncomfortably in my seat. I thought about that day in the student center when Halle had mentioned my hairy legs, the way she was with Sarah Hoffstedt. There were things I would never divulge to

Halle, that I would never say to her. I still didn't trust her—or anyone in that crowd, for that matter.

"Yeah. I know what you mean," she responded, looking away before she pulled her gym bag into her arms and rummaged through it. I wondered in that moment if she was hiding behind a shield too.

For the next couple of weeks, I walked around with a hollow in the pit of my stomach. I watched my mother make piles of things she was going to take to California. I watched her pack.

"Hey, wanna come keep me company?" she called from her bedroom whenever she saw me in the hallway. I ignored her, still believing that maybe it would all just go away. In the mornings, I left home without saying goodbye, and when I came home late, sometimes she was waiting up for me, a sad smile on her face.

"Looks like you're having fun with your new friends," she'd say, or "I missed you today. How was school?" I looked at her blankly before I went to my room and fumed at her.

"She's delusional, Dad. You have to stop her," I said to my father, but he just shook his head.

"I'm trying everything I can, Tara," he told me. There was a sadness in his eyes I had never seen before.

And then a couple of days before Halloween, I realized that *I* was the one who was delusional. My mother had made up her mind. She was leaving to go to California.

The day of my mother's flight, I intentionally made plans to go to Nick's house after school to work on our egg-drop project. By now, late October leaves were accumulating on sidewalks, patchwork pieces of red and orange waiting to be swept away by the wind.

My mother had booked her ticket for California for the day before Halloween, and it made me think about how carefully (and yet poorly) she would sew all my Halloween costumes when I was little, how we would spend weeks deciding what candy we were gong to distribute, how we would open up fun-size packs of M&M'S and she would eat all the reds and browns and I would eat the oranges and greens. We would split the blues and yellows.

I stopped at home to drop off my books, knowing that I would run into my mother, intending to behave as though I didn't care. The kitchen lights were on when I arrived, and she was standing over the counter, an apron around her waist, her hair tied in a loose bun on top of her head. She was making dinner.

"It's a red-eye. I don't have to leave home till about nine. I thought we'd have a last meal together before I take off. Tara . . . please talk to me," she said, and when I heard her voice crack, I broke, but only slightly.

"I can't," I told her, coolly. "I have to go to Nick's. We're working on a project together for AP physics."

She didn't argue. She was wearing a red dress, a dress I had seen her wear only once before, years ago when we lived in New York.

"I know we've never been away from each other for more than a day," she said.

"I don't want to talk about it," I cut her off.

"I just need you to know that I'll miss you and love you. I wish there were another way, but I have to . . ."

"You *wish* there were another way?" I yelled. "There is another way. It involves you staying home!"

"I think I used to dance to escape it all. I loved that feeling of dancing without abandon, no thoughts in my head except where my feet were, the line of my body. But now I can't stop thinking . . . about all the possibilities, everything that happened, everything that could have happened. I don't know how to make it stop. Lately I wonder if I spent all these years trying not to think about the past, trying not to look back. I need to . . . unpack everything that's happened to me over the course of my life," she said. "And I need to do that alone." The way she looked at me, I knew I wasn't going to change her mind.

I felt something for her then, some precursor to the longing for her that I knew would beset me when she left. I wanted her to be my mother again, for just a minute. I sat down on the counter before her and picked at the slivers of radish and carrot she was chopping for a salad.

"I can't stay for long. I should head out in half an hour or so."

She nodded. "How was swim practice?"

"Good. Swimming always makes me feel better," I lied. Usually I did feel at home in a pool. The familiar humidified scent of chlorine, the cool splash of water underneath my arms, the echo of whistles and voices in the distance—there was nothing like it. But today, it wasn't enough. Nothing was enough to make me feel better today.

"I birthed you in a pool, you know. Because you're a Pisces."

"I don't know what that means."

"It means you're a sensitive soul. An old soul," she said, looking at me with tears in her eyes. "I'm sorry I'm going to miss your birthday this year," she added.

I looked away. "What else does it mean?" I asked.

"It's not just your sun in Pisces, but your Venus and your Mercury too. It makes your Mercury debilitated."

"What does that mean?" I asked, not that I cared about my Piscean Venus or my debilitated Mercury. I felt debilitated as it was without the planets mocking me. I just wanted to talk to my mother again. It would be nearly the end of the school year the next time I saw her. I would be a year older. Green leaves would be sprouting on trees.

"It means that you sometimes struggle to express yourself, to say the things you really want to say," she said. "But I suppose we all do."

I had been wondering more and more how my parents had ever ended up together. My father lived in a world of questions and answers. Obstacles could be scaled. Problems could be unpacked. My mother was different. She lived in a world of spirits and tarot cards, moons and suns and Piscean debilitations. It wasn't entirely a surprise that she was capable of leaving home because of the discovery of a planet in a distant solar system.

"And your moon, it's in the twelfth house," she added. By now, the tears were streaming down her face. "It means you feel separate from me, always at a distance."

This, I wanted to disagree with, and vehemently. I had never felt separate from her till now, and the feeling ripped through me, searing me in half.

I couldn't tell her how much I missed her and loved her, how badly I wanted her to stay. If she said no, if she refused to stay, I knew I would never recover from the rejection of it, of my own mother telling me she had better things to do than be with me. And so I left it alone, uncertain of what untangling that ball of yarn would bring.

She was right that I was sensitive. It didn't have anything to do with houses or planets or moons. It was because my mother didn't seem to want to be my mother anymore. And what could I say to her about that on the eve of her departure? It was a moment where I felt terrified of what the stars could reveal if I looked too closely at them.

SEVENTEEN

I stopped on the curb a block away from Nick's house so I could lean against an old sycamore tree and cry. The days were getting shorter now, and it was almost dark. I had always hated daylight savings, especially in the fall, when the days felt trimmed in half and there was less time to actually do things, but somehow more time to think about all the things you had done wrong.

Was there anything I could have done to make her stay? If I had been nicer to her, instead of not speaking to her after she announced that she was leaving, would she have changed her mind? But it was the last question, the one that I had to arrive at slowly, that made me cry the hardest, the kind of crying that reverberates through your entire body. *Why didn't my mother love me enough to stay?*

I took a deep breath, trying to calm myself. What would the

Other Tara do? I asked myself. What would she tell me to do? I imagined her as just like me, but better in almost every way. Smarter, wiser, all-knowing. *Pull it together*, she would maybe say. *You just need to get through today, okay? Go to Nick's, work on your project, get through this evening. There's nothing you can do to change your mother's mind.* I wiped my tears away with my hand.

I had to pull it together. There was no one I could talk to about what was going on with my family. I couldn't imagine sitting down with Nick and Halle and telling them that Terra Nova had somehow forced my mother to pack her bags and move to California. I thought about what Halle had said that day at Pizza Post. *How damaged would you have to be to leave your family?* I didn't even want to imagine what they might think of me if they knew.

I remembered my father's words to my mother about me when they were arguing: "This is going to have an impact on her for the rest of her life. It'll change her." It made me wonder if a seed of impending struggle had been planted within me— just as it had been planted in my mother. Would it grow and grow and take half the rest of my life to uproot? Had the damage already been done? Was I going to be fucked up forever, no matter how much things changed on the outside? These were the kinds of thoughts that plagued me in those days. It never occurred to me that I might be worried about all the wrong things.

~

Mrs. Osterman opened the door when I rang the doorbell. Her gray bob was freshly cut, and she was wearing a red cardigan and black slacks.

"Hello, dear. Halle and Nick are already in the kitchen. I put out some snacks for the three of you. An egg-drop competition! Can't believe they still do those kinds of things in school."

I followed her into the kitchen, wondering if she could tell that I had been crying, but she seemed not to notice, or knew better than to say something.

"Look who it is!" she announced to Halle and Nick as we walked into a large country kitchen.

"Tara Krishnan! We missed you." Halle smiled.

"Ta-ra. Do you know what your name means?" Nick asked. I had always loved the way he said my name. "*Hey, Tara.*" "*Ask Tara what she thinks.*" "*Hey, Tara, can you . . .*"

Halle cut him off immediately. "Obviously she knows." They both looked at me from the large wooden table in the center of the room. They were seated next to each other, and I settled into a space across from them on a large bench.

"Yeah. It means 'star,'" I said, pulling my book from my satchel.

"See, she knows," Halle told Nick. "Linda was just telling us that she studied Sanskrit in college," Halle said.

"You did?" I turned to Mrs. Osterman.

"Well, linguistics. Did you know that Veronica's mother was my roommate at Smith?"

"I heard," I told her.

"The two of us . . . we visited India . . . God, probably six times together in our twenties. We trekked through all of Asia the summer after we graduated. Have you ever been to India?"

I shook my head, feeling strangely exposed, even ashamed.

"Well, you must at some point. Most amazing experience of my life! Anyway, I baked some cookies, and there's hummus and muhammara and veggies, and Cokes in the fridge. I'm going to go play tennis with Hester. Nicky, if there's a problem, call your dad."

"Oh, Mrs. Osterman?" I asked.

"Yes, dear?"

"Since you studied linguistics . . . what do you think about these radio broadcasts that are coming out of Terra Nova? About the linguists studying speech patterns?"

But it wasn't what I really wanted to ask her. I wanted to know, what did a normal, regular adult think of Terra Nova? Did she wonder about another version of herself on another planet? "I heard about that!" she exclaimed. "Well, who hasn't? Who could have ever thought their *language*, of all things, would be so similar to ours! You know, Noam Chomsky has this quote about when he was a college student—something about how he thought linguistics was a lot of fun, but after we've done . . . I think he said 'a structural analysis of every language in the world, what's left?' It was assumed there were basically no puzzles."

"This is a serious puzzle," Nick said, reaching for a celery stick and mashing it into the red-pepper dip before him.

"Exactly! I think that's one of the best things about the discovery of Terra Nova. We go about our lives assuming we know essentially everything we need to know, but there's no end to the mystery of the world. It's brought back a feeling of sheer wonder. By the time all of you are my age, well, who knows how much we'll know about these . . . people? Maybe we'll even have a chance to talk to them ourselves."

I looked at Mrs. Osterman now, wishing she were my mother, someone who could feel wonder and excitement without turning her entire life upside down. I didn't even want to think those words, the horrific ones that reverberated through me like a heartbeat since my father had mentioned it during one of my parents' arguments. *My mother's gone and joined a cult.*

"Have fun at tennis, Mom," Nick called out after Mrs. Osterman.

"Have fun . . . dropping eggs, I suppose," Mrs. Osterman tossed over her shoulder.

"Screw that," Nick whispered once she was out of earshot. "It's not due till next week, and Adam Schulman did it last year and he said to just pack an egg in peanuts and tie a parachute on and it should be fine."

"Peanuts?" Halle asked.

"Yeah, like packing peanuts."

I shrugged. "That's what I was going to suggest. Or, like, puffed rice. Or grapes."

"See? Tara knows what's up. Anyway, my dad just bought a telescope, and you can see Terra Nova's sun. Wanna look?" he asked.

Halle glanced at me. "Sure." I shrugged.

We followed Nick to the deck behind his house. The sky was dark now, an endless black tarp with a million tears of light.

"Fancy telescope," I said, inspecting the shiny contraption before us.

"It's all set. It's pointed right at Terra Nova's sun. My dad looks at it, like, every night when he comes home from work. And he's been reading all this poetry all of a sudden."

Halle raised an eyebrow at him, and I could feel a frown forming across my face as I tried to discern the correlation myself.

Nick sighed. "He was an English major in college. Says he wanted to become a poet, but then he had to make money. Now he's all wistful that two paths diverged and all that."

I nodded. "I know what you mean," I said, but I couldn't bring myself to say any more.

Halle shrugged. "My parents are in Belize right now. I think they couldn't care less about Terra Nova. They're about as terrestrial as it gets."

"Look, you can see it right here," Nick said, showing us an astronomy app on his phone. He held it up to the sky, arrows pointing at the Big Dipper, the Little Dipper, Sirius, and Terra Nova's sun—Pinder-17, named after the scientist who had discovered it.

"Is that really the space station?" I asked, pointing to a smaller light on Nick's app.

"Yeah, pretty cool, isn't it?"

"You guys look. I'm going to go get a snack," Halle said.

I glanced at Nick, and he gestured to the telescope. "Go ahead," he said. I put my hand on the side of it, my face close to the lens. "Do you see it?" Nick whispered.

"Why are you whispering?" I whispered back, and we both began to laugh. He placed his hand on the small of my back then. "See it? It's right there," he said, looking into his phone. His face was two inches from mine, but neither of us turned.

"Oh yeah. It's pretty big. I mean, it's just as big as any other star, maybe even . . . bigger. So we knew that the sun was there, just not Terra Nova? Because the light of the sun was obscuring the planet?" I could feel Nick's thumb as it trailed along the waistline of my jeans.

"Yeah, we discovered the star a while ago, but it's hard to see planets because they're so small, and the light of the stars makes them difficult to see. They get lost in the glare, so astronomers look for a transit—that's, like, when the light of the sun dims by a fraction when a planet passes it." He was still whispering, and I could feel a trail of goose bumps on my back as he latched his finger into my belt loop. My heart was racing, and I couldn't move for fear of what might happen if I did.

"But it was out there all along."

"Yeah. We were bound to discover it sooner or later."

"Do you still think there's a different version of us out there?" I asked.

He was quiet for a moment. "Another version of you and me standing on a deck on Terra Nova, looking for Earth . . ." he mused.

Inside the house, the TV clicked on, authoritative voices talking about something that couldn't nearly be as important as this moment.

"I like that we're on the same team together," he said. "Here, I mean. Maybe on Terra Nova too."

"Yeah. Me too."

"Remember when we were the Obamas?"

At this, I burst out laughing, moving away from the telescope to look at him. He was grinning at me.

"You think we might have been the Obamas on Terra Nova? Honestly, I thought it was super racist that I was forced to play Michelle."

"You were *not* forced to," Nick laughed. His hand was resting on my waist now.

"I totally was! Mrs. Patterson made me, that horrible racist wench. You just don't remember."

"No. *You* just don't remember. Patterson had nothing to do with it. You were Michelle because I asked you to be."

I thought about it a moment and realized it was true. He *had* asked me. I had forgotten that part. "Why'd you ask me?"

He shrugged. "I guess I had a crush on you."

I opened my mouth to say something, but nothing came out. We stood there for a moment, under an umbrella of stars, an eternity of possibilities just above us. All I could think to do was reach my hand toward him. It came to rest on his chest, and his breath quickened.

"I . . ."

"Guys, you have to come in. The interview's on . . ." announced Halle from the door.

I jumped, my mouth still ajar, my hand recoiling from the shock of Halle's words.

"Oh hey, Halle," I said. My voice was a little too shrill, but when I looked at her, she seemed unperturbed by either the story, whatever it was, or by the fact that Nick and I were standing inches from one another in the dark.

"What interview?" Nick asked, following her in.

"You know, that Japanese lady from the picture."

They were both halfway across the kitchen by the time I turned to join them.

I stopped at the threshold of the doorway and looked back to that spot. The spot where Nick Osterman had confessed to me that he once had a crush on me. *Had*, I reminded myself, before I followed them both to the living room, where the TV was blaring, another wave of breaking news. Halle and Nick settled on the couch together, in front of the TV. I hesitated a moment before I sank into a chair off to the side.

It was her, the lady from the bitmap image. MICHIKO NATORI, read the banner beneath her face.

"And when was it that you identified yourself in the image distributed by NASA?"

"My friends forwarded me the picture. E-mail after e-mail . . . text after text . . . friends and family asking, 'What are you doing on Terra Nova?' It was like a joke, but it's not funny. She looks exactly like me, but she's not me."

"And what do you make of that?" the reporter asked as the camera panned out. AN EDWARD COPELAND EXCLUSIVE INTERVIEW, read the banner across the screen.

"That's the guy who cried on the air," I said, thinking about how his tears had elicited disdain from my father.

"Shhhhh . . . I want to listen," Halle said, her voice a little too harsh.

"I don't know what to make of it," Michiko Natori told him. "What would you think if it was your face? If it was you? What if you knew for certain there was another you out there? Someone who wore a different coat this morning? Someone who chose a different route to take to work? Or maybe even bigger things . . . a different wife? A different career?"

"I don't know what I would think of it." Edward Copeland shook his head. "I think it would . . . make me go a little crazy," he said.

But I already knew how I felt about another me on Terra Nova. Something about it was comforting. And yet that question *what if?* was like a virus. A small infection—so negligible that initially, I had ignored it, while all around, it had already become a global epidemic. And of course, I had always asked myself questions like that: *What if we had stayed in New York? What if I hadn't walked down Hillside Road that day? What if I had stayed home instead of going to the restaurant the night Veronica was dining there?* But now there were bigger questions. *What if there was a version of me on Terra Nova who was with a version of Nick? What if Nick was my boyfriend instead of Halle's?* I felt a mild euphoria as I thought of it.

We watched the rest of the report in silence. I thought about my father driving my mother to the airport. I thought about how she would check in her luggage, take off her shoes at security, collect them on the other side of the X-ray machine. At eleven fifteen, she would board a flight. JFK → LAX. She would land tomorrow morning in another world. A world of sun and fake tans and people who hike through the Santa Monica Mountains.

And here I was, in Nick Osterman's living room, my eyes glued to the TV, Halle and Nick in my peripheral vision, his arm around her shoulders, hers resting on his leg. I alternated between excitement and frustration, trying not to think about what could be. But mostly, I tried not to think about what he had said to me, what I felt for him, or the fact that he didn't look my way again for the rest of the evening.

EIGHTEEN

"A road trip, that's what we need!" Halle announced. We were sitting in her BMW SUV, Alexa and me in the back, Veronica in the passenger seat. It was a Friday afternoon in mid-November, and by now, the cold had set in. Trees arched their skeletal branches into the street, begging for a taste of light. Instead, they got rain and haze. There was no snow yet, but the skies hinted at it, that orange early evening glow, and so I was prepared, wearing a green coat, white mittens, and a white beanie.

"I detest road trips," Veronica intoned. "Everyone fights, people get sick. Sometimes people die."

Alexa and I burst out laughing. "Why would anyone die?" I asked.

Veronica shrugged. "Seriously, it's the premise of, like, every horror movie. Camping is even worse. Are you guys campers?"

"I'm Indian. We don't camp. My dad says in India camping is poverty. Tents, malarial swamps, shitting by the side of the road." We were cracking up now.

Halle had insisted on having dinner together tonight. Her parents were out of town again, this time in Italy. It was becoming clearer and clearer to me that Halle's extended family was the staff at her estate—a housekeeper, a butler, a gardener, her father's driver. I had never, until I got to know her, seen her as someone who might be lonely, but now I wondered if spending all that time alone was what had made her so precocious.

"You guys, seriously. I don't mean, like, now, but maybe in the spring. We could drive up to the Cape, or my parents have a house in Nantucket. We could spend a weekend there. What say, Tara?" She turned for a minute to look at me, flicking a strand of her hair out of her eyes. She was dressed in an ivory Burberry coat and looked like the quintessential New Englander with a matching Burberry scarf around her neck.

"So it would be, what, us and Nick? Do you want to invite Jimmy or Hunter?"

"No Nick, no Jimmy, no Hunter. No boys allowed."

"Jimmy's going to be disappointed. He might show up in Nantucket and try to roofie Tara." Veronica turned and mock-frowned at Alexa and me.

"Yuck! Don't ever use the words 'Jimmy' and 'roofie' in the same sentence."

"You haven't noticed that he's all over you, like, all the time?" Veronica asked.

"Tara's got a lot of admirers," Halle said in a deadpan voice.

"Don't be jealous, V. Hunter still loves you. He told me he'll wait for you till the end of the Earth. Hey, maybe on Terra Nova, you're in love with him?" she teased.

I saw a flash of anger in Veronica's eyes, but she hid her emotions well. "I don't date morons."

"He's a handsome guy," Halle pressed. "So you won't date morons, or handsome guys, or . . ."

I could see Veronica about to say something, but it was Alexa who cut Halle off.

"That's mean," she said. "You're all lucky to have admirers."

"Aaaawww, poor Alexa feels left out. You can have Hunter if you want." Halle looked at her. "I'm sure Veronica'll let you have him. He's not her type."

"Seriously, you can have Jimmy," I told her to diffuse the tension.

"Take Nick too, while we're at it," Halle said.

"Whatever, Nick completely doesn't fall into that category," I said to Halle, but even as the words came out, I sensed that they touched a nerve in her, and I wondered if I had unconsciously sought to do this. I had noticed that she and Nick were spending less time together, and Halle had been insisting on "girl time" regularly since the day of our egg-drop preparations. Sometimes Nick would call while we were all together, and Halle would simply ignore her phone.

I would say I tried not to think about this too much, but the truth was, it was all I ever thought about, curiosity about their relationship growing within me like an incorrigible weed. This was only compounded by the other questions I pondered day and night: Had Halle heard us talking on the deck that evening? Did she know what Nick had said to me? Did she care? Did it even matter? *Had* was the word he had used. I *had* a crush on you. Before Halle. And then I would feel that twinge of disappointment in the pit of my stomach. Halle Lightfoot: 500,000, Tara Krishnan: 0. I knew you weren't supposed to feel this way about your friends, but I did.

Most of the time, I liked Halle. When we were hanging out or grabbing pizza or talking about books. But then I'd return home and start to resent her again. She was so perfect, it was kind of infuriating. She still always knew the right thing to say. She was still a stellar student and star of the track team. She still came to school every day looking as though she had just walked off a runway. And Nick was still in love with her, even if I wasn't certain she felt the same way.

"Do you want to invite Nick for dinner?" Veronica pressed Halle. "I could call him right now," she said, reaching for her phone.

Halle reached for her wrist to stop her, but on her face was a smile. "No," she said firmly. "Just us." Then her tone softened. "Can we, like, pick a place for dinner and then talk? I'm starving."

"It's five o'clock, Halls."

"I'm up for an early bird special. I just ran eight miles. Can we go get Indian food?"

"The restaurant isn't open for another hour," I told her. I didn't want to go to the restaurant with Halle, Veronica, and Alexa. I didn't want to run into my father, didn't want to witness the awkward tension of him waiting on our table, or worse, Halle leaving behind a tip for him.

"Really?" her eyes widened. "Well . . . can't you maybe call in favors or something? I mean, I guess we could do something else, but . . . I would, like, *love* Indian food right now, and you would be my hero."

I hesitated for a moment, but Halle continued to smile like she wasn't asking. "I guess. Okay, let's head over. Amit will let us in."

"Who's Amit?"

"He works at the restaurant. They're probably prepping right now. We can have them make us something."

"Wait, that really cute guy?" Halle asked. "He's, like . . . a sophomore in college?"

"Yeah . . . he's the one."

"He's super tasty," Halle said, reminding me how much I hated that expression.

Amit unlocked the door for us, looking frazzled and annoyed. "You know we're not open yet, right?" The radio was blasting loud gangsta rap.

I shrugged. "We were hungry," I said, adopting that same indifference to other people I had seen in Halle and Veronica at times.

"Okay, just go sit over there," he said to us like we were a bunch of recalcitrant kindergartners. "I'll see what we have ready. Your dad's not here yet."

"Could you maybe bring us some of those really delicious lassis?" Halle looked at Amit wide-eyed, a smile on her face. "They're my favorite."

Amit looked back at her, disarmed by her charm. "Sweet, plain, or mango?" he asked.

"What do you think? I think maybe mango? I'm Halle, by the way."

"Amit." He smiled, reaching for her extended hand. "Mango's my favorite," he said with a smile that made me cringe.

"Mango for everyone then, I guess," Halle told him.

"I'll do a plain," said Alexa.

Amit turned down the radio. "Oh . . . don't tell your dad, okay? We were just . . . prepping."

We sat down at a corner table by the window, and Halle sighed, looking nervously at her phone.

"What?" Veronica impatiently remarked, spreading mint chutney on a papad.

"Hypothetically speaking . . . it's normal to kind of get bored after a while in a relationship, right?"

"Are you saying you're bored?" Veronica asked.

"It's just that . . . Nick is so . . . happy all the time," Halle said.

"He's a happy guy," Veronica said.

"And why wouldn't he be? He's cute and smart and president of the student council and a star soccer player and everyone likes him . . ." I cut myself off, realizing that I was getting weird.

"You're exactly right, Tara. Everyone does like him." Then she looked around at us and shrugged. "It's like that story with Socrates and Plato . . ."

"Do tell." Veronica's eyes widened, and she mockingly leaned her chin on her fist.

Halle rolled her eyes. "Plato asks Socrates, 'What's love?' So Socrates sends Plato out into a field of wheat and says, 'Find the best stalk you can, the most magnificent stalk, but you're not allowed to turn back and get one you saw earlier, you have to keep walking forward, and if you find the best stalk, you've found love.' So Plato goes, and he comes back empty-handed. Socrates asks, 'Why didn't you bring anything back?' and Plato says, 'I saw some awesome stalks in the beginning, but then I thought there might be better ones up ahead, so I kept going, but turns out the early stalks were the best ones,' and Socrates says, 'Yup, that's love.'"

"That's your story?" Alexa raised an eyebrow.

"There's more, Alexa," Halle responded with irritation in her tone. "So then Plato asks Socrates, 'What's marriage?' and so Socrates sends Plato out into the woods and says, 'Find the tallest, most beautiful tree, chop it down, and bring it on home.'"

At this point, Amit, carrying plates of food in his hands, interjected. "And then Plato brings back a shitty tree, or at best, it's mediocre, and Socrates says, 'What the hell is this piece of shit?' and Plato says, 'I know it isn't the best tree around, but I didn't want to miss out on having a tree because of what happened in the wheat field, so I just . . . picked one.'" Amit placed a plate of naan and a plate of tandoori chicken before us. "Oh, the samosas are coming. Is four okay?"

"None for me," Alexa told him.

"I'll have yours," Halle said before she turned to Amit. "You know all about Socrates and Plato?"

"Yeah, I'm a philosophy major."

"I didn't know that," I said. "I thought you were, like . . ."

He cut me off. "What? An Indian computer science stereotype? Thanks, racism toward one's own," he said, making me blush.

"No, just . . . I didn't know."

"So what's the moral of the story?" Veronica asked.

"That's irrelevant. It's more of, like . . . a question. How do you know if someone is your stalk? Or your tree? I'm just asking." She turned to Amit with wide eyes again. "I mean, did they teach you that part? In college?"

Amit looked at her for a long moment before he responded. "Not . . . not quite, no. But I know what you mean," he said. He lingered for a minute longer, making the whole thing really uncomfortable.

"Thank you," Halle said, touching his arm. "I thought you'd understand."

Veronica and I exchanged glances, but it was Alexa who broke the weird spell.

"I don't think you should break up with Nick."

"I do," Veronica said. "I mean, if you're not into it anymore."

"So it's nothing he said or did. You're just looking for the perfect stalk of wheat?" I asked.

Halle sighed. "You're right . . . he's great. I just . . . I'm bored out of my mind. I'm allowed to want more, aren't I?"

"Then for God's sake, break it off with him," Veronica moaned.

"No one is talking about breaking up," Halle said. "Besides, I can't. I feel like it might crush him."

"It probably would," Veronica said. "But then he could move on and find someone who wants to be with him, his own stalk of wheat or tree or whatever." I took a deep breath and picked at a samosa, breaking its edges into small crumbly shards, a tiny wisp of hope in my heart growing, wanting to burst out of its cage.

"I just wish someone would take him off my hands. I'd be happy for him, really."

Veronica raised an eyebrow, and Alexa shifted uncomfortably in her chair. Amit was immune to all of this. He simply showed up at our table again, a silver pitcher in his hand.

"Who wants tea?" he asked with a grin on his face.

NINETEEN

MY father never came to the restaurant that night, and when I saw his car parked in the driveway, I assumed something was wrong. When I walked through the front door, I was startled by the dark. There was only one light on, in the kitchen, and my father was sitting in the living room, reading the *Economist* in the thin, jaundiced light that made the entire house look older, more weathered, and cheaper, if that was even possible. John Coltrane's *Blue Train* was playing on the turntable. He didn't hear me coming in, and didn't look up till I switched on a lamp.

"We dropped by the restaurant, my friends and I. You weren't there." I sounded like a peeved adult scolding a child.

"Amit seems to be running things quite efficiently these days. They don't really need me there."

I sat down on the sofa next to him. "Of course they need

you, Dad. Did you even leave the house today?" My father was dressed in shorts and a T-shirt in the middle of winter. He hadn't shaved in days.

"I'm fine, Tara. You don't have to worry about me, okay?" He sounded irritable, as though he wanted to be left alone, as though he wanted to regain a modicum of authority. "Your only job is . . ."

"I know . . . get good grades and act like everything's normal. But it's not. Mom's in California, you're hanging around here, completely depressed, and I . . ."

"Who said I was depressed? I just felt like taking a day off. When do I ever take days off?"

"Never. That's why I'm worried about you."

"I'm the parent here, remember?" he said, but he hadn't really been acting like a parent in the past few weeks. He had been spending a good deal of his time on the living room sofa since my mother's departure, filling the indentation she had left behind.

I looked at my father, at the purple circles under his eyes. He looked tired, exhausted, really. Was it from a lifetime of what my mother thought of as a compromise? Just thinking about it made me sad.

I wondered, as I regarded him, if misfortune was contagious. It wasn't myself that I was worried about, but my father. Seeing him here, alone in a darkened house, made me think of my mother, every year on the anniversary of her parents' death.

"Dad . . . did Mom really . . . join a cult?" For a second,

I thought verbalizing it might make me feel better, but the moment it came out of my mouth, I realized that some things were better left unsaid.

My father slowly shook his head. "It's not a cult, it's some sort of spiritual seminar. She'll be back in a few months, completely refreshed." But he sounded unconvinced, and this only inflamed my anxieties. Now that I had unsuccessfully prodded at the Pandora's box, I couldn't give up.

"Dad . . . do you feel like you compromised too?"

"Whatever made you say that?" he asked, looking at me in shock.

"Because . . . Mom said that we weren't . . . happy . . . that you had both compromised."

My father put down the *Economist* and looked at me. "Your mom . . . she's having a crisis. Almost everyone goes through times like this, when they're uncertain, when they're questioning the decisions they've made."

"Yeah, but most people don't just pick up and move to California. They don't just leave their families behind."

"It's a strange time. Strange things are happening all around us. And sometimes at times like these, people feel the need to make drastic changes. But your mother's choice—it's not permanent, and it has nothing to do with you, okay? I want you to remember that. She's doing this because she feels she needs to, but I know that you are her greatest accomplishment, her greatest joy."

"That's you, Dad," I said.

"It's me too." But his answers were like molasses, slow and

thick and syrupy and lacking nutrition. I wanted to know things, understand him and my mother, like those people who send away saliva samples to learn what kinds of genetic predispositions lay hidden like land mines beneath the surface of their skin.

"Dad . . ." I slowly said, knowing that I was about to ask him the question I most wanted to ask.

"Yes?"

"How come you don't want to make drastic changes? Didn't you want to be a physicist? Isn't there a part of you that wants to be at the center of all of this? You could have discovered Terra Nova. You could be one of the scientists working to learn more about it."

What I really wanted to know, what I was ashamed to ask, was whether those seeds of complacency lay hidden within me too. It would have been a relief to learn that my father wasn't complacent, but I knew that to believe this would require a grand leap of imagination. My mother's words were like invisible ink—"We're not happy," she had said, and only now was the truth becoming evident, in the aftermath of her departure, in my father's unshaven face, in his old torn T-shirt.

I understood now, as I watched him, what had brought my parents together, and what had driven them apart. She was like a child. She always had been. She brought light into his life and made him laugh. And he was the responsible one, the one who grounded us, made us feel like we had something solid beneath our feet. But in the last few years, my father rarely laughed. And based on my mother's decision to leave, maybe she looked down at the ground beneath her one day and felt that her feet had been shackled to it.

"You'll understand when you're older," he said. "Sometimes you just choose a path and keep walking along it. You don't realize that there are going to be unhappy patches ahead. But there are unhappy patches in any path. They're patches."

"Do you wish you had taken another path?" I pressed. "Don't you wonder? Doesn't Terra Nova make you wonder about another version of you? What if the other you chose another path?"

"Wishing and wondering can be dangerous things, Tara. Of course, when they first detected that signal . . . I wondered. I thought about how I had given up a career in science. I fell in love with your mom, and all I wanted was to be with her. Maybe that's why I tell you to study, to work hard. I do want you to find what you love and to be able to do it. But the thing is . . . I made every decision in my life with open eyes, whether it was coming to this country, marrying your mother, moving here. There's still time for me to do the things I want to do."

"When? When will you do the things you want to do?" I asked. It had never bothered me before, but today it did. My father wasn't old, but he wasn't young either. I wondered if he realized this. Then again, what did I really know about time? My hours were broken into periods, blocks of English and physics and gym classes that occupied a few semesters.

"Don't worry about me, Tara. I'll be fine. The only thing I'm sad about is that we've been separated as a family. But I don't think this separation will last."

"How do you know?"

He shrugged. "Because all of these people driving themselves crazy, telling themselves there's something better out there, or that they've been arbitrarily trapped in this particular life . . . it's just silly self-flagellation. This life is all we have, and it's a good one. If we want to make changes, we should."

"But that *is* what Mom did."

"Well, no. Ideally, we should make those changes without disrupting other people's lives. We should think about the consequences of our choices. But maybe your mother didn't feel she was in a position to do that . . ."

I went to my room that night feeling worse than before. I had wanted something from my father, but I wasn't even sure what. I could tell he was unhappy, even if he claimed he wasn't. How could he possibly be happy running a restaurant when he could have been building a space probe? Discovering new planets?

At least my mother was running free toward her dream, cutting off the umbilical cord and finally making a choice in life, even if it meant hurting everyone around her. My father was this sad man left holding the bag. Honorable, maybe. But then, what was honorable about giving up your dream and pretending you were okay with it? I didn't know why, but it made me angry with him, and I went to sleep, a red haze underneath my eyelids, my teeth gritted in a rage.

TWENTY

IT was a grainy black-and-white transmission, but you could make out the image. A slightly stout man and an elderly woman facing each other. The man was wearing horn-rimmed glasses and a houndstooth jacket. The woman had distinctive features—a prominent but beautiful nose. "An intelligent nose," my father would have called it. But my father didn't call it anything that night. He merely stared at the TV, dumbfounded. A banner across the screen read: BCB NEWS, 10 FEBRERIUS, 1961.

"Ms. Wool, author of twenty-five novels, university professor, women's rights and antiwar activist, thank you for being with us today." The man smiled.

"Why, thank you for having me."

"Why don't we start with you telling us a little bit about your work these days?"

"For most of my life, I've been a writer. But these days, I also teach and work on behalf of women."

"You run a foundation, do you not?"

"Yes. It's called A Room for One's Own. It provides women writers with a stipend to write their first novel."

"And it is Britainnia's most prestigious prize in literature. You're also actively involved in the antiwar efforts in Americus."

"I was deeply affected by the two wars we had in Europa. After the second war, I nearly lost the will to live, and so when I first heard about Americus's intent to pursue a war in Nam Viet, I urged all writers and artists across the world to join me in protest. This, of course, came to be known as the Great Protest. I was amazed at the power of words to influence the world around us. In the end, it wasn't just writers and artists but people from every walk of life, from every corner of the world, protesting the act of war. This was followed by the global boycott of Americus's goods. Of course, the young in that country were already protesting, but once Americus saw the universal hatred for the war they were planning, just how much it would tarnish their image, the economic implications, they decided not to pursue it. I can't take credit, of course—there were countless other factors that went into Americus's decision. Perhaps they realized that they could never win this war, that many lives would be lost trying. Either way, I believe that antiwar efforts need to be global. Perhaps it takes an entire planet of people to shut down a war, but so be it."

"How do you still find time to write, with everything else that you do?"

"My writing is still, to me, the most important thing I do."

"And your writing has evolved over time, has it not?"

"It has, as I imagine any writer's work does. In the past twenty years, I feel as though I've entered another era of my life."

"Tell us a little about that."

"The earlier part of my life was difficult. Much of what I wrote about was loss. I experienced loss in the form of losing my parents, abuse from an older half brother, two wars, the loss of friends, and, during the darkest times, what felt like the loss of my own sanity. This allowed me to produce the kind of work that I did in my earlier life."

"The experimental nature of your work . . ."

"That's what people say I am known for, but I write the way I think. I write as the words come to me. I hear words all the time, wherever I go, wherever I am, from both outside and from within."

"You once said you heard birds singing to you in Greek . . ."

"It was a period of madness. For many years, I suffered from mental illness."

"You've spoken a bit about the incident twenty years ago . . ."

The woman nodded. "I had finished the manuscript for *In Between*, and I was horribly depressed, as I sometimes am when I finish a novel. My house in London had recently been bombed. Life felt unbearable. I wrote Leonard a note, put on a large coat, and made my way to the river . . ."

The interviewer adjusted his glasses, discomfort evident in his face. "What happened then?"

"I was walking along the bank of the River Os, about to do it. I put rocks in my pockets. I was waist-deep when I heard a voice. It was Leonard. 'Virginia!' he was yelling. He came after me and dragged me out. 'You mustn't do it,' he said. 'There's still so much for you to live for, still so much you need to do.' You see, Leonard always had a difficult task before him—every day, he made sure I slept and ate well and regularly and didn't have too much excitement in my life, and often I felt as though I was a burden to him, but all those years, every day, he saved me, and then he saved me yet again . . . I was so close to taking my own life that day."

"But that day changed everything . . . your work has been deeply influenced by this event . . ."

"It has . . . I still think—what if Leonard hadn't been there at that moment? Everything would have been different. I began to think of the endless possibilities of my life, how we are all interconnected . . . What if Leonard had missed the train from London? Or what if he hadn't found the note I left for him? What if he hadn't seen my cane on the riverbank? I simply couldn't stop thinking about such things, and so I began to write about them. I also began to wonder . . . about that particular version of myself who waded out into the River Os. I feel as though there was a part of me that *did* die that day, a version of me that just as well might have, and it made me strive harder in my own life."

"And today you are here, and Leonard . . ."

"Leonard passed away more than ten years ago. And yes . . . I am still here. Unbelievable, isn't it? I miss him terribly every day, and I am grateful for every moment I had with him."

"For our viewers tuning in, we're speaking with Ms. Virginia Wool—poet, scribe, university professor, and Britainnia's strongest advocate for the rights of women."

The screen cut to static.

A shiver went up my spine. I had been standing in the kitchen, a plate of kitcherie in my hand, and I had to sit down on the counter. For some reason I felt the urge to cry, and I began to.

"This is Edward Copeland, reporting on a video that NASA received and decoded just today. It's an interview with a poet and writer on Terra Nova who appears to be very similar to our own Virginia Woolf, who died in 1941. As you can see, some of the language they use on Terra Nova is different from our own . . ."

My father came over, placing a hand on my shoulder. He didn't say anything, and this frustrated me. I was overwhelmed with what was happening, in the world and in our own small life.

"She's alive up there . . . or at least she was in 1961. She didn't die. She lived. She stopped a war! And her words reached hundreds and thousands of people. They reached *us!*" I said to him.

My father nodded.

"How can you not wonder, Dad? About what all of this means?"

He was quiet for a long time before he responded. "I do wonder," he said. "I wonder all the time. I don't blame your mother," he added. There was a sympathy in his voice that I didn't understand, didn't want to. "She's just trying her best to make sense of a completely absurd world. We all are."

TWENTY-ONE

"NICK, can you tell me what a karass is?" Bucknell asked.

"It's a group of people linked in a cosmically significant manner, even if on the surface, they don't have a lot in common. Like me and you, Mrs. Bucknell," he said. "Oh no, wait, you and I are a *duprass*."

Bucknell giggled in response. "Thank you, Nick." Nick flirted with all our teachers, and they all loved it. Bucknell continued her interrogation as Nick tossed me a note written on a wad of lined notebook paper. I opened it. "I think Bucknell likes me," it said, and I couldn't help but laugh. It was the type of funny note Nick passed to me in class often, the kind of note that literally made my day. "Tara, can you explain to us the basic tenets of Bokononism?"

"I, uh . . ." I looked up, Nick's note still in my hand. I began to talk, but that familiar shrill wail silenced my words, red and white lights flashing all around us. It was the sixth fire alarm in four weeks, the tenth that year. They still hadn't caught the person who kept pulling the alarm.

"Not again," Bucknell sighed as we scrambled to gather our things. "Okay, everyone form a line, we're going to head to the fire exit together . . ."

"Ugh, I hate these things," Veronica said to me as she quietly slid her bag over her shoulder and made her way to the back exit. "Maybe we can sneak off campus till this thing is over."

Bucknell was so busy lining people up, she barely noticed us. I looked back at Nick. He was still putting his books into his backpack. I lingered for a moment, waiting for him to join us, but clearly Veronica had no intention of hanging out with him.

"What are you waiting for, Tara? Let's go!" She looked at me with her impatient face, and I realized that now that we were friends, I would occasionally have to endure her scoldings. I followed her through the back door of the classroom, turning to look at Nick one more time. He was still stuffing his books into his backpack as we turned the corner out the corridor through the student center.

"Hey, where are you going? Stay with your class leader!" Mrs. Leonard called after us, but we were already making our way to the glass corridor.

"Let's go this way . . ." I said, pushing through the crowds, into the front courtyard of Brierly. The sky was a dour New England white, the kind that makes your eyes tear. It made me want to live someplace else, someplace where everything and everyone wasn't monochrome. We dodged through a motley crew of students crowding the front lawn, clogging up the sidewalk, their backpacks clipping us on the shoulders, their familiar faces grimacing in the cold.

"God, all these fire drills!"

"I know, this is, what? Like, the tenth one? It's like one a week now!"

"I heard someone's pulling the alarm. And that graffiti outside the science wing? Did you hear about that?"

I shook my head.

"Nick told me. They called an emergency student council meeting over the weekend. Painted it over on Sunday before anyone could see it. Some sort of cryptic message about overthrowing all institutions. People are acting super weird. It's that Virginia Wool." Veronica shook her head. "Starting a revolution here on Earth."

But the fire drills had begun well before any of us saw the video. There had always been small acts of vandalism at Brierly—names carved into desks, the occasional pulled alarm. Last year Carter Anderson had called in a fake bomb threat and was expelled from Brierly, but Veronica was right, this was an unusually high incidence of weird behavior.

"Hey, you guys, wait up!" I heard a voice and turned.

"Oh my God, I can't believe she has the audacity to talk to us," Veronica mumbled. It was Sarah Hoffstedt. She looked as uneasy as I felt at the sight of her. She had all but disappeared since our confrontation in the student center. Veronica looked into the space above her head, as though she couldn't see her.

"I just . . . I wanted to say goodbye."

"Are you hurling yourself off a cliff, Sarah?" Veronica asked calmly.

Sarah ignored her. "I'm leaving Brierly," she said to me. "All this Terra Nova stuff, and that thing you said, Tara . . . I'm not a racist. I'm not closed-minded. Or at least, I don't want to be. But I've been living in this tiny town my entire life, and I'm sick of it. I want to see the world. So Moira and I are going backpacking across Europe and Asia."

"Who's Moira?" Veronica asked.

I looked away. Who would have thought that Sarah Hoffstedt, one of the most popular girls at school, would befriend Moira, who had spent half her life in the Brierly library? Then again, who would have thought that I would be having dinner at Veronica Hartwicke's house on a regular basis, or doing my homework with Nick and Halle?

"When do you leave?" I asked. I felt an unexpected pang of envy when I thought of Sarah as free—free of Brierly, free of Greenwich, free of all of us.

"After Thanksgiving break. I'm taking a year off. My parents were really upset about it at first, but then they realized I wasn't going to back down. And they thought it might be good for college. Hey, didn't your friend Meg go away for the year?"

Just the mention of Meg's name filled me with dread. What would I say to her when she returned next semester? Halle's crew had accepted me, but that didn't mean they were going to accept Meg. And then another thought occurred to me: I wasn't sure I wanted them to. I wanted to leave Meg behind, in the past, just as she had wanted to leave me behind when she left for Argentina.

"Yeah. Listen, Sarah . . . about what I said that day . . ."

"It's okay." Sarah looked at me. "I was upset, but it really made me think. I don't want to be stuck in this tiny little world anymore. Brierly is like a blip in the middle of nowhere—all our stupid little dramas, our dumb fights. But when you're here, you think it's everything. And it's not," she said. "I know that now. But for the record . . . I didn't hit that dog."

"Okay, whatever, Sarah." Veronica waved a hand in the air.

"No, seriously. I didn't. There's no reason for me to lie about it."

As we watched Sarah walk away, I couldn't help but wish that I were in her shoes. She seemed happy about her decision. She seemed carefree. She was going to see the world, and I was still stuck here at Brierly. Veronica turned to me and lit a cigarette.

"I give her a week before she flips out and comes back," she said.

"I don't know. She seems pretty . . . self-assured."

"Now's the time to do all the crazy stuff you ever wanted to and blame it on Terra Nova. Maybe you should use this as an opportunity to go after Nick."

"I don't know what you mean . . ." But I could feel my cheeks getting hot. Of course I wanted to be with Nick. I thought about Virginia Wool on Terra Nova. Maybe my fate didn't have to be tragic either.

"Oh, come on, don't act dumb with me," Veronica pressed.

"I see the two of you together, passing notes, giggling constantly. What are you doing, Tara?"

"Look . . . I know he's with Halle, okay? And I'm not going to break up a couple. If they have problems of their own . . ."

"That's not what I meant."

"What did you mean, then?"

"Stop being second wife."

"It's not like that."

"Of course it is. She's going to break his heart anyway, you know that, don't you? Are you just waiting to pick up the pieces when she does? Because that's a terrible strategy. Do you want to be his pathetic rebound, wiping away his tears?"

Of course the thought had crossed my mind, but it did sound particularly pathetic when Veronica put it that way.

"Do you have a better suggestion?"

Veronica placed a hand on her hip. "Maybe you need to take a page from Halle's book. She's strategic."

". . . and he loves her," I finished. "And no amount of strategy is going to change that." But I wondered for a moment if it could. I couldn't hear the conviction in my own voice, and by the way Veronica was looking at me, I could tell she could sense the lack of it too.

"Don't you see how she is? How she manipulates people to get whatever she wants? Nick, you, me, even that guy at the Indian restaurant?"

I had seen Halle work her charm from time to time, but then Nick was charming too. The thing about him was, it never seemed as though he had some sort of ulterior motive. Nick just liked making people laugh—Hunter and Jimmy, teachers, all of us. With Halle, I wasn't sure what exactly she wanted, what she was seeking. I knew that her charm sometimes did feel manipulative, but in ways I couldn't necessarily articulate.

"That thing she did with Sarah—putting you on the spot like that. That was really uncool. And making me disinvite her from the party? And that thing she said about wishing someone would just 'take Nick off my hands.' I mean, what do you think that was about?" Veronica made a face like she was trying to piece together a puzzle.

"I thought you said that Halle didn't know about my crush on Nick," I said.

Veronica shrugged. "She doesn't. But it's kind of weird, isn't it? I mean, why doesn't she just break up with him?"

"Because she doesn't want to break his heart?"

"She's afraid. She wants to look like she has it all together. The image is more important to her than anything." Veronica shook her head. "You're the only one, Tara. You're the only one who understands what I'm talking about. You can see it. I can tell. Nick and Halle, they're my friends, but they're totally self-absorbed people. They'll take what they want and leave you with the crumbs. That's just what they do."

I sensed that Veronica wasn't going to let this go unless I threw her a bone, but truthfully, I also wanted to confess my feelings about Halle to someone. "Sometimes . . ." I hesitated.

Veronica turned to me.

"Sometimes I just don't feel like I can totally . . . trust her, I guess."

It was such a tiny admission, and I felt strange bad-mouthing Halle, but something about it felt good too. Especially since it was the truth. I didn't trust Halle. I had never felt like I could tell her my secrets. Then again, I didn't feel like I could tell anyone my secrets. I couldn't even imagine having a conversation with anyone about my mother, for example.

"Exactly. Because she's not being real with you. Or with me, or with anyone. I'm so glad someone else notices it too, finally!"

All around the globe, things were changing so fast, it was hard to make sense of it. Some said it was because of Terra Nova. That it had somehow changed the way we saw ourselves. That it made people question the very order of the world. Here, at Brierly, Veronica was beginning to do the same, and she looked at me as though I was an ally. I didn't understand why she was so angry with Halle—what had happened between them beyond that vague explanation she had given me at the party: that she was sick of Halle, sick of knowing her so well, sick of being her best friend all these years.

The wind whipped through my hair, and I buried my hands in my pockets, feeling exposed. "I want to go back in," I said. "It's freezing." But there was something else I felt in that moment, something that made me uncomfortable—it was the dangerous side of possibility. Halle was manipulative, but at least she was artful about it. Veronica's approach lacked that finesse.

And yet, as we walked down the street, I felt a mixture of guilt and release. Talking about Halle behind her back felt like a welcome sacrilege. There was something heady and exciting about it, and yet it also felt tinged with an unfamiliar danger.

"Let's go get some hot chocolate at that coffee place on the Ave," Veronica said.

"Ugh, do we have to? I'm already sick of you," I joked, but it wasn't a joke. Veronica laughed, gently shoving me into a bush.

"No you're not. You love me," she said, still laughing.

TWENTY-TWO

"BABE, I've been dying to catch up with you!" my mother declared. Her voice sounded cheerful and relaxed, as though she had just emerged from a spa. "It's wonderful here—you would love it. California's beautiful, and we meditate every morning. The cafeteria food is so good—all vegan and organic. We take turns working shifts to keep this place running."

I was quiet, and she said, "Tara, I keep calling and e-mailing, but you won't respond to any of my e-mails! There's so much I want to tell you . . . and there's this event in the spring. I'd love it if you and your dad could come out to California and visit!"

I wanted badly to speak to her, to tell her about Nick, about my new friends, to ask her about that newest video transmission and what she thought of it. But when I heard her voice, cheerful and calm, my anger returned. What right did she have to be cheerful? What right did she have to ask me questions about my life? My mother wasn't entitled to an answer, to any answers. If she wanted to know about what was going on with me, she should have stayed.

"Do you want to talk to Dad?" I asked coolly.

"Tara, next week we go into a month of—it's called 'cleansing.' We just meditate and talk to people here at the church, but I won't be able to call home and talk to you as much . . ."

"They can make you do that?" I asked. "And they call it *cleansing*?"

"Well, it's part of the process."

"Oh, the 'process'—that's what it is?" I practically spat out, feeling a wave of outrage cresting within me. "You should ask yourself about this 'process' of yours where people can tell you to stop calling home, and you listen. And they give it the same name as a juice diet to make it sound innocuous."

"Tara, I . . ."

But I didn't give her a chance to respond. "I'm handing the phone to Dad," I said and held the receiver out to my father.

I listened to them talking, my father's voice soft and tender. He even laughed a few times, fueling my rage. Had he forgiven her already? How could he have? My anger boiled as they chatted away, as though everything was fine. After about twenty minutes, my father got off the phone and turned to me. I was sitting on the kitchen counter, doing homework. It was a rare evening that I had decided to stay in.

"She misses you," he said.

"Well then, she should have stayed," I said, without looking up from my textbook.

"She says you would like it out there. She suggested we go out west in the spring, spend some time in LA. What do you think?"

I slammed my book shut and looked at my father incredulously. "Have you gone crazy?" I exclaimed.

My father flinched. "Tara, she's your mother. You can't stay angry for—"

"I can stay angry for as long as I want. And for you to even suggest going out there? It's ridiculous. She's broken this family, and we're supposed to reward her for it? Let her rot in California by herself. She's a selfish, horrible woman!"

My father looked at me, shocked. "I know you're extremely upset right now, but . . ."

"But nothing. The hell we're going to California!" I said, gathering my things before I marched into my room and slammed the door. I buried my face in my pillow, hot tears pouring out of my eyes.

The first snow of the year fell on Thanksgiving. It started early in the morning, the first flakes melting into the ground, sacrificed soldiers dropped from the sky along the beaches, making way for the others.

Because we had no large extended family to host, no elaborate dinner to prepare, the day usually lingered on, porous, its boundaries shape-shifting to embrace the only loose annual traditions we had, a net cast into the sea, catching whatever waited in the depths below.

There were a few staples, placeholders to mark the occasion. A walk on Tod's Point. My father's turkey curry and rice. Our dining table set with an indigo batik-print tablecloth and a few white candles, my parents sharing a bottle of wine. But that wouldn't happen today.

The conversation I had with my father that night when I returned home and he was sitting alone in the dark was a litmus test I returned to again and again, inspecting that strip of red in my head. It was an alarm, a warning, an early signal, a precaution. While I couldn't seem to muster up any sympathy for my mother, and couldn't understand how he could, I felt an affection for my father now like never before. I felt as though my father was like a child, a little helpless, a little uncertain. Our lives were like a Jenga set, and my mother was a critical center piece, now removed. Everything hung in the balance. I would have to anticipate unpredictability; I would have to be the stable piece. And so, on Thanksgiving morning, I woke up and put aside my rage and decided to be there for my father, wondering if this very choice was a partial answer to that question "What will this do to Tara?"

I didn't know what the answer to that question was, what or who I would grow into, what buried rage and unrequited love and not fully trusting your friends and being the only Indian person at Brierly and the discovery of a mirror planet and thinking constantly about another version of yourself out there in another world did to the shape and form of one's soul, but then, I didn't know yet that these wouldn't be the only defining incidents and qualities of my junior year. I couldn't have suspected that there was more to come. Perhaps I was too scared to even wonder beyond a certain horizon.

And so I kept my fears to myself. I went to the Church of the New Earth website every morning, looking for photographs of my mother, but I didn't find any. What was she doing? Was there some sort of induction ceremony? Did she have to wear a uniform? Did she eat lunch every day in that cafeteria she mentioned? Did she spend her hours hiking with the tan Amazonian women who graced the website? I wanted to know all these things, but I still didn't want to speak with her.

But what I learned, what stunned me, wasn't something I found on the Church of the New Earth website. I was scouring the Internet looking for new goggles to wear at swim practice when I came upon a small sports-equipment manufacturer based out of LA. For some reason the photographs on the site looked familiar. Blond people hiking through mountains, looking cheerful. My blood went cold.

"Dad!" I yelled. *"Dad!"*

After the second call, he ran into my room.

"Dad, look!" I said. He stood behind me and peered at the cheery image. I could tell by the way his face fell that he recognized it too.

He took a deep breath. "Let's deal with this later," he said, nervously running his hands through his hair.

"Deal with this *how*?" I asked. "It's a stock image! That means the photographs on the site aren't even real. They're not real people! Who knows what's actually going on there!"

"Let's go for a walk. Our annual walk, Tara. She's on that cleanse, remember? We won't be able to reach her anyway, and there's not much we can do right at this moment."

"Are you kidding?"

"What would you suggest I do?"

"Call the police!"

"And tell them what? That my wife, your mother, voluntarily went to California to join an organization that's using stock images on its website?"

I glared at him for a minute. "Fine. I'll get my shoes. We'll just walk on the beach like everything's normal," I said.

When we returned from our walk, my father checked on the turkey curry. I reminded myself that he missed my mother too, that this was hard for him too. I sighed and brought out the white ceramic pasta bowls we saved for special occasions. I had just brought the bowls into the living room and set them down on the coffee table when my phone rang. UNKNOWN CALLER, it said. My mother never called my cell phone. She knew better. The thing was, I was scared and worried after what I had discovered that day. I picked up the phone with a sense of dread in the pit of my stomach as I waited to hear her voice.

"Hello?" I asked.

"Why, hello," said a voice that was distinctly not my mother's.

"Who . . . who is this?"

"It's Barack Obama, calling to wish you a happy Thanksgiving."

My anxiety dissipated before it re-formed into anxious excitement.

"Hey, Nick."

"Hey. Are you having a good Thanksgiving?"

"Yeah, we're just about to sit down and eat."

"Oh yeah, you probably eat at, like, a normal time. We start dinner at four around here, for my grandparents and all the little kids."

"Kids?"

"My nephews—my sister's kids—and cousins and . . . it's a huge event, like, thirty of us. Had to escape."

"It sounds like fun. I'd love to have a big Thanksgiving," I said, realizing my father could hear me. "Actually, could you hold on a sec?"

"Yeah, take your time."

"Dad, do you mind if I take this? It'll be, like . . . ten minutes."

My father smiled. "Go ahead. I'll be here."

I went to my room and closed the door.

"I didn't know it was you . . ."

"Oh yeah. We have a blocked number. My dad hates getting work calls at home. I think he hates work, generally. Anyway, how's your Thanksgiving going?"

"Mellow. We took a walk on the beach, and we're about to have dinner now."

"I'm not interrupting, am I?"

"No, no. Of course not," I lied. I noticed I didn't mention a word about my mother. I was getting used to doing that. Never speaking about her or her departure to anyone, keeping the fact that my family had broken apart solely to myself.

"Yeah, well . . . I guess I was just sort of . . . in the mood to talk. It gets lonely, a few days out of school, you know? You guys are kind of like my family at school."

"It feels that way sometimes, doesn't it?" I said.

"Yeah. I'm really glad you started hanging out with us this year, Tara. It's hard to believe that in just a year and a half, we're all going to go our separate ways."

"It's a whole year and a half away, Nick. Don't start waxing nostalgic just yet."

"But it goes by real fast. Or at least, that's what people tell me."

"People?"

"My grandparents. They met in high school. Kind of romantic, huh?"

"Yeah. That barely happens to anyone anymore."

"It still does, to some people . . ." he said, and I smiled, wondering for a moment if it could happen to me. "But we'll all remember each other, right?"

"Yeah, of course. We'll have memories of parties at Halle's and road trips and . . ."

"Road trips?"

I hesitated, wondering what was wrong with me to have let that slip. "No, just hypothetically, if we decide to . . . you know . . . but yeah, we'll have tons of memories."

"Except Halle. She's going to forget all about me." He laughed a little, and I didn't even have a chance to recover from my relief over his not dwelling on the road trips comment. I hesitated for a moment before I responded, uncertain of what I was being lured into.

"Why would she?"

"I mean, we've been fighting a lot. We never used to fight, and I don't understand what's going on. I tried calling her today, but she's not picking up. She barely ever picks up. I can never tell what the deal is with her, she's so hot and cold . . ."

"Have you tried to talk to her about it?" Why was I always encouraging communication between other people and Halle?

"Of course I've tried. She's impossible. Have you ever tried arguing with her? She always wins. Listen, has she said anything to you about . . . us? Like, is she upset with me, or did I do something to piss her off?"

I thought about Halle's discussion of Socrates and Plato that night at the restaurant. "She hasn't said anything to me," I lied again.

"Oh, okay. Just thought I'd check. It's just . . ."

"Just what?"

"You're so easy to talk to. It's like . . . we have this flow. I wish it was like that with Halle."

I nodded as though he could see me.

"Hey . . . what do you think we're doing on Terra Nova today?" he asked, his voice playful again. At the beginning, we asked these kinds of questions a lot. It was a game, a distraction, a way to escape. When things got bad, people asked,

"What do you think is happening up there?" or "Maybe I won the lottery today on Terra Nova," but it didn't change anything here. Our feet were still planted on our own Earth. On that day, I wondered if my mother had left home on Terra Nova too. I didn't say this to Nick.

"Wandering around Rome, probably."

He was quiet before he answered abruptly. "Listen, I should let you go have your dinner. I'll see you on Monday?"

"Yeah, see you at school," I said, wondering what I had said to upset him.

"Bye, Michelle."

"Bye . . . Barack."

I hung up the phone and looked out my window, watching small heaps of snow accumulate on windowsills and rooflines. I sat there a long time, thinking of Nick, of my mother. What *were* our other selves doing on Terra Nova today?

My father was eating rice pudding from a cracked porcelain bowl when I returned to the kitchen. I looked at it. There was a gossamer veil of silver paper across the top.

"I can reheat the curry," he told me. "It's not a problem," he added, even before I had a chance to apologize. I could see that he was trying too. He smiled. "I'm glad you have friends who care enough about you to call you on Thanksgiving," he said.

TWENTY-THREE

"HE left his wife and two kids," Veronica said. It was Monday after the holiday, and we were walking to Paesano's to get sandwiches—Veronica, Halle, and I. Alexa was at the nurse's. She was always at the nurse's, always lightheaded, or exhausted, or doubled over with cramps.

Earlier that morning, a substitute teacher had covered for Mr. Grover.

"Mrs. Emerick," she wrote on the whiteboard. Then she turned to us, her lips forming a straight line.

"Mr. Grover will not be returning to Brierly for the rest of the year. I will be filling his place for the time being." The room buzzed with whispers of speculation. Unsurprisingly, Veronica had the answer. She had a pipeline into gossip like no one I had ever encountered in my life.

"Just like that? Quit his job and everything?" Halle asked.

"My mom goes to the bookstore on Shore Road where his wife works? And she told my mom that he told her he wasn't in love with her anymore. That he had reconnected with his college girlfriend via Facebook, and he was moving to Florida to be with her. It's all this stuff with Terra Nova. It made him wonder about the college girlfriend, what their life could have been like—his *alternate* life. I think it was because of the Virginia Wool video. I mean, that was pretty crazy."

I shoved my hands into my pockets and looked away.

"What the hell is Grover even going to do in Florida?" Halle asked.

"I don't know, Halls. But they do have high schools there. And physics," Veronica quipped.

Halle was quiet.

"Anyway, it's pretty awful, don't you think? What kind of person just ups and leaves their family like that?" Veronica asked, and I felt a sinking feeling in my stomach. *Someone like my mother*, I thought.

At Paesano's we placed our orders for sandwiches—turkey on rye with cheese for Veronica, steak for Halle, and veggie and cheese for me. Veronica left us to go to the bathroom, and Halle turned to me, pulling her long hair into a ponytail.

"Listen, don't tell V or Alexa, but I'm breaking up with Nick."

"You're *what*?"

"I know. We've had a good run, but I'm just pretty over it. I want to get it done before Christmas—I don't want him to get me presents and stuff. And that way we don't have to see each other over vacation. I just decided, you know, now or never."

I nodded slowly, trying not to betray my excitement, but every part of my body buzzed with delight. *Halle and Nick were breaking up. Nick would be single.* For a brief moment, I felt bad for Nick, wondering how he would handle it. But I rebounded quickly, like a rubber ball smacking the Earth for a fraction of a moment before bouncing back into the air.

"How come you don't want to tell Alexa or Veronica?"

"You know how Veronica can be. She's just bitchy about everything these days. And Alexa'll try to convince me to stay with him. Not that it matters. I've already made up my mind, but just the thought of that conversation with Alexa and Veronica . . ." Halle made a face like she was about to throw up. I laughed. "And also—and seriously, you can't tell *anyone*—but I met someone. It's just the beginning, so I don't want to jinx it, but I have to give it a fair chance. But there's no reason for Nick to know that. He'd be *devastated*."

Veronica returned from the bathroom to find us still standing by the counter. "Did you get us a table?"

"Not yet, we were just chatting," Halle told her.

"What about?"

"The usual. God, that Grover! I seriously can't believe it!" Her tone was light. She had already moved on, from Nick, from our conversation, from all of it.

"I know. Who does that?"

"Seriously, that's messed up," I said, and they both turned to look at me. There was a defensiveness in my voice, and once the words were out of my mouth, I felt like I had no choice but to continue. "All this Terra Nova stuff. It's just an excuse for shady behavior." I was still thinking about my mother. What would Halle and Veronica think if they knew I hadn't spoken to my mother in two weeks, or that she was living in California now, in dormitory-style housing? Or who even knew what kind of housing she was living in? The photos on the website weren't even real.

Halle shrugged. "Or a reason to make some changes," she said.

I could barely eat, my thoughts alternating between despair over my mother and the thrill of Halle's confession. When would it happen? What would she say? How would he react?

"Don't turn into Alexa on us," Veronica commented when she saw my half-eaten sandwich.

It wasn't till we started walking back to school, still talking about Grover and the fire drills and Alexa, that I realized something: Halle had confided in me—told me something neither Alexa or Veronica knew. *Nick* didn't even know yet. And the thing about it was—I felt privileged in some way. Chosen, even. A wave of shame washed over me. I was embarrassed at how little it took for me to feel special, but this was temporary too, just like my concern for Nick had been in the moments after Halle told me what she was going to do.

How easy it was for Halle to be the sun. How easy it was for the rest of us to stay in her orbit.

TWENTY-FOUR

"I am not a messiah, or a voice from another planet. I cannot tell you what your future holds or what you should do with your life or who you should be with. I cannot identify your mistakes. I cannot be held responsible for the choices you make. I am just one person. I am not a god," Michiko Natori insisted, desperation in her voice. "This is the last press conference I will give. The last interview. I have nothing more to say. I just want to be left alone."

But nobody wanted to listen.

She had become a part of it, a symbol. Her life had become intertwined with this story.

And besides, people believed what they wanted, rejected what they had come to hate. Decisions had become more decisive, more absolute. Things that had merely been bearable, day in and day out, now began to suffocate and chafe, to strangle spirits and lives.

Perhaps this is what being alive was, had always been, even without the discovery of a planet, but the edges had become sharper. Kind of like the rings of Saturn, not meteorite junk spinning through the sky, billions of little pieces that make no sense, but a sleek pattern, a crisp ring. We could see ourselves in a way we never had before. From a distance. But that doesn't mean we could see ourselves clearly.

"She's, like, a rock star. I mean, serious cult status. Since that image showed up, people have been lining up at her door, like 'You are the messiah, tell me what to do,' and she's totally freaking out, like 'I'm no messiah. I'm just an architecture student living my life. And I don't want to be a messiah. I don't have any answers for you,' but people are asking her what they should do with their lives. They think she's like a god or something," Nick said. I was perched on the stone wall outside campus, my knees drawn up to my chest to ward off the cold. We were waiting for the fire trucks to arrive, even though by now, we knew there was no fire. There never was.

"Hey, Tara, scoot over." Jimmy grinned and sat down next to me, thigh to thigh. "I like your bracelet," he said, reaching for it, brushing my wrist with his fingertips. I ignored him. All I could do was watch Nick. He had no idea what was about to happen, no idea what Halle had told me earlier in the week. He was regular Nick, all enthusiasm and cheer, excitedly talking about Michiko Natori.

"That's insanely messed up." Veronica shook her head.

"Nick can't stop talking about her." Halle rolled her eyes at Veronica and me.

"Seriously, Halls, can you imagine how crazy it is for her? It's like she's some modern-day Jesus or something. I hear she can't even go to the grocery store. All these people are constantly following her, won't leave her alone. Like, people who are sick are asking her to cure them."

Halle didn't respond. She was looking away, her mind already somewhere else.

"That sounds miserable," I said. Nick took a step closer to me, almost closing the circle around us. I felt a thrill as he did this. He looked at me, his eyes bright. "Sarah and that chick— what was her name?"

"Moira?"

"Yeah, I wonder if that's where they're headed. They told Melanie that they were going to Southeast Asia," Nick said.

"I thought it was Europe?" Halle said. She was biting her fingernail. She was still looking away.

"Who knows? Weirdos, just leaving school like that." Nick casually leaned his elbow on my shoulder, the way I had seen him sometimes do with Halle. It made me smile, but Halle didn't even seem to notice.

"Is Alexa still at the nurse's?" Veronica asked.

"Probably," Nick responded. "She looked awful this morning. Didn't want to be at school."

"So what is she going to do?" I asked.

"Alexa?" Nick asked.

"No—that Japanese woman—Michiko Natori . . . about all the people standing outside her door?" I asked.

Nick shrugged. "What can she do? She didn't do anything; she didn't ask for it. Sometimes I think that's just how it is. You don't have a say in your destiny. People just make decisions for you, and there's not a whole lot you can do about it."

TWENTY-FIVE

"IT'S a secular tree," my father said, holding it up.

I shook my head. "It's a pity tree." The tree matched the state of our lives. It was the sad one left behind on the lot on Christmas Eve, the kind of tree that would appeal to my father's sensibilities. It sat, crooked and slightly limp, by the bay window, shedding needles that would eventually find their way into every crack and crevice of the house, only to be discovered months later.

On Christmas morning, I eavesdropped on my parents Skyping while I decorated the tree with threads of silver tinsel and handmade ornaments from the box we kept in the basement.

"I'm so glad they let us talk to our families on Christmas! It was such a *thing*! Had to get special permission and everything. I miss both of you today. How is Tara doing?" my mother asked.

"She's . . . well, you know. This isn't easy for any of us," my father responded, diplomatically as ever.

"Ask her about the photos," I said from across the room.

My father frowned, but then he turned back to the screen. "Jennifer . . . Tara thinks . . ."

"I don't *think*," I told him. "I *know* they're using stock photography. Ask her why," I said.

My mother must have heard me, because she smiled. "Tara! There you are! Are you talking about the website? They use stock photography because the organization's so new. I'm part of their first class. But those photographs approximate what it's like here. Next week, I'm going into an interview process. Now that I'm 'cleansed'—you know, from the vegan diet and the meditation and minimal contact with the outside world—they're going to assess whether I'm ready for the next step."

"What's the next step?" my father asked.

My mother grinned broadly and shrugged. "I don't know, Sudeep. But I'm really excited."

I looked at the tree before me, the tinsel in my hand. It was surreal, hearing my mother's voice on a computer screen on Christmas. Christmas had always been my mother's favorite holiday. She'd make her own wreaths with branches from trees and kumquats and holly and ribbons. She would hang cards on bits of string attached to doorframes. Cheerful bowls of pinecones, apples, and walnuts sat in the living and dining rooms. On Christmas Day, she would roast a chicken with lemon and rosemary and garlic in her lime-green Dutch oven and bake chocolate walnut cookies. My mother grew up without traditions—she had no rituals, except this one. And this year, there wasn't even that.

When the phone rang at two in the afternoon, I thought it might be my mother again, calling to apologize, at last. Calling to tell us she had come to her senses, that she was leaving Santa Monica and coming back home. But it wasn't my mother calling.

"Merry Christmas, Michelle!" He sounded cheerful, even though I knew that Halle had broken up with him. She had told me about it just before break.

"He was bummed, but I think he took it better than I expected," she had said.

"Hey, Nick." I smiled now at the sound of his voice. At the knowledge that he was unattached and yet still managed to sound as chipper as always.

"What are you up to right now?"

"Right now? Not much."

"Did you get any good presents?"

"Some money, some books. Nothing super exciting. You?"

"Want to see what I got? I'll pick you up in ten minutes," he said.

"Wait, Nick . . . where are we going?"

"You'll see . . ."

It was one of those planes that you can fly with a remote. It was shiny and silver, fresh out of the box.

"It's a Corsair—it's modeled after the planes they flew in

World War II." He didn't say a word about Halle, about their breakup, none of it.

"I had no idea you were such a nerdboy." I laughed.

He grinned. "Wait till you see it."

We parked his car outside Tod's Point, jumping the fence, and climbed the jagged boulders that lined the lagoon in front of where Mr. Tod's house once stood, situating ourselves in a grassy patch from which Nick launched the plane, clumsily flying it over trees, over fences, over the few electric wires in the vicinity.

"I'm still learning how to fly it."

"Yeah, I can tell." I laughed, watching that anomalous silver streak in the sky, a tentative mechanical bird. It was sluggish at first, dodging the highest branches of trees, but still oddly mesmerizing.

It took about fifteen minutes before it began to dive and turn. I laughed in delight. "It *is* cool," I said, watching as it zipped over the horizon, turning this way and that.

"See? I told you. Want to try?" he asked, but I shook my head, lying back in a patch of dead grass. I looked toward the empty land before us, a rolling hill that once contained an estate, now razed to the ground.

"It's kind of messed up, isn't it? That he donated his land to the township, and in return, they tore down his house?"

Nick's eyes were still on the plane. "It was a tax burden. Too much upkeep, or at least that's what my dad told me."

"I know, but they could have done something cool with it."

"Like what?"

"I don't know, made it an artists' colony."

Nick laughed. "An artists' colony in *Greenwich*? That's a lot to ask."

"Just saying," I said, my feelings slightly hurt.

Nick picked up on it and took his eyes off the plane for a minute to look at me. "Let's pretend it's an artists' colony. We're flying our plane over an artists' colony."

"What kind of artist are *you* supposed to be?"

"Don't sound so skeptical. I'm a highbrow photographer . . . super successful . . . very dashing." Nick grinned as the plane circled over us, over the phantasmic rooftop of our mythical colony. "Who flies planes in his free time. What kind of artist are you?"

"A painter," I said, watching the red plane soar through the gray sky above.

"Nah, that's too predictable."

"Okay . . . what sort of artist am I?" I asked.

"A sculptor."

"Really?"

"Yeah. Just pretend," Nick said, landing the plane at my feet before he joined me in the grass, lying down beside me.

"You love to pretend." I turned to him, laughing.

"You have the best laugh," he said. And then, under the gray skies of our imaginary colony, Nick Osterman kissed me.

TWENTY-SIX

IT was freezing, and we laughed as we undressed each other.

"Your hands are way too cold." He reached for me, touching my neck.

"Oh my God! Yours too." I giggled.

Then his body enveloped mine. His hands intertwined with mine. I could see the heat rising off him, and we were both quiet for a minute.

Nick broke the silence, his voice tentative, shaking. I couldn't believe he was nervous. "I've wanted to do this for so long," he said, and my body arched to meet his, my fingers entangled in his hair.

"Me too," I whispered.

"Have you ever . . ."

I shook my head. "But I want to." I took his hand. "I want to with you." I slid my thumb between his lips, parting them.

"I really do," I said, and then his hands were running down my back, over my thighs. His breath was cold, and the taste of his mouth—familiar and yet a revelation. I kissed him again and again, feeling the stubble of his chin scratching my neck, my cheeks. We were a secret in the cold of the woods, our legs braided together, our ankles knotted against each other. My breath quickening as he kissed me harder, with an intensity I had never before seen in him, a kind of hunger.

He was a different Nick. Not all laughs and lightness, but ardent and fierce. It was as though underneath that cheerful facade, there was another Nick—dark and alluring, fixated, obsessed.

"I can't believe this is actually happening," he said to me. I looked into his eyes and kissed him harder, recognizing that right there, with him, I was a different Tara. Not trapped in my head, all logic and rationalism. I was open and vulnerable in a way that I never allowed myself to be—all thoughts erased from my mind. Replaced by nothing but desire. All I wanted was him, enough to risk everything in that moment.

I couldn't have known till then the things that unlock between people in the dark, who we are underneath our masks. I realized that he, like me, was caught too, held prisoner by who he appeared to be. But I could glimpse so many sides of Nick in his fervor, all those energies not yet harnessed, not fully integrated within him. Yet they were there. They always had been. Just as this part of me had always existed: unguarded and bare.

Afterward, he held me against his chest and stroked my hair. He was tender, his arms encircling me. He told me stories about other places, his voice a barely audible whisper. I wondered, as he held me, if maybe our world wasn't so bad after all. Maybe *I* was the lucky Tara, a better Tara. Maybe this Earth was the one where people finally got the things they had always wanted.

It was dark by the time we left, running down the gravel path to the entrance, just as the gate closed behind us, a delirious laugh escaping my lips. I couldn't remember the last time I had laughed like that, felt like that, entirely without abandon.

"I'll call you," he told me, kissing me in my driveway. His hand was on my knee. There was a possessiveness in his voice. I traced his jawline with my finger.

"Okay," I said. I didn't want him to leave. If it had been up to me, we would have stayed there just like that forever.

TWENTY-SEVEN

On Wed, January 1, 2016, at 12:14 PM, Megan Stevens <meganstevens@gmail.com> wrote:

Tara!!!

Guess what?!? I'm back! Argentina was great, but in the end, I got so homesick. And Ernesto and Clara really started getting on my nerves. And talking in Spanish all day is really hard. Plus being around snobby Argentinian girls all day got really annoying.

But I'm so glad to be back! When can we hang out?!? I already left a message and a text for you. And I called your home phone too. Where are you?!? What did you do for New Year's?

Call me!

Megs

On Wed, January 1, 2016, at 2:19 PM, Jennifer Krishnan
<j.krishnan@gmail.com> wrote:

Hi, Sudeep! Hi, Tara!

Happy New Year! May this year bring you peace, love,
and the resolution of all challenges in your life. Hope
everything is going great for both of you. Have some
really big news to tell you in the next few weeks, but
just wanted to give you a heads-up. In two weeks, I go
into "Internal Reflection." It's much more intense than
cleansing. This means that I'll be cutting off contact
(temporarily! Don't worry!) for two months with the
outside world. The purpose of this is to harness my
inner power. Here at the Church, we believe that if we
all do this, it's almost like if you download an app on
your phone that beams a signal into the cosmos. Now
imagine if thousands of people do this. Okay . . . now
imagine if the entire planet did this! Amazing, right?!
Anyway, at the end of it all, we'll have a big celebration.
More news to come in the next few days (whoops, hope
I didn't give too much away!). Love you both! Miss you.

Mom/Jennifer

"Dad, she's beginning to make no sense," I said to my
father. " 'Internal Reflection'? Cell phone apps?"

"It's probably nothing," he responded. But I could hear it—
the uncertainty in his voice.

$\sim$

I got a text from Nick the day after Tod's Point. **Going away for a few days after X-mas. Will call you when I get back**, it said.

Talk to you soon! I responded right away. I would come to lament that exclamation point, the immediacy of the response. Cringe at the thought of it. In the days that followed, I wanted to run miles away from that exclamation point. It betrayed the fact that my heart crackled with glee, like a colorful foil chocolate wrapper, the moment Nick's name appeared on my phone.

Then again, what was wrong with that? For the first few days after Christmas, I told myself that maybe this was how things were always meant to be. I had always wanted him, for as long as I could remember. In that moment, he was there offering himself up to me. How could I have said no? *Maybe I can trust Nick,* I remember thinking. *Maybe he knows what he's doing.*

But then he didn't call after Christmas. Or on New Year's. I thought about picking up the phone and calling him myself, but I found that with each passing day, the part of me that had opened up that afternoon at Tod's Point was closing, paralyzed with fear. Something that had felt so easy just a few days ago— picking up my phone and tapping in his number—felt more and more impossible in the aftermath of what had happened. *He said he would call,* I chastised myself every time I reached for my phone, *you just have to believe him.*

But what did it mean that he hadn't? That in seven days, Nick hadn't called me? To distract myself, I spent the remainder of winter break in front of the TV, listening to NASA scientists talking about building a space probe that would travel to Terra Nova.

On the first day of school after winter break, Nick was nowhere to be found. Neither was Halle. By first period, that mild anxiety I had felt for days dilated to overwhelming dread.

"Who wants to explain to me the three-body problem?" Emerick scrawled "three body problem" across the whiteboard and turned to look at us. No one raised a hand. I was doodling in my notebook, trying to quell the rabid, aching panic within me. Halle never missed school. Nick rarely did either. *That didn't necessarily mean they were out together*, I told myself. *Or did it?*

"All right, since it looks like no one did their reading over the holidays, I'll simply tell you," Emerick said in a condescending tone. "The classical three-body problem is the movement of a planet with a satellite around a star. Did anyone read the chapter about Newton's laws of motion?"

Silence.

Maybe Nick was just running late. Some sort of emergency. Maybe Halle was traveling with her parents.

"Can anyone tell me what else the three-body problem pertains to?"

Love, I thought. All of a sudden, I realized that I was in the most intractable kind of three-body problem, the kind that was driving me to insanity right at that moment. It was probably nothing. He was always late to stuff anyway.

"All right, let's just stick to Newton then. Right after

Newton solved the differential equation for the two-body problem, which shows us why a planet moves in an elliptical orbit around the sun, he moved on to the three-body problem for the sun, Earth, and moon. What happened then?"

Just having to be in this class, looking at the empty seats where Halle and Nick usually sat, made me want to scream. *Maybe Halle was really upset about it. Maybe she had even tried to convince him to stay with her. But why would she do that? They were broken up. She had another boyfriend now, right?*

"Tara? What happened?"

I was tapping my foot rapidly against the leg of my chair, the tap-tap-tapping inadvertently drawing attention to myself, I realized. "He couldn't solve it," I said quickly, more to shut her up than anything.

"Why?"

"Why?" I repeated, looking up at Emerick from my doodle. *For God's sake!* "Because the three-body problem . . . makes no sense. Its behavior is inherently unpredictable."

"Thank you, Tara." Emerick smiled at me.

"Mrs. Emerick?" I asked, raising my hand. "Can I go to the nurse's? I'm not feeling well," I said.

"Can it wait till after class?"

Why did teachers *always* ask that? "No. No, it can't," I insisted. If I had to sit here a minute longer, I would lose it. One more second talking about the three-body problem and I would tear my hair out or run out of the classroom in tears. I had no idea what I was capable of.

What would the Other Tara do? I desperately asked myself.

She'd be cool and calm. Not agitated and driving herself crazy thinking of Nick. She'd be looking forward to seeing him. She'd be light and happy and excited.

I couldn't shake it, the belief that all the answers I was seeking lay with her. That's the thing about desperation—it's like those fish that swim against the tide for miles just to spawn. I refused to believe in something easier, continued to hang on to the idea that there was a solution to my loneliness, my feeling of isolation, all my frustrations with the people around me—my mother, Halle, Nick—even if that solution was billions of miles away. In that way, I wasn't so different from my mother. Maybe I was worse. She had traveled across the country to "psychically commune" with her parents. I couldn't go anywhere, but I still felt strongly that there *was* another me up there, the only person who could possibly understand how sad and lost I felt.

But I couldn't talk to her. And now, on the first day back at school, all I wanted was to get away from Brierly and never come back.

TWENTY-EIGHT

THE moment I arrived in the student center, Treem accosted me.

"Tara! I was going to call you into my office today. Do you have time now?"

"I was heading to the nurse's. I'm not feeling so well."

"It'll only take a minute. It's important," she said. She was the last person I wanted to see, but I followed her to her dank office.

"Sit, sit," Treem said, flashing me that familiar toothy smile. "As I'm sure you know, there have been a handful of incidents of 'vandalism' around campus," she said, making air quotes.

I nodded. My heart was racing at the thought of Nick. *Where was he?*

"Well, the faculty has decided to put together a safety committee to ensure that incidents of this sort don't happen again.

It's considered vandalism, you know, tampering with school property, pulling a false alarm like that. And we still haven't been able to find the perpetrator. We're going to ask students to volunteer to man all the fire alarms during their free periods for a couple of weeks to show solidarity . . ."

"Mrs. Treem, I'm not sure how any of this concerns me . . ."

"Well, it's about the committee. It was just formed, and it's composed of parents and teachers. I'm the president." She beamed. "But we need a student representative." At this, she smiled again, that toothy, aggressive smile that always made me cringe. "The Safety First committee—that's what we're calling it. And I suggested you as our student representative."

I sat in Treem's leather chair, a chair that was far too nice for either this dingy office or for Treem. "Why me?" I asked, distracted by the chalkboard behind her. Someone had written "twat waffle" in the tiniest letters in the corner, making me smile involuntarily.

"Well, we're hoping the student representative can rally students and enlist them to voluntarily man the alarms. And we're still searching for the perpetrator, so we thought you'd put out feelers among your friends and fellow students. Anyway, your peers have a great deal of respect for you, Tara . . . You're most likely going to be salutatorian of your class, you're editor of the yearbook, on the swim team, and you bring . . . well, you bring diversity to the student body."

"Diversity?" I repeated.

"Well, I have to tell you . . . I've been reading this book." She rifled through the paperwork on her desk and produced a copy of *Battle Hymn of the Tiger Mother*. "I just think there's so much we could learn from you, from your culture!"

Treem had said a lot of stupid things to me in the past, but this was way past just stupid. "That . . . that's not my culture," I said, pointing to the book.

"Forgive me . . . that came out wrong." She smiled before she continued. "What I meant to say was that I feel like your culture emphasizes a respect for authority that the students here could learn from."

I felt a rage pulsating within me that couldn't be controlled. "You want me to find out who did this and then turn people in to you because . . . I'm brown?"

"Tara, well, I would hardly put it that . . ."

"How would you put it, Mrs. Treem? Would you ask anyone else? Would you ask Halle Lightfoot or Veronica Hartwicke or . . ." It came out like one of those sneezes, uncontrolled and harsh.

"I asked you because—"

"You asked me because of the color of my skin, Mrs. Treem," I said, and I could feel the outrage welling up within me as I said it. "You want me to say yes to the shittiest job in the world, and you want me to be grateful you asked? You want me to ask people to *volunteer* to man the fire alarms? During their free periods? And you want *me* to be a snitch?"

Treem crossed and uncrossed her legs uncomfortably. "That's hardly what I'm asking of you, Tara."

"That's exactly what you're asking of me." I raised my voice, looking away from the chalkboard scrawl to face Treem for the first time. Whatever hidden switch there was within me that needed to be flipped, she had found it, to her own detriment. I opened my mouth and realized, in that moment, what happens to buried rage. *What will this do to Tara?* my father had asked, and Treem was among the first to find out the answer.

"First of all, your 'Safety First' committee," I said, using air quotes, "is the stupidest idea I've ever heard. Congratulations on being president of some completely moronic circle jerk. Second of all, why the hell would anyone volunteer to man the fire alarms? Man your own damn fire alarms. Or hire security. We're not slave labor . . ."

"Well, that's why it's voluntary . . . Tara, perhaps we've gotten off on the wrong foot. I thought you'd see this as an honor, and I . . ."

But I cut her off before she could say more. "An honor?" I laughed aloud, a laugh that made Treem shrink in her chair. "You picked me, the quiet model minority, because you think it might make me *happy* to be your little pet. To sit at your feet, saying, 'Oh, yes, pick me! Please, me! Let *me* do your dirty work. I can gather students together to do the shit job of manning your fire alarms! I can start a whisper campaign to find out who pulled the false alarm!' And then you can pat me on the head and say, 'Good Tara! Good model minority! You did the right thing!' Seriously, *fuck that*!"

Treem looked back at me, and something clicked within her, a shameful recognition of the truth in her eyes. "I can see you're very angry, Tara, and what I don't understand is . . ."

"What you don't understand is that I don't want to be your

bitch, Mrs. Treem. And I consider your asking me to be on your stupid-as-fuck committee *racism*. I seriously think that you're a racist." The word rang. It seemed to make the room vibrate, and Treem shifted uncomfortably in her chair again. "And given that you know nothing about my 'culture,' maybe I *can* teach you something. When the British came to India, they got a handful of rich Indians to do the kind of shit you're asking me to do. And that was the start of colonialism." I was going out on a limb now, and I knew it. "But I doubt you would know that, because you don't teach anything but Western history at this school."

"Tara, I . . ."

"If you want to switch me to a different counselor, go ahead, because the truth is, I don't want to be reminded of your insulting question every time I walk into your office in the future. But let it be known," I said, standing up and pointing a finger at her, "that as far as I'm concerned, you're a bigot." I threw my bag over my shoulder and opened the door to her office. "And by the way, it says 'twat waffle' on your chalkboard," I said, pointing to it before I slammed the door shut behind me and walked out.

TWENTY-NINE

"HEY, Tara! What are you doing here? Don't you have physics right now?" It was Alexa. She looked startled to see me.

"Hey, Alexa. I just—I was feeling kind of ugh, needed to step out. And then I had this whole thing with Treem. Hey, do you know where Nick is? He wasn't in physics this morning," I said, all in one breath.

"They're probably late getting back from their trip," she said.

"You mean his family?" I asked, my heart beginning to race.

"Halle didn't tell you? They went away right after Christmas. Decided to spend a week at Halle's parents' house in Nantucket. Anyway, they were supposed to be back last night, but they must have gotten delayed. I'll text her," said Alexa, pulling out her phone.

"Nick and Halle?" I asked, feeling the dread in my stomach

before it filtered down to my arms and legs, leaving them numb. "A whole week?"

"Yeah. I think they had some stuff to work out. Well, you know. It was Halle's idea, which surprised me. She's usually such an avoider."

"So it was just . . . the two of them?" I asked, my heart sinking.

"Yeah, I think so. Halle's parents don't care, obviously, and I think Nick told his mom he was going away with Hunter and company. They're probably on their way back now. Halle hates missing school . . . here's her response. They're here! They just parked. They'll be in the student center in a minute."

I got up abruptly, pulling my bag over my shoulder, clutching it tightly to hide the fact that my hands were shaking. He had been with Halle this *entire* time?

"Are you okay, Tara? You look a little pale."

But before I had a chance to answer, I heard that all-too-familiar voice, that cheerful lilt that made my heart sink.

"Look who it is! I was hoping we'd run into you both!" I looked up, feeling my face flush with heat as Halle approached our table. She was wearing her ivory coat and sunglasses, her hair up in an aristocratic bun. Nick was by her side, wearing a navy North Face, his hair disheveled as though he had just woken up. I could feel the blood draining from my face the moment I saw them.

"Hey, you guys! How was Nantucket?" Alexa got up to hug them both, but I sank into the table, my feet frozen into the ground.

"We completely lost track of time! You know when you're

just out in the middle of nowhere and you're like, 'We're going to leave at six P.M.' and then you look at the clock and it's already past midnight. Total accident . . ."

"No such thing as accidents!" Alexa said.

"I'm pretty sure accidents exist, Alexa." It was Veronica. I could tell from her tone that she was in an unusually good mood. "You are such a weirdo, but I still love you," she said as she hugged Alexa. "I missed you guys," she said, embracing Halle and Nick and then me. "How was vacation? What did you guys do over Christmas?" Veronica looked at us.

I looked away, willing myself not to cry as I thought about my Christmas.

"Good, awesome. Just hung around here. How was your New Year's?" Nick asked Veronica. *Just hung around here?* I felt a wave of humiliation at his answer, followed by outrage.

"Super boring. How was the trip?" Veronica asked.

"Nantucket was awesome. It's so empty this time of year. We went ice skating and just hung out and made a fire every night," Halle said. "Anyway, what about you, Tara? How was your New Year's?" she asked, and they all turned to look at me. I opened my mouth, but no sound emerged.

Finally, it was Alexa who spoke. "She's not feeling well, poor thing. Listen, do you want me to take you to the nurse? Or I can drive you home if you want."

"It's okay, Alexa. I can just call my dad . . ."

"You're sure?"

I nodded. Veronica sat down next to me as we watched Alexa saunter off.

"She's such an idiot savant," Veronica whispered. "Sometimes I think she knows way more than she ever lets on, and sometimes I'm like, 'Uh, what is going on in there? Is the malnutrition affecting her brain?'"

Halle laughed. "I have no idea what's going on in her brain, ever." And Halle and Veronica began to gossip, about how Melanie Carter was apparently considering changing schools, about something Hunter had said to Veronica about junior prom.

"And I was like really, Hunter? You're asking me now? It's January!" Veronica exasperatedly exclaimed.

I tuned it all out, running my fingers over the seam of my bag, wanting desperately to escape. When I looked up, Nick was watching me, a tentative expression on his face. I looked away and pulled my bag over my shoulder.

"I think I'm just going to take off. I'll see you guys later."

"You poor thing," Halle turned to me. "Is it bronchitis? I heard it's going around."

"I'm not sure what it is," I said, trying not to cry.

"I'll call you later tonight," Veronica said.

"Yeah. Me too," Halle said before she pulled me aside. "Oh, and Tara—I just wanted to tell you—you were right."

"About what?" I asked.

She put an arm around me. "That thing you said? About people using Terra Nova as an excuse for bad behavior?"

At first I thought it was an accusation, that she knew what had happened between Nick and me. But then I realized she was talking about herself. "Thank you. I had a good hard think about everything," she whispered to me. "You were right. I was just being stupid . . . about the other guy. It was just a . . . a pointless fling," she said, her arm still around my shoulders.

I could see Nick watching us, his jaw tensing for a moment as he strained to listen to our conversation. I turned to him, and he held my gaze for a moment. Why was he subjecting me to this? What did he want from me? I couldn't tell, but the moment he averted his eyes, I *knew* it in the deepest part of me. Nick wasn't going to be my boyfriend. He loved Halle. Halle didn't know what had happened between us. She didn't know any of it, my feelings for him, whatever feelings he might have for me.

"Thank you," Halle whispered to me. "For keeping my secret. You're a really good friend."

I swallowed hard. "You too," I said as calmly as I could muster. "But listen, I really have to go. I feel . . . terrible."

And then I turned and saw her. She was sitting alone in an empty section of the student center wearing jeans and a fitted jacket. She was pretending to read, but I could see her watching me. Our eyes met for a moment before I broke the gaze. I had never responded to Meg's e-mail. Or her multiple calls. Or her multiple texts. And the truth was, I didn't even want to think about that right now.

Here I was, in uncharted territory, floating through space, no Earth beneath my feet. I wanted to be rescued—like Moira had been rescued by Sarah Hoffstedt, like Virginia Wool had been rescued by Leonard, like my mother had been rescued by the Church of the New Earth. Could a belief rescue you?

Because all I had was a belief in someone I had never met, someone who couldn't come and take me away from the mess I had made.

I didn't start crying till I got home. Till I had walked through the threshold of my crappy little house, till I had made my way to my crappy little bed in my crappy little room. I couldn't even blame Terra Nova for what had happened. I did it all myself, and now I was paying the price for it. But the worst part of it, the part that makes me cringe, the part that I'm still ashamed of, even today, is that the reason I hated myself most of all was because Nick Osterman didn't love me.

THIRTY

IT was late in the evening when the news broke. They played the footage on loop, again and again and again. Riots had broken out all over Tokyo. Buildings burned. People ran through the streets screaming. Overnight, a peaceful city had turned into a war zone. Who could have thought that an innocent woman, now dead, would be at the center of it all?

They said she knew something was coming. She could sense that her world had become dangerous. For weeks, she had been reaching out to authorities, bureaucrats, the local police, asking for help. She asked for a bodyguard, relocation, a temporary safe house. She felt unsafe. People were leaving strange messages on her phone. People were following her wherever she went. She couldn't sleep. She was a nervous wreck.

I wonder how she felt when an angry mob knocked down the door of her house in the middle of the night, dragging her out of her bed, still in her pajamas, and into the streets of Tokyo. She must have been terrified as they pulled her through those avenues, when they threw her into the middle of the road and doused her with lighter fluid. I have to close my eyes when I think about that moment when someone lit the match.

Bystanders watched, horrified, screaming. She was screaming too. They said it happened so fast, they couldn't help her.

The news commentators called it a tragedy, but a tragedy is when someone dies of cancer. A tragedy is Halle's dog accidentally getting hit by a car. Michiko Natori's death wasn't a tragedy. It wasn't an accident. It wasn't like some evil wind swept through her home, breaking windows, overturning chairs. It's easier to think of her death as sad and inevitable. But it wasn't.

Those responsible for the act called her "a symbol of Terra Nova," a symbol of everything wrong with the world. They called her a false prophet, an imposter, something that needed to be destroyed.

Some even called it a "Terra Nova–related crime." But Terra Nova didn't make people kill Michiko Natori.

And those people who called her a symbol? You have to wonder about that too. Because Michiko Natori was a person well before she became a symbol. Not a person I knew, but she could have been. She could have been anyone.

Michiko Natori was killed because people were afraid. Not of her, but of what she meant, what she symbolized. And what she symbolized was that there were things about the world we didn't fully understand, couldn't fully make sense of. But getting rid of her couldn't change that fact.

THIRTY-ONE

On Wed, January 5, 2016, at 12:04 PM, Jennifer Krishnan <J.Krishnan@gmail.com> wrote:

Here's the big news I was telling you about! I really hope the two of you will participate. I know there have been some terrible things that have happened in the past couple of weeks, but I truly believe that Terra Nova is pure good. We just have to learn to manifest the power of it to become empowered ourselves. Sending you so much love!

Mom

For Immediate Release
Church of the New Earth to Host a Night of Communion with Terra Nova

| Santa Monica, CA • January 5, 2016 |

At midnight PST on the evening of April 4, more than 2,500 "Mirrors," as members of the Church of the New Earth are called, will gather at various positive healing energy vortices across the Earth to commune with their mirror selves and with the energies of Terra Nova. The Mirrors will raise their hands to the sky and pray to their counterparts on Terra Nova, harnessing the healing energy of their higher selves.

In honor of this historic occasion, the ecclesiastical leader of the Church of the New Earth and chairman of the New Earth Board, Mr. Andrew Sadakis, will travel to Honolulu, HI, to lead the ceremony.

Members of the public are welcome to join us in prayer on the dawn of a golden era.

Santa Monica's state-of-the-art New Earth Facility provides visitors with an introduction to the Church of the New Earth. The Public Information Center contains more than 100 films and texts that present the beliefs and practices of the New Earth religion and the story of founder Robert Bennington. To learn more about our global human rights program as well as the New Earth Volunteer Minister program, visit our website to get involved with Church-sponsored philanthropic and humanitarian programs.

New Earth Churches now stand in such world centers as Berlin, Copenhagen, Johannesburg, London,

Madrid, Melbourne, Mexico City, Moscow, New York, Orlando, Quebec City, Rome, San Francisco, Santa Monica, Tel-Aviv, and Washington, D.C.

For a complete list of New Earth locations, visit www.ChurchoftheNewEarth.org.

———————————————

The Church of the New Earth religion was founded by actor and mystic Robert Bennington in Santa Monica in 2015. The religion has since expanded to more than 200 registered churches in 18 countries.

THIRTY-TWO

I don't know why I needed to go back, but it was as though it was calling out to me, like a voice in the dark.

I thought of the Sirens. We studied them in Greek mythology in the ninth grade, and for my final project, I memorized Margaret Atwood's poem "Siren Song." I could recite it now if you asked me. And so I did recite it to myself as I pulled my bike out of the garage and rode to Tod's Point through tiny side streets in Old Greenwich. It was already dark out, but the moon was full, illuminating the sidewalks and fences, making lone trees look particularly uncertain and somber. I repeated the words over and over again, pedaling down Sound Beach Avenue, banking right on Shore Road.

This is the song everyone
Would like to learn: the song

That is irresistible:
This song
is a cry for help: Help me!
Only you, only you can,
you are unique

It took on a new meaning now. "Help me! Only you, only you can, you are unique!" I said to myself. I knew exactly who the "you" was. And on that day, I still believed she really could help me. That she was the only one. After all, who else was there? My mother had gone to California, my father was despondent and confused. Meg wasn't even my friend anymore.

The realization was like that feeling of belly flopping into a pool, the water slapping you into another level of consciousness: There was no one in *this* world who could help me, and the only person who could understand me, understand what I was going through, lived in another world. A world I would never see, never travel to. A world so far away that it may as well not even exist. The desperation grew within me the longer I rode. I pedaled harder, past the stately homes that sat on the shoreline, all of them looking ghostly and pale in the moonlight.

The gate to Tod's Point was locked, but the fence was low enough for me to climb over, and I did, without thought or worry, as though in a trance. I had heard that people do crazy things during the full moon, but I had never been one of them. People blamed things on Terra Nova, but I knew the truth. The real reason I slept with Nick had nothing to do with Terra

Nova. I slept with him because I loved him. Just the thought of this made me cry. How could I have been such an idiot? To let my guard down like that? I was better off eating lunches in the library, keeping to myself.

I couldn't stop crying. Over me and Nick, over Michiko Natori. Over my mom, who was halfway across the country, about to go into "Internal Reflection," right when I needed her more than I ever had.

A silver sheen of gossamer moonlight shimmered over the surface of the sea.

I walked along the sand and through the woods till I reached Mr. Tod's invisible house, the ghost of a house perched on a cliff. I squeezed through the low hedges and brambles till I made it to the lawn—the lawn where Nick had flown his plane. The imaginary artists' colony where we had kissed.

"Mr. Tod, I'm sorry to be trespassing on your lawn," I said before I laid down in the grass.

It was freezing cold. I don't know why I hadn't felt it while I was on my bike, but now I could see my breath fogging up the stars, the cold pressing down on my chest, making it hard to breathe.

Help me! Only you, only you can, you are unique. I reached my arm toward the sky.

My mother had written me an e-mail, talking about how strange it was in California. "The ocean is on the wrong side!" she declared. "I'll never get used to it."

But I knew in some part of me that she would. That one day,

California would feel more like home for her than Connecticut ever had. I didn't know how I knew this, but I did.

And then I realized it: Ever since they had found the new planet, being on Earth felt like being on the West Coast, the wrong coast. Every day something felt a little off, a little wrong. Things didn't make sense. Maybe they made sense on Terra Nova. Maybe when they looked at their ocean, they knew it was on the right side. Maybe when they looked at their lives, they felt the same way. Maybe we were the ones on the wrong side entirely. A shoddy duplicate of the real thing. A distorted mirror image, everything in reverse, and somewhere in our hearts, we knew it. We felt it, every day, all the time.

Only you, only you can.

"Tell me what to do," I cried, the tears pouring down my cheeks, frozen and salty. It was a plea, a prayer, a desperate cry.

"*Please,*" I begged, stretching my fingertips to the sky.

"Please," I asked again of the void, of the sky, of my twin, my ghost ship sailing away without me.

And from the void came nothing, only silence.

THIRTY-THREE

"I brought you flowers. And juice. They're from my mom's greenhouse. The tulips. Not the orange juice. That's Tropicana." It was Sunday evening, and Alexa was standing at my doorstep.

I had been home an entire week now, feigning illness, avoiding phone calls, and watching *Roman Holiday* no less than five times, eating my father's mulligatawny soup. Nick left twelve messages, all starting with "Tara, please, you have to call me. I need to talk to you," or "Tara, I know you're upset. Just call me," or "Listen, Tara, I know I'm probably the last person you want to talk to, but I really would appreciate it if you could just . . ." I deleted them all, telling myself that this was what resolve looked like. Then I cried some more.

"Oh, good, you look like you're feeling better. Let's go for a drive," Alexa declared now.

I was so shocked that I conceded, throwing a coat over my pajamas and sneakers over my wool socks.

We drove toward the Riverside Yacht Club, but halfway there, Alexa pulled her car to the side of the road.

"I've been sad lately," she said. "It's the malaise. It hits every year around this time, right after the New Year. Can you feel it?"

That was New England winter. The days melded together, indiscernible and gray.

"You call it the malaise?"

She nodded. "Veronica has it too," Alexa said. "It makes her bitchier than usual. So if she snaps at you, that's why. Halle's the only one immune to it. I think she's incapable."

"Incapable?"

"I sometimes think Halle is immune to sadness."

"That's not . . . possible. No one is immune to sadness," I said to her. I thought for a moment about the day Halle waited for me in the locker room.

"Do you want to tell me why you're sad?" she asked tentatively.

"I don't know what you're talking about."

Now Alexa looked at me with sympathetic eyes. "I'm not an idiot, you know," she said. "Look, I wouldn't even ask, but you were out of school for a week, and you haven't returned anyone's phone calls. And . . . I don't know . . . I just got this feeling." She shrugged. "I'm sensitive. I was going to say something that day at school, but I thought you might want to be alone."

"It's . . . nothing. I was just . . . having a bad day."

Alexa nodded. "You're my friend, Tara. I don't want you to be sad."

That was all it took, a tiny kindness for me to double over. Within minutes I was tearing up. Alexa handed me a Kleenex.

"How about I guess . . . and you nod if I'm right." Alexa took a deep breath before she asked me. "This is about Nick."

I hesitated for a minute, and then slowly, I nodded through my tears.

"You like him, it's obvious. Did something happen with you two?"

I nodded again, and Alexa looked at me carefully before she asked her next question.

"Did he kiss you?" she asked, her eyes wide. Either she really was an idiot savant or I was more transparent than I thought, but either way, it all came out in a slurry of tears and snot. Alexa listened to me describe seventh grade and Michelle and Barack Obama and Halle's party and Nick's deck and the telescope and his toy plane and our kiss. I told her everything. Everything except the part I couldn't bring myself to say to anyone, the part that kept me up late at night, sobbing into my comforter. How Nick was the first person I was ever with. How it meant everything to me and nothing to him.

"This is Nick's fault," she said at the end. "I can't believe how . . . dodgy he's being. You have to say something to him . . ."

"I can't!"

"Then you have to tell Halle."

"NO!"

"But if you don't, it's just going to eat at you, Tara. It's all lies. Their relationship, your relationship. How can you stay friends with either of them?"

"I guess I just have to. I have to act as though everything's fine. And besides, this is my own fault. I shouldn't have gone with him to Tod's Point. I should have stayed home on Christmas. It was all a huge mistake. Just . . . when Halle told me they were broken up . . ." At this, I stopped, realizing I had just revealed Halle's secret.

"Wait . . . Halle and Nick broke up? When?"

"I don't know . . . before Christmas. And besides, they're back together now."

"I can't believe she didn't tell me!"

"Promise you won't tell anyone," I asked Alexa, and she promised, a series of concerned creases across her forehead.

THIRTY-FOUR

"HEY, girl! Feeling better? I was worried," Veronica said. "You didn't return any of my calls."

"Or mine," Nick added, but I ignored him.

"I was just resting. Needed a few days off. But I'm much better now. Any idea what this emergency assembly is about?" My voice was calm, but my hands, in my pockets, were shaking.

"Beats me. Probably Pessanti wasting our time."

"Food drive for the indigent of Terra Nova," Nick joked, but I avoided looking at him. I sat down on a seat farthest away from him, next to Jimmy.

"Wait a sec," Jimmy said, and he reached for my cheek, his fingers sweeping under my eye in a C. The gesture was so intimate and so gentle that it startled me.

"You had an eyelash," he said, holding it out on the tip of his finger. "Here," he said, reaching for my hand as though he was helping me board a raft. He placed the eyelash on the back of my hand. "Make a wish," he said. I looked at him tentatively. He was grinning, and for a moment, I thought he was having fun at my expense, but I slowly realized that he was being genuine.

I looked down at my hand and quickly blew the eyelash into the air. I didn't consciously make a wish, but it somehow managed to slip from my heart, speaking as though on its own. *I want my mother to come back home. I want Nick to love me. I want so many things I can't have.*

As if on cue, Jimmy opened his mouth. "My mom always makes me do that. Wish on eyelashes." I nodded, my face turning red.

I saw Veronica grin, but she didn't look up from her binder. "Bushnell's totally going to quiz us today. Pop quizzes are so philosophically flawed." She shook her head.

"I know. That whole 'in life, you don't get to prepare' idea is so pointless. It's not life. It's school," Nick said, and he pulled up a chair between me and Jimmy.

"Then again, you can always wish on an eyelash for an A," Veronica said. I looked at the bemused expression on her face.

"I tried calling you, like . . . fifty times," Nick whispered. Veronica looked over at us, raising an eyebrow, but then returned her gaze to her notes. "I get it if you're mad at me . . ."

"Not mad, just . . ." I shook my head. "I don't know. Listen, I can't talk now . . ."

"You have something more important to do?"

"It's more like . . . I don't want to talk to you," I told him.

"I'm heading over to the auditorium," I said aloud, and Nick grabbed his backpack to follow me.

"Oh. Okay. See you guys later," Jimmy said.

We were already by the stairwell when Nick spoke again. "Listen, Tara, it got complicated. She wanted to go up to Nantucket . . . she wanted to get back together. And she's my . . . girlfriend."

"Funny, you seemed to have forgotten about your girlfriend at Tod's Point on Christmas," I said, picking up my pace.

"We were broken up. Now we're not. What was I supposed to say to her?"

"How about 'I slept with your friend Tara on Christmas,'" I said.

Nick dodged the crowds packing the glass corridor in order to keep up. "You could tell her too, you know?"

"Do you want me to?"

"Would *you* have wanted that? Would you prefer it if everyone knew?"

"I don't know, Nick. I just don't want to talk about it with you, okay?" I said as loudly as I could before I stormed off. I caught a look at his crumpled face before a group of freshmen stepped in front of him, obscuring my view of him. He looked as though he hadn't slept in days. I hated myself for feeling a tiny flash of sympathy for him.

I found a seat in the back of the auditorium and threw my bag on the ground, falling into my seat with a thud and profanity.

"Nice kicks," I heard. I knew the voice even before I turned. "Looks like a lot changed while I was away in Argentina."

It was the last thing I wanted to deal with in that moment. I turned to look at her. Meg had changed too. Her eyes were heavily mascaraed, and she was tanner. Her hair was longer. It fell all the way to her back now. But even if I physically looked the same as I did a semester ago, I knew that I must have seemed to her a different person.

"Yeah," I responded. I could hear the weariness in my voice. "I guess it has."

She squinted at me, her eyes an accusation. "I saw you guys. On the first day back. You and . . . Nick and Halle and Veronica and Alexa? You were all palsy in the student center."

I thought back to that first day back at school—that moment when I learned that Halle and Nick were returning from their reunion-moon in Nantucket. To anyone on the outside, it was a lovely tableau. We were figurines in a dollhouse, acting out some sort of play. Halle with her arm around me, Veronica in a good mood for once, Nick watching, all of us . . . friends.

But the reality lay buried in the tiniest of gestures, the most fleeting of glances. You had to be on the inside to understand how much between us was unspoken, to know that nothing really means what you think it does. What to me had been a grotesque moment might have looked lovely, even enviable to Meg.

"Looks like life is treating you pretty well these days," she said. "I mean, why would you want to return any of my calls or e-mails when you've got a whole new popular set of friends?

I hear you've been hanging out with them all year." There was hurt in her eyes, and my instinct had always been to make Meg feel better.

"Look, I'm having a day, okay? I just need to get through this assembly," I said to her. The casual brush. I had seen Halle and Veronica do it so many times to so many people.

Meg changed her tack, as though she believed that chumminess would bring us closer. "It's something about this moronic Safety First committee. Pointless waste of time. If people want to pull alarms, they'll find a way to. They're always fighting the tide."

I was the one fighting the tide. For whatever reason, I couldn't seem to escape the hamster wheel of my life. I looked at Meg. It had been hard being an outcast, but I wondered if this was harder, pretending that I didn't care about Meg, that I didn't want to know about her semester abroad, pretending I was mad at Nick when all I wanted was for him to apologize and declare his love and tell me he had made a mistake, that he wanted me, not Halle. Pretending that Halle was one of my friends when secretly I just wanted her to go away. I was always pretending. And yet it still never seemed to do me any good—the things I wanted felt so far out of reach.

Pessanti made her way to a podium, and the auditorium went silent. "As all of you are aware, in early September we had an incident of vandalism on the Brierly campus. Since then, we've had nearly a dozen false fire alarms and more graffiti outside the science wing. We still have not been able to identify the perpetrator or perpetrators, but we know that it is most likely a Brierly student who is responsible for these acts. Incidents like these waste our time, they endanger students and faculty members, and they are a waste of taxpayer money."

There were some snickers across the audience, but Pessanti continued. "In response to the incident, we have decided to put together a Safety First committee. We're asking students to man the alarms for the next week as a show of solidarity. It's symbolic, but it shows the perpetrator that we, as a community, will not be messed with."

"This is so insanely stupid," Meg said.

"And now I'd like to introduce you to the student representative of the Safety First committee, Halle Lightfoot."

"Seriously?" I whispered.

Meg made a face as Halle got up in front of the podium, shaking Pessanti's hand. I looked at Meg. She had always observed Halle as though she were a starlet on the cover of *Us Weekly*. But now, that admiration had been replaced by distaste. I wondered how much of it had to do with the fact that Halle and I were friends now.

Halle looked out into the crowd with that typical Halle confidence. She was wearing skinny black leather pants, an oversized white gossamer T, and a checked scarf around her neck. Her hair was blown out.

"Hey, guys!"

"Hey, Halle!" a handful of people called out.

"So when Mrs. Treem and Mrs. Pessanti asked me to take on this position, I was like, 'Hmmmm . . . do I really want to be the student rep of the Safety First committee? Do I really want to be urging people to man the fire alarms?' Is that really the best use of our time?"

"Fuck no!" someone screamed out, causing an avalanche of laughter in the crowds.

Halle laughed too, which made her seem even more charming than usual, if that was possible. "Come on, you guys. This isn't about the incident, and it's not about the alarms. This is about solidarity. We, at Brierly—we're a community. We're a family. We have to look out for each other. We have to . . ."

But I couldn't sit through any more of this nonsense. I collected my bag and slid down the aisle.

"Hey, where are you going?" Meg called out, but I didn't turn back. I made it to the door, but Mrs. Bushnell was blocking the exit.

"Tara, you can't leave. We're all required to be here for this."

"I need to leave right now, Mrs. Bushnell." I had learned that when you looked directly at someone's eyes and spoke with a particular tone of authority, it didn't matter who you were speaking to or what they were trying to make you do. Bushnell opened the door and let me through.

I was halfway across campus when I heard her voice again.

"Tara . . ." Meg was following me across the quad. "Listen! Wait up . . ."

She ran behind me, and we quietly walked together to the edge of the woods. It was freezing cold, and with the snow we had gotten over the holidays, by now a carpet of icy black sludge was piled up in every corner. I trudged through murky pools of decomposing leaves and branches and finally found a tree stump to sit down on. Meg stood there, watching me.

"She's your best friend now? Halle?"

"No," I said to Meg. "Honestly, Meg. What do you want me to say?"

"I want to know why you couldn't even send me an e-mail when I was away, during the hardest semester of my life. I want to know why you didn't return my calls. I called you, like, twelve times over winter break! I want to know why or how they're now your friends, and I'm not . . ."

"YOU were the one who went to Argentina to become a better person. YOU were the one who insisted that we'd grow apart."

"Yeah, and looks like we did," Meg said.

"What was I supposed to do? Wait around for a year for you to come back so you could tell me you're all cool and cosmopolitan now because of your year in Buenos Aires?"

"It wasn't a year, and honestly, it sucked. And now . . . this sucks. This sucks more than anything." Her eyes began to tear, and she sat down next to me.

"I don't have an answer for you, Meg." I felt guilty, but I couldn't take on Meg's desperation. My own desperation was enough.

"They're all bullshit, that crowd. I can't believe you're friends with such liars. They're all full of shit," she said, lighting a cigarette and passing it to me.

I looked at it, hanging off the tip of her fingers, a wisp of smoke slowly dissipating into the air.

"When did you start smoking?"

"Since I stopped caring about anything."

"That's original," I muttered.

Meg brought the cigarette back to her lips. "You don't know anything about them. And the whole thing with that alarm . . . God, if that idiot Halle chick only knew who it was . . . what does it matter anyway? They're all bullshit. The teachers here, Pessanti, your crowd. You used to think so too."

I looked at Meg, the girl who used to come over to my house for sleepovers in the seventh grade in her flannel pajamas and her glasses, and I wondered if I should tell her that I still thought it was all bullshit. I felt a wave of shame wash over me. Did Meg think I was bullshit too?

"What is it like, hanging out with them, being friends with them?" There was curiosity in her eyes, and when I looked at her face, I realized that she assumed I was still an outsider, looking in. To her, I wasn't one of them. And even if that was exactly how I felt too, I was angry at her for sensing it.

I took a deep breath. Maybe I wasn't like Halle and Nick, but *we* were different now too, Meg and I. She didn't know about my mother leaving home, my father's moods. She didn't know about what had happened between Nick and me. She didn't know how I really felt about Halle or about the nights I spent awake in bed, thinking about another Tara on Terra Nova. It had all changed, and one thing was clear: We were most certainly not the same, not anymore.

"They're my friends," I said. "Things changed, Meg. Everything changed, and you weren't here."

THIRTY-FIVE

VERONICA had rage in her eyes when she arrived to meet us at the diner off Post Road. "Why didn't you tell us . . . about you and Nick? That you broke up?" she asked Halle. I looked at Alexa, who averted her eyes.

"Who told you?" Halle asked.

"Nick told Hunter. Hunter told a bunch of people, including Melanie. We're supposed to be friends, Halle. How come we're finding stuff out about you from Melanie Carter, of all people, who isn't even in our group, who isn't even our friend? How come she knows what's going on with you, and you don't even bother to tell us?"

"God, you always have to be first to know all the gossip, Veronica. It was private. And besides, we're back together now. This is stupid. I don't get why you're mad."

"It's not gossip. And of course I'm mad! You're always keeping things from us. I thought we were friends."

"We *are* friends. And I tell you everything."

Is that what the definition of friendship was, I wondered. What kind of friend did that make me, then? But I already knew. I could rationalize it in a multitude of ways—that I hadn't known Veronica and Halle and Alexa that long, that I still felt like I couldn't trust Halle . . . but that didn't change the fact that I slept with her boyfriend. And Halle—she had confided in me. I was the only one she had told about her breakup with Nick. She had acted like a friend. I knew that I hadn't.

"You didn't tell us you signed up to be on that stupid 'Safety First committee,'" Alexa said.

Halle looked at Alexa and burst out laughing. "Treem asked me. I couldn't say no. And whatever, am I supposed to let you know, like, my entire schedule of extracurriculars?"

"You could have said no." Alexa moved a piece of tandoori chicken around her plate.

"I thought it would look good on my college applications. Besides, she asked Tara first."

"She told you?" I asked.

"She said she asked you and that you declined."

I shrugged. "Yeah, I did." I hadn't spoken to Treem since the incident. In fact, a week later, I found a note in my locker instructing me to go see Mr. Tuttle, my new guidance counselor.

"This is totally not what we're here to discuss," Veronica cut in.

"What are we here to discuss?" Halle asked.

"You being a crap friend."

"I have been an awesome friend . . . to all of you," Halle insisted. "I don't know what's going on with you, Veronica. Why don't you tell us why this bothers you so much? Are you jealous of me and Nick?" Her fork was suspended in midair over a plate of chole. She was looking at Veronica with concern in her eyes, like Veronica was sick or misguided or something. Her tone—patronizing and a little haughty, like she felt sorry for Veronica—put me on edge.

"Why would I be jealous?" Veronica's voice was shrill. "I don't want to be with Nick."

"But you're jealous that I spend so much time with him."

"Please. Don't flatter yourself, Halle. I don't think it's right that I'm finding out about my best friend's life through strangers."

"All right. In the future, I will keep you abreast of any developments in my life, large and small. Are we all good then, guys?" she asked us. Alexa and I glanced at each other.

"Yeah, we're good," Alexa quickly said. There wasn't going to be any sort of resolution to this conversation, at least not the kind Veronica was looking for. It was easier, somehow, to hold a grudge than to confront Halle head-on.

"Okay, awesome. Because I want to talk about something way more important than this stupid shit." She turned to me, burying Veronica's confrontation as though it was irrelevant and old news. "I just rented a house in Cape Cod for spring break. You guys, you have to see it!" she exclaimed as she pulled up her phone. There was such audacity in the announcement that it caught us all off guard.

Veronica glanced at me. "I don't know that I can get away for spring break," she said coolly.

"You can figure it out," Halle said. "You have . . . what? Exactly two months till mid-March."

"Yeah, my birthday falls on that week . . ." I said.

Halle put down her phone. "You guys, seriously? When in life are we ever going to have a chance to be young and in high school and drink on the beach in Cape Cod? Come on, Tara, we'll celebrate your birthday there, just the four of us. I promise it'll be the best birthday you've ever had. Please, please, please think about it, you guys!"

"I don't know," Veronica said, looking away.

"You promised, Veronica. You said if Tara agrees, you'll come."

"When did I even say that?"

"In the car, a couple of months ago. Remember? We were on our way here."

"That's the thing . . . I don't know if I can . . ." I said. I thought about my mother, about the Day of Prayer. Even though I was still mad at her, we hadn't heard anything from her since she sent that last e-mail. I was worried about her. I wondered whether it was a good idea for my father and me to visit her.

"I won't hear it!" Halle was smiling, and she reached for my hand. "You guys are my best friends," she said. "Please. I'll take care of everything. It'll be the most memorable week you've ever had. Let me at least make it up to you for this entire . . . you know, this whole misunderstanding," she said to Veronica.

It sounded like a terrible idea given that just two minutes ago, Veronica and Halle were fighting. *Everyone secretly has issues with Halle. I'm not the only one.* I looked at her now. I wondered what she really thought about us, about me. That was the worst part of it. She really did seem to think that we were her friends, that we had her back.

"You guys, I'm going to go to the bathroom. When I get back, I want you all to say yes, okay?" She gave us all a look before she got up and ventured to the back of the restaurant.

Alexa sighed, resting her chin on her palm as she sipped on her lassi. "She's not going to let up till she gets her way."

"I really don't think I can get away . . . it's my birthday," I said, fully aware of the fact that this wasn't a real excuse.

"Have you ever tried saying no to Halle?" Veronica snorted.

"It's totally weird. Not to mention . . . you know." Alexa gave me a look.

I glared at Alexa, annoyed that she would hint at my thing with Nick in front of Veronica. But Alexa merely looked back at me, a helpless expression on her face. "You might as well tell Veronica . . ."

"I already know," Veronica told me. "Don't be mad at Alexa. I forced it out of her. I knew you weren't really out sick. Halle doesn't know, I promise."

"Guys! Alexa, you weren't supposed to tell!"

"Were you actually going to keep it from me? Seriously, you

think I didn't see it coming with you and Osterman? Besides, it's just a kiss. God, I won't tell her, okay?"

My stomach churned when Veronica said that. *It's just a kiss.* What would happen if they knew it wasn't just a kiss? I swallowed this thought before I spoke. "So we're all going to go up to Cape Cod hiding things from one another, feeling resentments that we've been carrying around . . ." I looked at them.

"It could be healing?" Alexa shrugged, but even she looked skeptical.

"Friendship shouldn't be this hard," I said, thinking of Meg. Everything was always so simple with her. Till now.

Just then Halle's phone rang. She had left it on the table. I glanced at the screen. It was Nick.

I took a deep breath. "I need to use the restroom too. I'll be right back."

I turned into the corridor, wondering how I could get out of this stupid trip, and just then I saw them.

I met someone, she had said.

There's no reason for Nick to know. He'd be devastated.

And he would have been if he had seen what I saw that afternoon. Halle and Amit, giggling in a corner, her hand on his arm in a way that was so intimate that they looked like a couple. It reminded me of how she used to be with Nick when they first got together.

I briskly walked past them to the bathroom, locking the door behind me. I stood in front of the mirror for a moment, looking at my reflection. My hands were shaking. I had no idea what I would say to her when I walked out. I slowly opened the door, hoping to slip back to the table without having to speak to her, and was relieved to see she wasn't lingering in the hallway.

Until I saw them, out of the corner of my eye. They were standing together in the storage room: Halle and Amit, pressed against the wall of the pantry, kissing passionately.

"That was quick." Veronica looked at me when I returned to the table. She was ladling lamb vindaloo onto her plate. I felt nauseated just looking at it.

"Where's Halle?" Alexa asked, her eyebrows furrowed.

I shrugged, my face flushing. I was filled with dread, as though I was the one who had done something wrong. And then I remembered that I had. I had slept with Nick, after all. Weeks ago, and it didn't even really matter. He was still in love with Halle, who was kissing Amit in the pantry of my father's restaurant. And yet, I didn't want to tell Veronica and Alexa what I had just seen.

"Are you okay, Tara?" Alexa looked at me.

I didn't get a chance to answer.

"All right then, have we decided?" Halle was back, a smile on her face, her hair pulled into a ponytail. "It's a yes, right? We're all going to Cape Cod? If I have to personally pack your bags for you and drag you out of your homes, I'll do it." She grinned that quintessentially Halle grin. She was immune to everything.

Alexa shrugged. "I guess I'll come."

Veronica sighed in resignation. "Okay. I'm in."

They all turned and looked at me. I was exhausted, but I also didn't trust what might happen if they all went without me, for my own secrets were scattered so precariously among them now. Days on the Cape, gossiping and talking. All it would take was for one of them to wonder, to lazily pick at that tight knot, to find the lurid and messy truth about me and Nick lurking just beneath the surface. I thought about what they had done to Sarah. I needed to be on guard.

"Okay. I'll come," I said, exhaling a shaky breath.

THIRTY-SIX

I couldn't have known the extent of it then, but my life had already been recalibrated by everything and everyone around me. Just like Virginia Wool on Terra Nova. It made you wonder: How much of our lives was just luck or good timing, and how much was actually choice? How could it be that tiny serendipitous events could change everything? And if lucky events could change everything, could minor mishaps have the same power? These were the questions we were all asking ourselves in those days, and it was only when I looked back that I would be able to see what an enormous difference minor shifts and small decisions can make. Time does that. It can make a pile of ice and rocks hurtling through the air look like a colorful tilt, the brim of a planet. It can even make the past look beautiful.

A week before my trip to Cape Cod, we learned about

Florida. My skin went cold as I heard the news. Hundreds of people—men, women, children, the elderly—all living in a cramped compound, all members of the Church of the New Earth, had, on cue, taken a mix of pills and fallen asleep, believing that they would be transported to the mirror planet in their slumber. A few children had escaped, running to the nearest neighbors, six miles away, to ask for help.

"Dad," I said. But it was all I could get out. My hands were shaking violently. I wanted to throw up.

"I need to go out to California and get her," he said. We spent the afternoon trying to call her, but she wouldn't pick up her phone. It kept going to voice mail, her cheery voice greeting us like a dead end.

"Hi, you've reached Jennifer Krishnan. Leave your message after the tone."

That evening, my father contacted the police. "I'm flying out tomorrow. She'll be fine. I promise you, she'll be fine . . ." he said. His eyes were glued to the TV.

"I'll come with you," I told him, but he shook his head.

"I don't know if it's the safest thing for you to come. Meg's back, right? Can you stay with her? Or at your friend Veronica's?" There was an urgency in his voice I hadn't heard in a long time.

"Yeah, of course . . ." I lied. I had no intention of staying at either Veronica's or Meg's. "I'll talk to them. But I'd rather come with you, Dad."

"It's not safe. And if anything happened to either of you . . ." His eyes began to tear. I started to say something, but he cut me off. "Tara, please don't argue with me on this one. But this 'Day of Prayer' thing that they're organizing . . . who even knows what it could be? I need to go there before it happens."

Of course I didn't talk to Meg. Or to Veronica. What was I supposed to tell them? I needed to stay over so my father could rescue my mother from the Santa Monica branch of the suicide cult that was all over the news? My father was too stressed out to even check in with Meg's or Veronica's parents.

On the news, they were reporting that some of the other chapters of the Church of the New Earth were disbanding, that supposedly there were factions forming within the organization and a lot of infighting.

The next morning, before my father was supposed to leave for the airport, there was a press conference airing from Santa Monica.

"My name is Robert Bennington, and I'm the leader of the Church of the New Earth. It's a difficult time for many of us, and I offer my condolences to the families of those we lost in Florida. It's a grave tragedy. But I formed the Church of the New Earth to help others find peace on our Earth, not sow the seeds of destruction. Our membership is stronger than ever, and I want to address these accusations that we are holding people within our organization's centers against their will. This is a blatant lie, and we still stand for the same values . . ."

I walked out of the room then. I went to my bedroom, buried my face in my pillow, and screamed.

My father put his hand on my back. He had followed me down the corridor. "It's going to be fine, Tara, okay? We'll get her back home."

I wished I could believe him. For the first time in my life, I wondered what my life would be like if I never saw my mother again.

"We'll celebrate your birthday together when I get back."

I didn't say anything.

"We'll be back by then, Tara. And we'll celebrate together, like we always do." I didn't like the tension in his voice, the way he kept repeating himself. "In case we're not, though . . . you should go up to the Cape like you planned. Go and try to enjoy yourself."

I remember thinking how ridiculous this directive was, given the circumstances. "Dad . . . what I really want is to come with you."

"I know. But it's best for you to be here. And if I'm not back by your birthday . . . have fun in Cape Cod. There's no reason why you shouldn't get to have a normal teenage life just because of everything that's going on."

THIRTY-SEVEN

I tried to keep myself distracted, I really did.

There were still days when I watched them from a distance: Nick with his arm around Halle, Veronica with her glasses on and her binder balanced on her knees, studying for a test, Ariel and Hunter trying to make everyone laugh.

I watched Halle as she explained something to Alexa and Jimmy. She was impenetrable, a complete mystery. Maybe she liked it that way. Then again, maybe she really wasn't affected by everything that happened between all of us, or even outside, in the real world.

On most days, Nick still waited for me after class, or sat down next to me in the student center in the mornings. I began to avoid him, leaving campus for lunch. Something about his perpetually cheerful disposition irritated me now. When I saw him approaching, I turned the other way. I avoided eye contact. I purposely didn't laugh at his jokes if I was sitting at a table with a group of people. He didn't know me. He didn't understand me or my life. How could I have once believed that he did?

But occasionally, I'd see him watching me in class, out of the corner of my eye, and I'd feel a pang of despair in the pit of my stomach, a precursor to the tears that I would force myself to hold back. I missed him. But I was so humiliated that I didn't want to be near him. And I felt guilty even thinking about him when my mother was possibly in danger.

I thought endlessly about Tod's Point, that day on his deck. I thought about his picking me to be Michelle to his Barack. I thought about his phone calls, the way he leaned his elbow on my shoulder. The jokes he made, the crush he had on me in the seventh grade. I thought about Halle making out with Amit in the pantry of my father's restaurant, about her sucking up to Treem and planning a spring getaway for us. I thought about the fact that my mother and I never even had a chance to eat cake for breakfast together. I was exhausted with the upsetting things that raced through my mind at all hours of the day, and yet, I couldn't escape any of it.

"She's so faux virtuous, like with this stupid committee that she's on," Alexa piped in.

"Did they catch whoever was pulling those alarms?" Veronica asked.

"No, but at least we're not hauling ass out of class every five minutes now," Alexa said. It was true—the alarms had stopped.

"I wonder if it was Laurie Hoffman," Veronica asked.

"That stoner chick? Yeah, I bet it was her," Alexa said, breaking a tortilla chip into three pieces.

"It's like Stockholm syndrome, being friends with Halle," Veronica said to Alexa and me. "I can't wait to graduate and get out of here."

We were sitting at a Mexican place on Greenwich Avenue, sharing a basket of tortilla chips, an unnaturally green-hued guacamole, and virgin margaritas. I could barely eat. Just the sight of food made me sick to my stomach.

"I've just . . . I've had enough of Halle. You guys . . . you're my real friends," Veronica said. "She's never been a real friend. Tara feels the same way, don't you, Tara?"

I didn't respond, but I had a cynical thought. Veronica was rallying the troops. We were the troops—Alexa and I. If the three of us broke away from Halle, she would be alone. This was the simple truth about democracy. The majority always won. All you needed was one more than your enemy, and even if Halle didn't know it yet, Veronica was no longer her friend.

"I think she can be difficult, and I don't think she's always honest with herself. But she's never wronged me, or you . . . or Nick, even," Alexa said.

I felt a tortilla chip scrape down my trachea, making me cough. They turned to look at me.

"What about that guy over the summer? She was seeing Nick when she was visiting tapas bars and going to concerts with that dude," Veronica said.

"Whatever, so she went to a concert with another guy. That

was nothing. You're fishing, Veronica." Alexa was too kind to tell Veronica what she was really trying to do. She was deposing Queen Halle, or at the very least, trying to strengthen the bonds between us so that she could depose her, if she ever wanted to.

"Seriously, why aren't you saying anything, Tara? You have total reason to be mad at Halle."

"I do?" I asked. I was barely listening to the conversation. But mostly, I didn't care.

I still resented Halle, but the truth was . . . I resented all of them. Their lives were so simple. How could they even understand what was going on with my family?

"She can be really . . . just insensitive toward other people," I said, feeding the flame, but all I was thinking about was my own hurt feelings, my own worries. Even in that moment, I knew that Halle wasn't the one responsible for hurting me. Nick was. My mother was. The Church of the New Earth was. But not Halle.

"Exactly! She's totally insensitive," Veronica said. "You see the way she treats you, don't you?" Veronica asked. "She doesn't see you as . . . one of us."

I looked at Veronica now, trying to wrap my mind around what she was saying, but I knew what she was saying. *Halle treats you differently because you're brown and you're poor.* What about the other things that made me different, the things they didn't even know? That my mother had joined a cult in California. That my father had gone there to get her out. That I was staying in my house by myself while I waited for them to come home. That I worried every night that my mother wouldn't return.

I didn't know if what Veronica was suggesting was true or not, but maybe it was. I thought about Amit, why Halle hadn't told anyone about him. Could it be because she was ashamed? Ashamed to be kissing a waiter at a restaurant? Someone who was brown and poor too?

And yet I also knew that Veronica was looking for a reason to throw Halle under the bus. That was how high school alliances worked. You didn't need an outright reason to cut someone. Years of resentment and jealousy and a false reason could suffice. I could have told them right then about what I had seen at the restaurant. It wasn't a real reason to hate Halle, to oust her from the group. It was a fig leaf of some sort, just as I was beginning to realize the dog had been with Sarah Hoffstedt.

I was fairly certain that there was still something going on between Halle and Amit. Halle's car was parked at the restaurant a few times when I rode by on my bike, and once, I saw them getting coffee together at the bagel place on Sound Beach Avenue on a Saturday morning.

She still acted normal around Nick—happier, even. Whenever I saw them together, they were either kissing or making plans for the upcoming weekend. Maybe people were happier in a world of lies. Then again, I was living in a world of lies and I was miserable.

Next week, we would go to Cape Cod together. We would all drive up in Halle's SUV to a clapboard house with four bedrooms and a chef's kitchen. We would bake cookies and eat lobster rolls and birthday cake and hang around in our pajamas and take pictures.

They would show those pictures at our graduation: Veronica and me in our glasses. Alexa wearing her retainer. Halle with her hair in two pigtails. They would play the song "Forever Young" by Bob Dylan in the background.

The four of us would notice how young we looked in those pictures—so much younger than we remembered feeling in so long. We would notice how content we looked, even though if you had asked us any of us then, we would have told you that we were resentful, filled with mistrust for one another, about to go our separate ways.

Still, as miserable as we all were, we would look back on those snapshots as a happy time, in that way that the past always appears happier than the present. That's the odd puzzle of time: It's a shoreline that keeps eroding. Every time you look, you're struck by the realization that once upon a time there was more—the more that you never really saw, because all you ever saw was the past.

THIRTY-EIGHT

"I'M staying at a hotel not far from the compound. There are a number of family members staying here, and the authorities have been alerted. I have a feeling they're planning a stakeout of some sort, but they're keeping it under wraps right now."

"Have you heard from her, Dad?"

"No. Her cell phone still goes to voice message. Calling the church is pointless. There's a receptionist who puts me on hold for hours on end. The FBI interviewed a number of us about what we know. Tara, a lot of people are on this, okay?"

"But you haven't spoken to her?"

"We'll get her out of here."

"How do you know?" I began to sob. I didn't want to say what I was actually thinking. *How do you know she's still alive?*

"I just know. Please trust me."

I thought about backing out of the trip, but then reconsidered, imagining myself alone at home for the entire duration of spring break, thinking about my mother.

And so on March 18, Halle, Alexa, Veronica, and I climbed into Halle's SUV and began the drive out to Cape Cod.

"I got you guys breakfast sandwiches and coffee. Oh, and oatmeal for you, Alexa, because I know you don't like egg sandwiches," Halle said, handing us each individual Starbucks bags, a crate of coffee cups sitting at our feet.

"Seriously, I can't wait!" Halle was wearing black jeans and boots and a Brierly track T-shirt. You could see her eyes smiling, even through her Prada sunglasses.

"How long is the drive up?" Veronica asked from the passenger seat. She was still in her pajamas. "I might take a nap."

"Four and a half hours, I think. You nap away. We'll chat." Halle turned to us. "And I put together a great playlist."

It was seven in the morning. I wouldn't have thought to put together a playlist, much less get everyone coffee or breakfast sandwiches (egg and cheese for me, egg and ham for Veronica; cream and sugar in my coffee, black for Alexa). This was Halle, thinking of every detail, as she always did.

The snow had melted, and snowdrops and daffodils were beginning to appear on freshly green lawns, tumbles of uncut forsythia painting the landscape yellow as we drove down 95, listening to an odd mix of early '90s grunge and Britpop.

"You guys are going to love this place! It's got a huge kitchen. I brought a ton of groceries and wine—I thought we could cook dinner at night. We'll stop at the local fishmonger and see what's fresh."

"This feels very grown-up," said Alexa, leaning back on her pillow. She had brought it with her, and her aristocratic curlicued monogrammed initials intertwined with the strands of her dark hair.

"It *is* very grown-up. I suspect adulthood will be like this," Halle said.

"What, full of five-day trips to the Cape?"

"You're always making fun of me, Veronica." Halle frowned.

"Not making fun. Just trying to understand what your concept of adulthood is, you freak." She added the last part with affection, but I tensed at the undercurrent of Veronica's hostility, knowing that this trip could be like a canoe ride down a particularly steep rapid.

"I hope it'll be more about doing what you love, with the people you love."

For us, adulthood was just as much another world as Terra Nova. It was something we couldn't see, something we could only speculate about. Kind of like that story I had once heard on the news about the Aymara tribe in the Andes. They believed that the future was behind them, the past before them. They were blind to the future, but the past they could see with open eyes. But what about the present? I know now that we don't often see the present as clearly as we think either.

"I don't think that's what adulthood is supposed to be," Veronica scoffed.

"You think it's a continuation of the misery we've suffered at Brierly?" I asked.

"Do you really hate Brierly that much, Tara?" It was the first time anyone had ever asked me that question point-blank.

I was quiet for a moment, trying to figure out how to respond. But it was Halle asking the question, and I felt like I couldn't tell her the whole truth. There were surface reasons why Brierly had been hard for me: My family was lower-middle class. I was the only brown person on campus. These were merely words, and they couldn't convey the discomfort I felt when I looked at the annual photograph of the swim team in the yearbook. When people assumed I was smart not because they knew anything about me, but because of the color of my skin. I had spent so many years feeling like I spoke a different language than everyone else, feeling like I existed on a tiny and remote island of my own. I ate different food, I had different stories, a different history, I spoke of different things, or I didn't speak at all. Mostly, I just watched and listened. I had spent so much of my time at Brierly feeling lonely. I felt desperate to connect, desperate to share, but I was afraid that no one would ever understand me. I was too different, and with each passing day, I became even more unalike.

"Brierly isn't the real world" was all I said in response to Halle's question. And I felt certain of it, for the first time, and also relieved, full of resolve: The rest of my life would be nothing like Brierly.

"No. Brierly's a holding pen," Alexa said.

"I just mean . . . I think it gets better as you keep going, I mean . . . I hope," I said.

"Not for everyone," Veronica said.

"I think adulthood is going to be way lousy for someone like Hunter," Halle said. "Have you seen the way swimmers look after they stop swimming? No offense, Tara."

"None taken."

"You're right. He's too handsome. It's all downhill for him," Veronica said.

"Maybe it's not about handsomeness," Alexa offered. "Maybe he'll be fat and happy."

We were all quiet for a minute, all of us wondering if Alexa was projecting her deepest wishes on Hunter.

"Maybe we'll all be fat and happy," Halle said, and even if she didn't mean it literally, I hoped she was right.

As we continued to drive, the tension between us seemed to dissipate for a while. Maybe Halle was right; maybe this was a coming together, an opportunity for us to recharge our friendship rather than tear it apart.

"I have a surprise for you, Tara," she exclaimed just after we crossed the Connecticut state line.

"What is it?" I asked.

"We're stopping to stretch our legs."

"That's a surprise?"

"We're stopping in Providence. I know you want to go to Brown. I wasn't sure if you've ever visited the campus . . ."

I shook my head. "No. I barely ever go . . . anywhere, really."

"Well, we'll get to walk around. I hear there's a great crepe place on Thayer Street. Anyone up for crepes?"

La Creperie was a tiny hole-in-the-wall with a cheerful yellow facade and what seemed to be a perpetual Bob Marley soundtrack. We ordered a handful of crepes to share and walked down Waterman Street to Faunce Arch. It was a bright and sunny New England day, the first in months.

"Let's sit for a bit," Halle said, spreading out the picnic blanket she had brought. "What do you think?" she asked me.

I can't describe how I felt, but it was a little like falling in love, my heart soaring at the sight of kids sprawled out on the main green, playing Frisbee or blowing bubbles into the air. There was a class going on, a professor sitting cross-legged among a circle of his students.

I was speechless. "This is it," I told her. "This is where I want to be," I said, and I heard the excitement in my own voice. It was frenetic, unbounded, almost like the euphoria people describe when they've just somehow escaped death.

It wasn't just the place I was describing, but a feeling, one that stayed with me the rest of the drive up to Cape Cod and the entire evening as we prepared a lobster dinner together, shrieking at the sight of live lobsters trying to escape the enormous pot we had located in the kitchen to cook them in. It stayed with me as we toasted each other with glasses of rosé at sunset, sitting on a porch that overlooked the bay. It stayed with me as we walked barefoot through the mud and sea grass and onto the shore, swatting away insects at our ankles and laughing.

I dove into the freezing sea with Alexa and Veronica and emerged to see a sliver of a new moon above us. The tide was high, but the ocean was fairly calm. I watched Halle, a lone figure sitting in the sand. She waved at me, and I waved back.

Somehow, Halle had been able to set the tone of our vacation, rather than Veronica. Veronica actually seemed to be having a good time, and so was I, a realization that surprised me. All I had needed was a good day, and my mistrust, my anger, seemed to have evaporated. I realized I wasn't even thinking about my mother or my father in California, and for a moment, I felt guilty. For the first time in months, I wasn't thinking about Nick either.

After a little while, I came back to the sand to join Halle while Alexa and Veronica walked across the beach. She handed me the joint she had been smoking, and I took a puff. I was shivering, and she put a blanket over my shoulders.

"Thank you," I told her. "It was nice of you, really nice, to plan this. And the trip up to Brown." I meant it too. Halle seemed different when she was out of the context of school. She felt like a real person, not the goddess of the Brierly campus.

She smiled. "You guys really are my best friends, you know that? You're like . . . family. And Tara, I know we only started hanging out this year, but . . . you three, you're like sisters to me. I'd really do anything for any of you," she said.

And then she did something I had never seen Halle do. It

was the kind of thing you saw children do with their mothers, a sign of vulnerability and affection, such a small gesture, and yet, for some reason, it transformed her into a different person, a real person. She put her head on my shoulder, and we sat there, together, watching Veronica and Alexa swim in the moonlight.

Maybe I understood it at that moment—the cult of Halle, why people loved and revered her. Why they forgave her, why, despite themselves, they wanted to be around her.

The endless discussions of time felt contrived at moments like this, only because they never touched on that most elusive and magnificent characteristic of it: that it had the ability to stop, to cease to exist. These were the moments when we were surprisingly, astoundingly happy.

THIRTY-NINE

THE sun was pouring in through the large windows that faced the ocean, and I turned to watch the mist rising over the water, everything an indiscernible blue and gray, all blurred lines. I was curled up under an airy down comforter and white linen sheets that enveloped me like a cloud. A bouquet of fresh pink hyacinths and lavender crocuses sat on my bedside table. Halle must have placed them there early in the morning while I was still asleep.

The whole house was white—white curtains, white walls, white linens—but not an institutional white. It was a peaceful, seaside white. I wondered if there was an entire industry of stylists and interior decorators devoted to finding the perfect shade of white for a house.

I was lying in bed, listening to the sound of waves crashing on the shore, when Alexa ran into my room, throwing herself on my bed.

"Haaaaappy birthdaaaaay, birthdaaaaaay guuurrrrl!" she yelled, and the others followed, laughing as they flung themselves over the covers.

"Tara's seventeen!!!"

"What are you going to do for your birthday, Tara?"

"Jimmy has a present for you! He told me. Spoiler: It involves him taking his pants off," Halle yelled.

"He wants you to make a wish on his eyelash." Veronica laughed.

We spent the morning gossiping in bed in our pajamas till Halle offered to make us breakfast. We accompanied her down the stairs to the kitchen, where a cornucopia of wrapped presents sat piled on the kitchen table.

Halle got to work making the French toast while Veronica juiced oranges and Alexa made coffee. I got up to help, but Halle wouldn't let me.

"No way, birthday girl. You're not lifting a finger today, okay? Today, it's all us."

There were windows throughout the kitchen, and the light was different here, misty but bright. The kitchen itself looked like a dream, something out of *Architectural Digest*, the stainless steel appliances gleaming in a way I thought was only possible with the use of Photoshop. You could smell the sea from here, salty and clean.

"I think Ina Garten cooks in this kitchen when she comes up the Cape," Alexa said.

"You watch *Barefoot Contessa*?" Veronica made a face.

"I like Ina." Alexa shrugged. "I like her pear clafouti."

"Do you think Jeffrey's having an affair?" Halle asked.

"Why would he be?" Alexa looked shocked.

"Because he's, like, always off in the city, and she's always at home cooking for him."

"That doesn't mean Jeffrey's a cheat, okay? They look seriously happy together. You guys are such cynics."

"So we are." Veronica shrugged, raising a glass of orange juice. "Happy birthday, Tara. Thanks for bringing us cynics to the Cape. You guys were right. This was a good idea," she mumbled.

"Wait, what was that, V? Could you, like, repeat that?"

Veronica rolled her eyes. "You were right, Halle! You are always right. Hail to the queen!" But it wasn't mean, the way she said it. There was actually a kindness in her voice. The French toast was caramelized on the edges, made with stale brioche bread and copious amounts of ghee and lemon and orange rind and cardamom and strawberry jam.

While we ate, I opened my presents: a gift certificate to the Strand, an IOU for lunch at Tarry Lodge, a Burberry scarf, a silver ring with an aquamarine stone, and finally, a box that Halle handed me. It was wrapped in silver paper, light in weight, with a black ribbon tied around it.

"Open it," she insisted. I looked at her, wondering what she was up to. I unwrapped the ribbon and tore off the paper. The box was unremarkable, but when I lifted the cover, I gasped.

It was the same sweater I had been wearing the first day of school, the turquoise cardigan I had to throw away.

"Now I know you probably don't want to be reminded about that day—but Nick told me that your cardigan was ruined. I, like, made him describe it to me in full detail, and I remembered I had seen something like it at Shores, that little boutique in Old Greenwich. Anyway, if it brings up bad feelings you can totally return it, but . . . I don't know, I thought you could get a fresh start with this one . . ."

I held the sweater up to the light, shaking my head in disbelief. It was the exact same one. "Halle, you are . . . kind of magnificent," I said.

"I just . . . I wanted to make it up to you. I'm really glad you were there for Mario . . . and I like that color on you."

I looked at the sweater and then at them, at the light coming in from the windows, the waves crashing on the shore beyond, and I remembered that day I had stood outside Starbucks watching a scene that seemed to have been art directed by someone who only loved beautiful people and beautiful things and beautiful landscapes. I knew I wasn't like Halle and Alexa and Veronica. I couldn't live that way, inside a photo shoot at all times. But I had to admit, to be inside of one for a day, for my birthday, no less, was kind of wonderful.

"You guys, this is the most amazing birthday, seriously."

"This is just the beginning, girl. You go shower, and we'll clean up. There are bikes in the garage—I have a whole day planned for us!" Halle exclaimed.

I checked my phone in my room while Alexa and Veronica and Halle cleaned. Birthday e-mails from Jimmy, Hunter, Ariel, and Janicza. One from Nick. A voice mail from my dad. I listened to the voice mail first.

"Happy birthday, my lovely Tara! I hope you're having a beautiful morning on the Cape. Hope all your wishes come true this year. Love you!" I heard him pause for a moment before he went on, "I have no new news, but I'm hoping I will soon. Try not to worry about her, okay?"

I saved the message, feeling a wave of anxiety that I chose to brush away before I scrolled quickly to Nick's e-mail.

On Sunday, March 19, 2016, at 9:05 AM, Nick Osterman <Nicholas.Osterman@gmail.com> wrote:

Hey, Tara,

Hope you're having a fantastic time on the Cape with the others. I just wanted to drop you a line and wish you a great day and a great year. Let's do a birthday lunch when you get back.

Nick

It was oddly disappointing, but then, I hadn't really spoken to him in more than three months. And today, I didn't want to think of Nick. It was almost shocking to me how little I cared about him today.

There was nothing from my mother. This shouldn't have surprised me, given the circumstances, but it felt eerie, not hearing from her on my birthday. I *was* worried, but I hoped my father would have told me if he knew something was wrong.

We spent the day biking around the coastline, stopping to get manis, pedis, and massages at a tiny storefront in the center of town, and then lunch at a French bakery in Hyannis, where we shared salads and pastries. Even the weather was a gift.

"It's like summer today."

"Global warming?" Halle asked.

"Maybe it has something to do with Terra Nova," Alexa said.

"You think everything has to do with Terra Nova." Veronica laughed.

After lunch, we biked down to the beach and stripped down to our bathing suits.

"You guys go ahead, I'm staying in the sand," Halle told us. Alexa and Veronica ventured to the water for a swim, but I stayed with her.

She had bought a gallon of lemonade from the bakery, throwing it into the basket of her bike, along with paperbacks for us to read, sunblock, mini-bar-sized bottles of tequila and rum, and Turkish towels.

"They're lightweight. They fold into my backpack," she said, spreading a few into the sand before she mixed tequila and lemonade together in paper cups. I watched her, in awe.

"I give up," I told her, sipping on a lemonade tequila cocktail. I was feeling particularly honest. "I don't know how you do it. You think of everything, and you do everything. You might just be perfect. I used to hate you for that, but now . . . I don't know. You're like Martha Stewart meets Angelina Jolie."

She frowned. "Both highly polarizing people." But it was

something else that upset her. "You used to hate me?" She looked genuinely hurt.

"Not hate exactly . . . but just . . . I envy you, Halle. But mostly because . . . you make it look so damn easy, all of it. All of this," I said, waving my hand in the air.

"It's not easy."

"It isn't?"

She turned and looked at me. "No." She shook her head. She sighed for a moment and took off her sunglasses, squinting into the sun. She was wearing a black bikini and a straw hat with a large brim. I noticed that the sunglasses had left indentations on the sides of her nose. She took a moment, wiping off the sand that stuck to her ankles, her knees, tiny diamonds of dust on her runner's thighs, lithe and slightly tan.

"I do everything because . . . my mother . . . she's never really around. That's the way it's always been, my whole life. It's like we're supposedly a family, but I don't even know what that means. I know it's stupid, I mean, I'm sixteen now . . . I should know better, but I can't help myself . . . I keep hoping that if I do everything right, get good grades and win track trophies, dress well and always say the right thing, the smart thing . . . that she'll finally see me."

Halle rarely spoke about her parents, and I wasn't sure what to say, so I sat quietly and listened.

"The thing is, she's never around to actually see me do any of these things. Never around to be like, 'Oh hey, good job on that test' and 'This bouquet is really pretty' and 'I like the

French toast that the housekeeper taught you to make.'" She wrinkled her nose. "But mostly, she's never around to actually be like, 'Hey, Halle . . . I like . . . actually being around you.'"

"I'm sure she likes being around you."

Halle shook her head. "Sometimes I wonder if anyone actually likes being around me."

I think we were both stunned to hear those words said. All this time, I had seen her as impenetrable, a mystery, incapable of sadness, of anything less than perfection, and yet, she wasn't.

"I think . . . they think I'm a terrible burden. I don't know if they actually even wanted kids. I wonder about that all the time. It's fucked up, I know, but you can't really get outside yourself, you know?"

Never in a million years would I have predicted this moment. Halle was insecure, just like the rest of us. She was uncertain of herself. She felt unloved. She just hid it so much better than anyone could have ever known.

"I want to be around you," I insisted, because it broke my heart, what she had said. "I totally want to be around you," I said, giving her a hug, and when she cried, I wiped her tears with my hand, leaving a trail of sand on her cheeks.

"I believe you, you freak," she said.

"My mom . . . she's not even . . . here," I told her, surprising myself as the words came out of my mouth. And then I found myself telling her everything, about my mother leaving home, about how close we were, about the Church of the New Earth, about how much I missed her, how hard it had been. How I was scared that she might not come back.

"She'll come back, Tara," Halle said fiercely.

"How do you know?" I asked her. I looked out at the shore-line. Alexa and Veronica were tiny dots bobbing on the surface of the ocean. "I haven't even heard from her today."

"She'll come back because she loves you. I promise you, she'll come back," she said, squeezing my hand.

It was the first time I really knew she was my friend.

"Okay . . . dinner. I'm making my famous lobster rolls," Halle declared.

"Do we have potatoes? I can make fries and cocktails. I think I saw a fryer in the kitchen," Veronica said.

"I'm baking the best chocolate chip cookies ever," Alexa said. And we all turned to look at her. "And then I'm eating, like, a whole tray of them."

We were quiet for a minute, and then Veronica spoke. "Whoa there. Let's go easy. It's not *your* birthday, okay?" We all laughed.

"Wait, what do I do?" I asked.

"You entertain us."

"I'm not an entertaining person."

"I don't believe you. You must have a skill that we don't know about," Halle said.

"I can tap-dance?" It came out like a question. My mother had taught me.

"I *knew* it!" Halle exclaimed.

"That I can tap-dance?"

"No. That you've been keeping secrets from us!"

I couldn't make eye contact with Alexa or Veronica, and there was only one thing I could think to do before anyone noticed the tension. I began to tap-dance across the kitchen floor.

"Seriously? How have you kept this from us all this time?" Veronica asked. She was doubled over laughing. And soon we were all cracking up, giving each other impromptu dance lessons. Alexa was the best of all.

"I used to be a dancer, all through elementary and middle school."

"Why'd you stop?" I asked her.

She shrugged. "It gave me serious body image issues."

I stopped dancing.

"I still struggle with all that stuff. Most days, I don't even want to be at school. I feel like everyone's looking at me and talking about me." She shrugged. "I mean, I know people talk about it at school. But I'm way better than I used to be."

I nodded. "I understand," I told her. Veronica and Halle glanced at each other before they looked back at me.

"The important thing is that we love you just the way you are, Alexi," Veronica said.

"I know that, you freak." Alexa smiled. "Now come tap-dance with me."

Veronica mixed martinis for us, and we drank them as we tap-danced and prepped for dinner. By the time it was ready, we were all pleasantly buzzed. We ate lobster rolls and fries and chocolate chip cookies on the back deck by the ocean, in our pajamas.

Afterward, Halle brought out a cake covered with

strawberries and flowers and seventeen candles. It said, "Happy Birthday to Our Favorite Star," and they sang and Veronica took pictures. I blew out the candles before I reached into the cake with my hand and smeared icing all over Veronica's face, making her laugh uncontrollably. In response, she grabbed a handful of cake and smeared it on Halle's face.

"Hey, what about me?" Alexa protested, and we all covered her face with cake, laughing and eating the rest of it with our hands, feeding each other icing and strawberries.

After we washed up, Halle suggested we light a fire. It might not have been the most prudent thing, lighting the fireplace while drunk. It had all the makings of an after-school special, trying to turn on the gas and asking each other if it needed more logs or if the logs inside the fireplace were real or ceramic, and laughing as we wondered if our pajamas were flammable and Alexa reminding us that flammable pajamas aren't really funny, but between the four of us, we managed to light a small fire.

We fell asleep in front of the fireplace that night, Veronica and I in our glasses. Alexa wearing her retainer. Halle with her hair in two pigtails. I still remember how I felt that night right before I fell asleep—completely present and completely happy, kind of the way I had felt that night at Halle's party. I wasn't thinking about another planet, or another me. I wasn't turning anywhere for answers. I actually felt, for the first time in a long time, as though I was among friends. Friends who loved me and understood me. Veronica took a ton of pictures that evening, but they don't really do that day justice. The snapshot I have in my mind is, to this day, still the best one.

FORTY

I opened my eyes. Someone was knocking on the front door. I had fallen asleep on the couch, head to toe with Alexa. Halle was fast asleep too, curled up on an oversize chair. Veronica was wrapped up in a blanket on a nest of throw pillows on the floor.

"Who would be knocking on our door at nine in the morning?" Veronica moaned. Her eyes were still closed.

"I'll go look," I said, slowly getting up.

"I'll come with you," said Halle in a hoarse voice, rubbing her eyes.

There were masculine voices coming from the front stoop. I recognized one of them even before we opened the door.

"Surprise!" Nick called out, throwing his arms up into the air. He was wearing a pair of Wayfarers, a white T-shirt, and jeans. Jimmy and Hunter were behind him, carrying six-packs of beer.

Halle's face fell. "What are you guys doing here?"

"We thought you might want company." Nick grinned and walked through the threshold, giving Halle a hug. She didn't hug him back. Jimmy reached for me right away.

"Hey, babe. Happy birthday," he said, kissing me on the cheek.

"Thanks. I didn't know you guys were coming..." I looked at Halle, and she was glaring at them, a hand on her hip, but Nick simply smiled, ignoring her expression.

They walked past us into the living room, trailing mud from their shoes through the foyer. Unease filtered through my veins, a toxic chemical sparking at nerve endings.

"What are they doing here?" I whispered to Halle.

She shook her head and made a face. "I never invited them," she said.

We watched as they entered the living room, yelling, "Wake up!" to Alexa and Veronica. Hunter jumped on top of Veronica to surprise her. I could have told him what a bad idea that was.

"What the hell! Get off me!" Veronica screamed, punching him in the stomach. "What is wrong with you, you freak? Why are you here?"

"Hey! Watch it! I just wanted to surprise you," he said, backing off. Veronica sat up.

"Who even invited you here?" she scoffed.

It was shocking how much we didn't want their company.

Something had changed between Halle, Veronica, Alexa, and me in just one day, some sort of tectonic shift, a delicate adjustment that if left untended could render an earthquake. The old mistrust was gone, but we needed more time to simply settle into ourselves and into each other, without the complications that these boys brought with them.

"You guys are trailing mud into the house." Alexa looked at the foyer.

"That's not a very nice welcome," Nick said, sitting down next to her, that perpetual grin on his face. "We wanted to surprise you guys. Didn't you miss us?"

"Not really," Halle said under her breath. She was standing next to the sofa where Nick was sitting now, looking peeved, but he ignored her, reaching for her, trying to pull her into his lap.

"Quit it, Nick."

"Baby, I'm just trying to kiss you. You're always mad at me."

"You guys knew it was a girls' weekend. I planned this for weeks!"

"Well, we're here now. We drove all the way up here from Connecticut to be with you. Let's get the party started."

It was unclear what exactly Nick was thinking, or why he had brought Hunter and Jimmy along as his lackeys. They were already beginning to goof off, punching each other and laughing, heading into the kitchen, opening the fridge to inspect and then consume the contents. There was something entitled about their behavior, the interloping masculine infringing on some sort of harmonious feminine that had been built in a mere day, still precarious, but extant. I started to feel it again, the need to escape. I didn't want to be around these people, I wanted to be home. I wanted to be with my mother.

Within a couple of hours, the boys had hijacked the place. A football game blared on the TV, and empty beer cans and bags of chips littered the living room floor. It was as though they had taken advantage of our shock to deploy an occupation.

Alexa, Veronica, Halle, and I huddled together in the kitchen.

"Halle, tell your boyfriend and his friends to get out," Veronica exclaimed.

"Why is this on me? You guys say something!" Halle said.

"Why does someone else always have to do your dirty work for you, Halle? I'm sick of being the bad guy! You be the bad guy."

"Maybe you're just better at being the bad guy than me!" Halle retorted.

"This is disgusting, you guys. They haven't been here two hours and they've turned the place into a frat house," Alexa said.

"Where is all this mud coming from?" Halle yelled at them.

"Oh, sorry, Nick made us go through the backyard to make sure we had the right house," Jimmy called back.

"Why would you guys have to go to the backyard for that?"

They all started laughing, slapping each others' backs.

"No, it's like, it's an inside joke. Nick just wanted to throw Hunter into the mud. By the way, you guys have a serious food situation going on out there," Jimmy said.

"What food situation?"

"Go look," Hunter said. I scanned the back deck through the window. The remnants of our lobster dinner and a destroyed cake were rotting in the sun, flies darting all over the mess.

"You should probably clean that up," Jimmy said. I looked at him. He was chugging a beer, a trail of potato chip crumbs all over his shirt. I watched his eyes as he turned from me to the TV.

"Holy shit, you guys! Look!" he said, pointing. I understood right then what people mean when they speak about those moments when everything goes into slow motion.

It was a news bulletin, interrupting the game. "Breaking news out of Santa Monica, California. The FBI has launched an assault on the Santa Monica compound of the Church of the New Earth. We've heard some explosions out of the compound, where cult leader Robert Bennington has been holding people hostage for the past fifty days. The Bureau of Alcohol, Tobacco, and Firearms also became involved in the investigation of the cult once they learned that the Santa Monica branch was stockpiling firearms and explosives. It is unclear exactly how many people are still inside the compound. It's too early to say if there have been any fatalities. We'll continue to bring you more news throughout the day."

I ran from the room, making it to the bathroom just in time, throwing up into the toilet.

"Aaaawww, that's bad!" I heard a voice behind me after a moment. Jimmy. He tried to touch my back, but I elbowed him away. I didn't want anyone touching me right then, especially him. I felt vulnerable on all fronts—it was physical, visceral, but there was also that overwhelming recognition that something terrible was about to happen. Something terrible was already happening.

"Here, let me help you," Jimmy said, pulling my hair away from my face, but I shook my head violently.

"LEAVE!" I said before another wave hit me. Beads of sweat formed on my forehead. I felt as though I was trapped on a train about to derail.

I took a deep breath. I cleaned myself up. "Mommy," I said, clenching my fists, "please be all right. You're going to come back home. You can't *not* come back home."

Outside, I could hear Veronica and Halle bickering again. *Be here*, I told myself. However bad *here* was, it was better than thinking about my mother. All I wanted to do was glue myself to the TV. All I wanted to do was call my father. *Why hadn't he called me?* But I couldn't. *She's coming home*, I told myself again. And I gathered up all my resolve until I believed it.

My head was pounding as I returned to the living room, where an epic fight between Nick, Halle, Veronica, and Hunter was unfolding. I sank down into the couch, and Jimmy took a seat next to me, touching my hair. I pushed his hand away.

"We drove all the way out here to see you!" Nick yelled.

"And NO ONE invited you. NO ONE asked you to do that! This was supposed to be a girls' weekend, Nick. And now you bring these two beer-swilling Neanderthals to the house . . ."

"Hey, you guys left a huge mess on the back patio, okay? There's, like . . . rotting cake out there!" Nick yelled.

"And it's OUR rotting cake! It's not our job to clean up after you! Why are you such a little kid, following us around?"

"Hey, we're only here to support Nick, okay?" Hunter said.

"Support Nick in what?" Veronica yelled back, and Hunter's face went pale. He had said something he knew he shouldn't have.

"Support Nick in what?" Halle asked.

They were all quiet for a moment before Nick responded. "I wanted to make sure you were actually out here with the girls, okay? And not with some guy."

We were all quiet. "Why would I be here with some guy?" Halle said, but I could see the corners of her mouth twitching nervously.

Jimmy reached for my waist at that moment. "Feeling better, babe?"

I pushed him away. His eyes were barely open, and I could see he was drunk. He pulled at me more aggressively this time.

"Hey, Tara," he said. I turned to face him, and just as I did, he tried to kiss me.

"Stop it, Jimmy!"

"What, I'm just trying to, like, make you feel better."

"Leave me alone!"

"Why are you being such a tease?"

"Stop it!"

"You're such a bitch!" he yelled. I gasped. Everyone turned to look at us.

"Leave her alone, Jimmy," Nick said.

"He's not the one you need to say that to," Veronica said under her breath, and Nick shot her a look.

Veronica glared at him. "Why don't you just come out with everything, Nick? You and everyone else. Everyone come clean, because this is bullshit," she said.

My heart started to race.

"Okay. Fine," she continued. "You're not going to be honest? Nick, Halle doesn't love you. She's pretty sick of you, actually."

"Really? Maybe Halle should tell me that herself. And while we're at it, why don't you tell everyone the truth about yourself, Veronica? Especially since you have personal stakes in my relationship with Halle."

Veronica was quiet.

"Really, you should do it, especially for Hunter's sake. Tell him why you'd never be interested in him," Nick pressed.

Veronica shook her head at him. "Why are you doing this?" Her voice was faint.

"Shut up, Nick. Everyone already knows, okay?" Halle said. "Everyone knows that Veronica's in love with me." We all turned to look at Veronica, and her face was flushed, her mouth agape.

"What? Is that true, Veronica? You like girls?" Hunter looked at her, but Veronica merely crossed her arms over her chest and shook her head, her eyes flashing rage. But when I saw how she looked away, how her cheeks flushed in embarrassment, I could tell that she hadn't wanted any of us to know. I wondered just then why she had chosen never to tell me, despite all the time we had spent together—all those dinners and study sessions at her house. Then I remembered my own secrets.

Halle turned to Nick. "Veronica's right, Nick. There's someone else."

"I knew it." He shook his head. "Who is it?" he demanded, and everyone looked at Halle. She didn't say anything, and I was surprised when I heard my own voice in response to his question.

"She's seeing Amit," I finally said. It came out almost too easily. As though all this time, I had been struggling to keep a flotation device under water with my own body weight. They all turned to look at me.

"Who the hell is Amit?" Nick asked.

"The guy from the restaurant," I said. I didn't even care anymore.

"You knew?" Halle looked at me. I nodded at her. "You saw us . . ."

"Wait, you knew and you didn't tell us?" Veronica turned to me.

"Why didn't you say anything to me?" Halle asked.

"I knew it. I knew you were a cheating liar," Nick said to Halle.

"Oh, don't even!" Alexa screamed at him. "We all know what you did, Nick!" She yelled. I looked down at my toes, realizing it was my turn.

"Tell everyone!" Alexa yelled.

"Fine. Tara and I . . . we . . . I . . . I slept with Tara."

"You did *what*?" Jimmy, Alexa, and Veronica cried out in unison.

"Seriously, dude! You knew I liked her," Jimmy said.

"But I don't like you, Jimmy," I said to him, and I didn't even feel a pang of regret as I said this.

"But you're interested in Nick?" Jimmy asked.

Nick interrupted, turning to Halle. "It happened on Christmas. When we were broken up. Ask her," he said to her.

"Is it true?" Halle asked.

I looked at Halle. But even before I could respond, Veronica stepped in.

"It is," Veronica said, turning to Halle. "Alexa and I . . . we knew . . . or part of it, at least."

"The two of you knew? And you guys kept it from me? So all of you—Nick, Tara, and the two of you—all kept this . . . secret . . . and you never said a word to me?" We were all quiet. "And you!" Halle pointed to Alexa. "Here I am *protecting* you! Signing up to be on committees so you don't get caught!"

"Wait . . . get caught for what?" Veronica asked.

Alexa pulled her knees into her chest. She didn't look at any of us. "I'm the one who pulled the alarm. Who kept pulling the alarm. I'm the one who graffitied the science wing. I'm the reason for that stupid Safety First committee," she said.

Halle sank into the armchair by the fireplace. She looked out the window at the ocean.

"Well, I guess it's all out now," she said. And then she buried her face in her hands and began to cry.

FORTY-ONE

THERE are endless variations on that particular second-grade math puzzle. In one of them it's a fox, a chicken, and a bag of corn that a man has to get across a river. In another version, it's a wolf, a goat, and cabbage. There might even be a version with a lion. The point is, the man can only take himself and one other item with him. The problem is he can't leave the fox and the chicken together, because the fox will eat the chicken. And he can't leave the chicken and the corn together, because the chicken will eat the corn, so it's a fairly lousy situation.

I still remember working on that puzzle, wondering how resolving it might ever serve me in real life. Who would have thought that a decade later, I'd find myself in Cape Cod with two cars and seven people who all hated each other?

Hunter was pissed off at Veronica for supposedly leading

him on. Jimmy hated me for supposedly leading him on. Halle hated all of us for keeping secrets from her. She hated Alexa for keeping things from her while Halle was trying to protect her from getting caught. We were all perplexed that Alexa was some secret vandal, lurking around school pulling fire alarms. Veronica hated Halle for outing her. Veronica also hated Nick for putting her in the position of being outed in the first place. I think Veronica might have also hated me for not telling her what I knew about Halle and Amit and for not telling her I had slept with Nick. I was definitely pissed off at Alexa for telling Halle about what had happened between us. Maybe Nick was too. Nick was pissed off at Halle, obviously, for cheating on him. But the weird, or maybe not so weird, thing was—I don't think Halle was mad at Nick for what happened between him and me. It was almost as though she knew. Or she didn't care. The secret upset her more than the fact that I slept with her boyfriend. And I was in a state of delirium, as though I was walking around underwater. I didn't care what they decided. I was frantically trying to call my father, who wouldn't pick up his phone.

Finally, I looked up from the end of the driveway, watching them standing on the gravel path by the door as they continued to bicker. Veronica was refusing to drive with Halle, and Halle was refusing to drive with Veronica. Nick and Veronica were at odds too, yelling at each other.

At the last minute, Halle shrugged her shoulders. "I'll stay here."

"Then I'll stay with you," Alexa told her.

"I kind of want to be alone," Halle said.

"Well, we can't fit all six of us in Nick's Jeep."

"Yes you can. Throw Jimmy in the back. Or take Amtrak. I don't care. I'm staying up here. By myself. You guys figure it out," she said. She looked at me, and I could tell that she knew I was thinking about my mother. She gave me a sympathetic look for a moment before she turned and walked inside.

In the end, Nick, Alexa, Veronica, Jimmy, Hunter, and I piled into Nick's Jeep, on what was supposed to be the third day of our vacation.

It hadn't taken long for everything to get tangled. It was like that peasant blouse from the '90s my mother had lent to me. It was white with a red ribbon stitched around the waist. It had been perfectly preserved in her closet for years until, one day after borrowing it, I accidentally threw it into the wash and it came out pink, strangled by the ribbon, which had disintegrated in some parts, wrenched itself into a ball in others.

"Turn on the radio," I said to Nick. And he did. I frantically scanned through stations. Every one was playing music. I checked my phone again, but there was nothing new about the raid. No clue as to whether or not my mother was okay.

For a while, no one said anything. Finally, Nick broke the silence.

"Why, Alexa?" Nick asked her.

"You know why." She shrugged. "I hate Brierly. I hate high school. I vomit every morning out of nervousness. I'm not a stellar student like all of you guys. People talk about me behind my back, say I have an eating disorder. I just want to be left alone."

I turned to her. "I . . . get it. Not the pulling the alarms part. But the rest of it . . . I get it."

She turned to Veronica then. "And you? Why didn't you tell us?"

"Because it's nobody's business. Nick knew, obviously," she said, nodding her head at him. "He's always known. I . . ." She took a deep breath before she continued, "I tried to kiss Halle, last summer. We were at a club in New York. Sarah was with us. She saw it. And she kept on making these homophobic comments afterward. I think that's why Halle wanted her out. Halle's . . . you know, a major pain in the ass sometimes. But she is my best friend. Whatever. You can't help who you love . . . and sometimes hate, in my case." Veronica shrugged. She turned to Hunter then. "Sorry, Hunter."

"You can't help who you love," Hunter echoed, shrugging.

"I'm pretty sure she gave Sarah the boot to protect you," Nick said. "Sarah has a big mouth."

"Did you ever talk to Halle afterward? About the kiss?" Alexa asked.

"No, of course not. I knew she didn't reciprocate my feelings, so what's the point? And . . . I don't know, I guess I didn't trust her enough to have a real conversation about it."

"Why didn't you trust her?" Jimmy called out from the backseat. But I already knew why. Because Halle was secretive. She was mysterious. She was hiding something, and none of us knew exactly what it was. So we suspected things, we made up stories about her. We made her a villain, a manipulator, a bitch. And she *was* manipulative, she was strategic, she was hiding a secret, but it wasn't that simple. She was hiding the fact that she felt unloved.

I thought of something then. "That thing that you said to me about . . . you know, how she sees me as different . . . she never said that herself, did she?"

"No," Veronica admitted quietly. "I just felt that . . . she's so heteronormative, and so . . . white, and so . . . 'came on the *Mayflower*, I'm a Pilgrim' . . . that she would, you know . . ."

I felt sick to my stomach again. We were passing the industrial skyline of Providence. It looked ugly and gray this time.

I turned to Nick. "Why did you get back together with her? Why didn't you call me and tell me?"

He shrugged. "I guess . . . because I didn't want to tell you. I mean, I knew I would have to, but I still liked you. And because I felt . . . bad."

"About sleeping with me, or about leaving town with Halle right after you slept with me?"

He shook his head. "Do we have to talk about this now?"

"Yes."

He was quiet for a moment. "I love her. I always have. Even despite all the shitty things she's done . . . like cheating on me. But I also really like you. Not just *like* . . . I feel like . . . in an alternate universe, you and I . . . we're probably together, you know?"

"Yeah. I know," I said, a sinking feeling in my stomach.

"No you don't. I wonder about us. All the time, actually. I think about you. But I also feel like Halle and me . . . this is going to make me sound like the biggest asshole, but I'm happiest when I'm with the both of you. Does that make sense?"

"It makes you an asshole misogynist," Veronica announced from the backseat.

"Lucky Tara. She gets to be Halle's sister-wife," Alexa said.

He shook his head. "But it's not like that." He turned to me. "You know it's not like that. I don't know how to express it to you, how to tell you this without sounding like a jerk. I can't stop loving her, and I can't stop wondering about us. Just the way she wonders about that other guy, I guess. Which is why I can't hate her. Even if I should."

The moon revolved around the Earth, and the Earth revolved around the sun. It was the natural order of things. But what did we actually know about the natural order of things? What did any of us know about anything? There was an Earth-like planet in the sky that contained an alternate version of each and every one of us. My mother was stuck in a compound in California that was being raided by the FBI. I was sick to my stomach wondering whether she was even alive. Till a few months ago, that wasn't normal.

"Tara? Why didn't you tell me about Halle?"

I turned to Veronica, grateful for the change of subject, because I didn't feel like thinking about Nick loving Halle for the rest of eternity, no matter what she did. I didn't want to think about my mother in a compound that was being tear-gassed either.

"Because . . . I don't know why I didn't tell you." It felt like it was *my* dirty little secret that I had kept from everyone.

"You should have told me," Nick said.

"Why would I have? You were a jerk to me," I said.

"But *I* wasn't! I was your friend!" Veronica exclaimed.

"Yeah, me too," Alexa said.

"You still are my friends. And you guys kept things from me too."

"Was I supposed to tell you that I'm some arsonist vandal who gets a thrill out of pulling the fire alarm every week?"

"Technically, you're not an arsonist," Veronica told her.

"Don't think I haven't considered actually setting Brierly on fire," Alexa said.

"*I've* considered it," Veronica responded. "Seriously . . . do you know what it's like to be a dyke in Greenwich, Connecticut?"

I had to smile a little. "Do you know what it's like to be poor and Indian in Greenwich, Connecticut? And I can't hide it either, okay? It's, like . . . right here on my face," I said to her, scanning my hand over my face until Veronica smiled back at me. It was a moment of levity, and I needed it.

"Tara, you underestimate yourself," Jimmy said. "And you underestimate me."

"Probably."

"And you overestimate Nick," Veronica said.

"Thanks, V," Nick replied.

"Everyone overestimates you, O Golden One," Alexa said.

"I thought Halle was the Golden One," Veronica responded. "I wonder what she's doing right now."

"This is the shittiest road trip on Earth. We're all a bunch of unloved liars and criminals," Hunter said.

"Technically, Alexa's the only criminal," Veronica responded.

"Yeah, and Hunter and I never lied about anything," Jimmy noted.

"And love is a maldistributed commodity," Alexa said, and we all turned to look at her. "No, seriously. It's a poorly organized, uneconomical thing . . . love."

"Do you think that's why we're friends?" Veronica asked me now. "Because neither of us belongs here?"

"What about me?" Alexa turned to her.

"You too." Veronica nodded.

"Who knows?" I asked.

We were quiet for a while till Veronica broke the silence. "You know, for a moment, just for that day, when we were all up at the house together . . . I felt like . . . *this is kind of amazing. We're not angsty or complaining or secretly annoyed with one another. We actually like being together.* We were like those matrilineal societies they taught us about in the ninth grade. And then these fuckers came up and ruined it all."

"It was not my intention to ruin . . ."

"Shut up, Nick. Your defensiveness is not welcome right now."

"I know what you mean." I turned to her. "It was nice. For a day."

Veronica shook her head. "Well, that's all over now."

"Yeah, but not because a bunch of guys showed up and destroyed your utopia. It's because you're all dishonest, deceiving, terrible people."

"Speak for yourself, Nick," Alexa said.

"I know I am," he said. "I'm a terrible person, you don't have to remind me," he said. And then he punctuated the conversation by switching the radio station. He turned it up when he heard it was Oliver Spiegel on the air.

"Now let's talk about some of the different theories that suggest that we live in a multiverse. Tessa Novak, you've likened the universe to a breadloaf. Explain this to our audience."

"Certainly, Oliver. Now, while Terra Nova exists in this very dimension, physicists have proposed that there might be many more dimensions to our world than we know of."

"And what would this mean for us?"

"Well, I like to think of it like this: What if our universe is one of many floating in a higher-dimensional space, much like a slice of bread within a grander cosmic loaf?"

"That's an interesting idea. Go on."

"Maybe these universes might line up like slices of bread in a loaf, but let's just say they aren't always parallel. If that's the case, they might slam into each other, and every time they do, it causes a Big Bang, a series of Big Bangs that reset the universes over and over again."

"Fascinating. And what about you, Adam Bryson? You also believe in the possibility of the multiverse, but you subscribe to a slightly different theory than Ms. Novak."

"Well, scientists don't know for sure the shape of space-time. Maybe it's a loaf, but some of us believe that it's flat and that it stretches out infinitely. So if space-time goes on forever, then somewhere down the road, it has to start repeating."

"Why is that?"

"Because there are a finite number of ways particles can be arranged in space and time. In this model, eventually, after looking far enough, you would encounter another version of you. And then another, and soon . . . infinite versions of you. Some that are exactly like you—down to the number of strands of hair on your head—while others will be, say, wearing a different shirt today. Others will have made drastically different choices in life. Perhaps they live in a different city. Or they're married to someone else, or have an entirely different career."

"And we have some more interesting developments in the field of science today, related to Terra Nova. Adam, would you like to tell us more?"

"In late fall of this year, NASA, in conjunction with the Korean Space Research Institute, the Soviet Space Program, the China National Space Administration, the Indian Space Research Organization, the UK Space Agency, and the European Space Agency, will launch the fastest space probe ever built. *Copernicus 1* will travel to Terra Nova in just eighty-five years. In the past, travel to the nearest star would have taken us some eighty-one thousand years, but given the commitment and resources of numerous world governments, in less than a century, our space probe will land on Terra Nova. Of course, most of us won't be alive in eighty-five years to witness this feat, but our next of kin will actually be able to see our sister planet," said Adam Bryson.

"God, what a bummer," Alexa said. "Eighty-five years! It means . . . we'll never meet them."

"But your children might. And their children," Hunter said.

"I know, but . . . what about us? We won't have any answers in our own lifetime," I told him.

"Maybe there are some things we're not ready for yet. Things we're not yet meant to know," Nick said.

"I don't know," Alexa responded. "It feels like a letdown. We'll never meet our Other selves. We'll never know what all of this means. It's just . . . disappointing."

"I wonder if we're all still fighting on Terra Nova right now," Nick muttered.

"Maybe we don't even know each other on Terra Nova," Veronica said.

"Maybe we do. Maybe we actually get along on Terra Nova," Nick responded.

I turned to look at him. We were still an hour and a half from home. It tortured me that he wasn't my boyfriend. It had tortured me for what felt like eons. And yet, despite my disappointment, despite my exhaustion, despite all of it, I sank into my seat with the knowledge that maybe somewhere in a parallel reality, we were together.

It was late afternoon by the time Nick dropped me off. I stood in my driveway, looking up into that clear spring sky.

"Please," I asked. "I just want everything to be okay. I just want my mother to be safe. I just want her to come home," I said.

I continued to stand there, as though I was waiting for an answer. Just as I was about to turn and go into my house, my phone rang. I pulled it out of my pocket, and I looked at it incredulously. It was a California number, one I didn't recognize. I hesitated.

"Please be good news," I said, but I couldn't hear any conviction in my voice. It rang again, and I took a deep breath, panicking.

Finally, after the third ring, I picked up.

I could hear someone sobbing. I knew it was my mother.

"Mom?! Mom! Are you okay? Where are you?"

For a moment she didn't respond. She continued to sob, her voice choking out the words, "I . . . I . . ." And then she broke down.

"Mom, please, where are you?"

"I got out, Tara," she finally said. "They just got us out. All of us. We're okay. We're safe. I'm going to fly home tomorrow. I'm so sorry. I'm so sorry for putting both of you through this!" She was crying and I was too, so hard that I couldn't speak. I don't remember what else she said, but after we got off, I fell to my knees in my driveway and buried my face in my hands, my whole body shaking violently.

"Thank you," I said, looking up at the sky. It was all I could say, again and again.

And then I thought about Halle. She had been right. My mother was coming home.

FORTY-TWO

SHE was gaunt, skinnier than I remembered her, when she walked though the door. I ran to her, and we held each other for a long time.

"I'll never leave you again, I promise," she said. In the days that followed, she told us everything. How it had started out fine. They all lived together in the compound, sharing responsibilities. There were orange and avocado and lemon and pomegranate trees and an overflowing garden. "We'd harvest our own food and cook it. There were classes—painting classes and yoga and meditation. It felt like utopia. Then it all changed."

As we all knew by now, they were asked to cut off communication with their families. Their personal possessions were confiscated. They were subjected to hours of interrogation in small rooms. "Kind of like a detainment. We had to get permission to go to the bathroom. Soon we couldn't even go out on the grounds. They questioned us for hours, telling us they were 'testing' our faith. None of us had contact with the outside world. They took our phones, our wallets, our credit cards . . . and then when Robert told us about the thing that happened in Orlando . . ." My mother shook her head. "All I could think was . . . I have to get back to you. I have to get back home alive."

My father was sitting next to her on the couch, holding her hand. She told us about how tear gas feels in your eyes. "It's the worst burning sensation in the world. And the gunshots! That was terrifying, the sound of gunshots. They had us locked in the cafeteria, and they had weapons—explosives, guns . . . I had no idea!"

My father jumped in. "The police had all the family members in one place. So many people traveled out to California in order to bring their loved ones home. We were watching the whole thing on a screen in some school auditorium, all of us, together. It was . . . terrifying. Jennifer . . ." his voice wavered, and she turned to him, touched his face in a way that I hadn't seen her do in years. "I don't know what I would have done . . . what we would have done if you . . ."

"I'm back, Sudeep. I'm back for good now," she said, and she reached for his hand again and squeezed it.

She apologized to me over and over for weeks after she came home. She seemed more fragile, her emotions closer to the surface. She had nightmares. Some mornings, I woke up and she was sitting on the edge of my bed, watching me.

"You were right," she said to me one day.

"About what?"

"About everything. About the whole Santa Monica thing. You were right. You were always wiser than I am."

I sat up. "But you missed your parents. You wanted to speak to them. You wanted to see them again. I get that. I get that now," I said, and her eyes filled up with tears.

"Can you ever forgive me, Tara?"

"Of course, Mom. I can't stay mad at you," I told her.

And it was true.

FORTY-THREE

THERE are these moments when you feel like you can finally exhale. That the world is a good and decent place again. I spent the next week with my mother, barely leaving her side for a minute. We couldn't stop talking. There were days when we talked the entire day, forgetting to eat, and by the time night came, I collapsed into bed out of exhaustion. A happy exhaustion, for once.

My father watched us, a perpetual smile on his face. He left snacks for us on the coffee table. He brought home pizza and kissed my mother and told her how much he loved her again and again. It reminded me of our days in New York, when we were a compact and unshakable unit. It felt good to be that way again.

The entire week, I didn't think about Nick. I didn't think about Halle or Alexa or Veronica. When the phone rang, I chose not to answer it. For the rest of spring break, I hibernated by my mother's side, and I couldn't have been happier.

On Monday, I didn't want to go back to school, but my father insisted. "Junior year, Tara. You know it's . . ."

"I know, I know," I told him, and I hugged my mother goodbye before I left.

Veronica accosted me just as I entered the glass corridor, panic on her face. She grabbed my arm. "We have to go over to the Lightfoots' right now," she said.

"What? Why? Class is starting in ten . . ."

"No, Tara, you don't understand . . ." Her eyes were tearing up. I had never seen Veronica this emotional.

"What? What's going on?"

"They want to keep it out of the press, but there's an investigation . . . She never came back. Halle never came back from the Cape."

I watched Veronica, trying to make sense of the words coming out of her mouth. "What do you mean, she never came back?" I asked.

"I mean just that. She never came back home. I called her cell a few times, but I just assumed she was mad at me when she didn't respond. So I called her house and talked to her housekeeper, and she hadn't heard anything either. My parents got involved. They called the cops, had them go over and check the house to make sure she was okay. And so they went to check out the house last night, and she wasn't there. She's still not there this morning. All her stuff is still in the house . . .

her shoes, her clothes, her contact lens case. Even her wallet and her keys . . . Why would she leave home without her wallet and her keys?" Veronica asked.

"Where could she be?"

Veronica shook her head. "I don't know," she cried. "No one knows. They've searched the area. The car's still parked in the driveway. Neighbors say that they saw an unfamiliar blond girl walking down to the beach the evening that we left, but that's it . . . that's all they know."

I could feel the blood draining from my face. "What do her parents say?"

"They flew back from London late last night. Obviously, they're distraught. And furious with us for leaving her up there alone. I talked to them early this morning. They called Nick too. The police are there now. They want to talk to us."

I drove Veronica's car to the Lightfoots' that day because she was sobbing so hard she couldn't drive. Alexa sat quietly in the backseat, her lips pressed into a line, her hands nervously searching her phone.

"I don't understand. How far could she have gotten without her car?"

No one responded to Alexa's question. We were silent the rest of the way there. The weather was odd for early spring. It was cloudy, but also unusually hot. The heat of the steering wheel seared my palms. Flowers wilted. The long road to Conyers Farm shimmered with dizziness. The sky looked as though it might rain. A dank humidity had seeped into every small space it could find—between bra straps and skin, between the pages of books, where the hairline meets the back of your neck.

The boys were already clustered by the pool at the back of the house—that spot where Hunter and Jimmy had played beer pong, where Halle had set up a turntable.

Halle's father, Walter, was standing with them. I had never seen him before. He was a large man, over six feet. His face was a perpetual red, and he dabbed at his forehead with a handkerchief.

I thought about my first time on the Lightfoots' estate, the way we had laid in the grass, Halle with a sarong around her waist, playing hostess. The way Veronica and I had laughed in that bathroom with a million first editions.

Walter silently guided us inside to where Bitsy sat on a sofa, talking to two police officers. She looked at us without acknowledging us, turning back to the officers.

"They're here now. You should speak to them. Do you suggest Walter and I go up there? Wait for her?"

"I think it might be best for you to stay here for now, ma'am, but we'll let you know if things change."

"Have you heard anything else? Is there any new news?" Alexa asked the room.

"They can't find her anywhere," Bitsy responded. "They can't find my Halle anywhere," she said. "I don't understand. She told me you were going to have a fun week on the Cape. Why was she there alone? What did you say to her? How could you have left her up there?" There was anger in her eyes, but it dissipated quickly. "I just want to know where she is!" Bitsy cried, and she began to sob. I thought about my mother, all those days I didn't hear from her, all those minutes and hours, waiting to learn how she was, whether she was even still alive. I looked away from Bitsy, swallowing the knot in my throat.

Veronica glanced at Nick and then at me. "It's what I told you on the phone, Mrs. Lightfoot." Veronica's voice was a whisper. "We did go up there for a fun week. To celebrate Tara's birthday . . . and we got into a fight. It was a bad one, and we . . ."

I watched Veronica try to explain to Bitsy and Walter and the police what had happened, but none of it made sense to me. That's to say: It didn't make sense to me that just a week ago, we were all together, up in a house in Cape Cod, and now we were here, and Halle was somehow gone.

FORTY-FOUR

THERE were rumors, most of them resembling conspiracy theories. That she took out her trust fund and that she's traveling the world. That the Lightfoots secretly know about it. But if you saw the state the Lightfoots were in that day we went over, you'd know that one isn't true. That she ran off to join one of those cults. But I know how she felt about those organizations. That she was the sole person on our planet who managed to commune with Terra Nova. That she was somehow beamed up there. And then there are the more sinister ones. That she was kidnapped. That she was murdered. That she drowned. Or that she drowned herself. That one makes me shudder. I remember how she hated pools. She hated water. I don't want to believe it. *It can't be*, I tell myself. *It can't be.*

~

April 4—the Day of Prayer—came, and there was still no word of Halle.

"We need to somehow subvert this, mark it, instead of ignoring it," my mother said. She took my father and me out to our front yard.

"I don't want to pray to commune with people on Terra Nova," she said. "I want to pray for people on this planet." And so we held hands and watched the sun set. We did it our way. I thought about Halle. I prayed that she was still somewhere on this planet, that she was safe. I prayed that she was happy. I prayed that she felt loved. I prayed for her to come back.

In the end, the Day of Prayer was peaceful. And apparently, many people did still gather at various energy vortices to look up at the sky, sending out prayer and goodwill. I wondered if anyone else bothered to look here, at us, at our little planet, our pale blue dot.

We don't really see things when they're right here in front of us.

Summer came and went, a long and sweltering one. Each day, I woke hoping for news. Good news. It never came. We checked in with one another, hoping that someone had heard something. There was a national campaign, her face on the news every day for a while. Whenever I saw Amit at the restaurant, he asked me about Halle—if I had heard from her, if I knew anything he didn't, and when I told him no, he nodded wistfully and walked away.

~

School started. We were seniors now. They held an assembly on the first day. People spoke of how talented Halle was, how exceptional, how brilliant, what a bright future she would have had ahead of her. She had been missing for close to six months. They talked about her as though they were sure she was dead. But to me she was still alive, she was still the Halle we knew—vibrant and pretty and brilliant and cool.

As people spoke at the podium, I thought about it again, the way I had nearly every day since she disappeared, what I could have said, what I could have done, those tiny little details that, we now know, can change the outcome of the whole. I could have stayed home instead of going to the Cape, I could have asked her, begged her to come home with us, and maybe none of it would have happened. I could have said no when I was invited to that party at her house, spent my junior year hiding in the library, and I wouldn't have played a role in our group dynamic. Maybe I could have trusted her more, treated her like a real friend. I could have chosen to stay home on Christmas. I could have said no to Nick. Maybe I could have stopped that fight.

"You can't blame yourself for this," my mother kept telling me, but I couldn't help it.

I thought about Halle's greatest fear—the one that superseded even her fear of water—that people didn't really love her, didn't truly want to be around her. That was the thing that I knew she felt on the last day we left her at the Cape, and I thought about how I was partially responsible for that.

She wasn't perfect. She could be patronizing, maybe she

was strategic, maybe she did maneuver people. She definitely kept secrets. But she wasn't a bad person. She thought of us as family, perhaps the only family she really had.

I just wanted her to come back. We all did.

I was walking home from school later that week when Nick pulled up at the intersection of Hillside and the Post Road. In the aftermath of Halle's disappearance, Nick had been inconsolable. He couldn't stop crying, not just at the police department and at the various meetings at the Lightfoots' but for days and weeks afterward. I would see him in class, looking at her empty seat, his eyes permanently rimmed with red.

I watched him now as he pulled up beside me and rolled down his window, his face blank.

"Hey, I want to talk to you," he said. He had lost that perpetual smile, that cheer I assumed would never go away. Now his eyes had constant dark circles under them; his lips were permanently pressed into a straight line.

I hesitated before I got into the car with him. I glanced at him, but he continued to look straight ahead at the windshield. I expected him to drive us somewhere, but he stayed parked on the side of the road and pointed to that spot, that spot in the road where we had sat waiting for the ASPCA.

"That dog . . . Sarah didn't hit him."

"What? I don't know what you're . . ."

"Listen to me, Tara . . ." He banged his fist in frustration on his steering wheel. "I hit that dog. I didn't want her to know, so I just let everyone think it was Sarah. But it was me. *I* hit

329

that dog. And then I didn't tell anyone, not her, not you, not anyone."

He burst out crying, leaning on his steering wheel. I sat next to him, watching him for some time before I reached over and stroked his hair.

"I knew," I said, unearthing another buried truth, one I had kept even from myself. I sat with him for a little while before I opened the door to his car and walked out. I knew I wouldn't speak to Nick again for a long time.

Love has its own strange velocity. The longer she was gone, the more he loved her. My love for him stayed the same, but Halle was an even stronger force in our lives now than when she was here with us. The difference was, I had come to accept it. I understood by now how fallible we are, the mistakes we make, the judgments we pass. I had watched her for so many years with a mixture of awe and envy, and I had formed a perception of her as a perfect ice queen. But she wasn't the cold one.

I was.

It had taken so long and so much to chip away at my own frozen heart. I was the one who held tight to my perception of Halle; I was the one who kept everything close to my own chest. And yet, she had always tried. She had become my friend, and just when our friendship became real, at least to me, *I* screwed things up. Not her.

Halle had asked me once what I was most afraid of, and I didn't want to tell her, but I was just as afraid of belonging as I was of not belonging. I hid behind books, didn't talk much, never had. I told myself I was a pariah; I had wished that I was someone else for so long. But even though I was lonely, I have to admit, most of the time, I preferred it that way. I was afraid of the messiness that closeness brings, afraid of friendships that turn to something else, afraid of my own petty jealousies and the monstrous things that can come of them. Afraid of letting people in. It was easy for me to distance myself from Meg after she had left. And it was just as easy keeping all my secrets to myself, never completely letting in Halle or Alexa or Veronica or even Nick either.

The irony was that I had spent all those months feeling like I couldn't reveal my entire self to these people because they would judge me for my difference, for my imperfections, and yet they were all flawed, just like me. It was easier believing that there was someone else out there, a mirror version of me on another planet who would understand me completely, but the friendship that Alexa and Veronica and Halle had offered me was real. I had just been too scared to take it.

Once senior year started, I never saw Bitsy Lightfoot around town. Rumor was that over the summer, the Lightfoots had packed up the estate and sold it, moved to a smaller house or permanently to one of their other homes abroad.

I remembered that thing Halle had said to me about her parents, *I don't know if they even . . . wanted kids.* Was it possible that now they didn't have any?

Then one day in October, after school had ended, I saw

Bitsy walking around the rim of Tod's Point. She was still wearing black, even all these months later. She had on the same sunglasses, the ones she always wore, the large ones that covered half her face. She was walking fast, trying to make it to the tip of Tod's Point, the clearing beyond the sailboat dock where there's a perfect view of the sunset.

She made it just in time. The entire sky was a luminescent orange that evening, one of those hazy and brilliant sunsets you sometimes get in New England.

I don't know what I was thinking, but I followed her in my father's Honda, parking it on a small bluff overlooking the Long Island Sound. I got out and stood about ten feet away from her. We were the only two people there.

She turned to look at me right away. She was out of breath, and she put her hand to her hips in a way that I remember Halle sometimes used to do.

"My daughter loved sunsets on the Sound," she said.

I smiled at her, nodded.

"I wish she had been able to see more of them," she added.

I often wondered if the Lightfoots looked up into the heavens with a hope that there was another Halle somewhere out there. And what if there wasn't? Would their grief be redoubled?

Symmetry is something that's always fascinated me, but lately, I find that it haunts me, keeps me up late at night. Is Halle still alive? And if she isn't, did we kill her? And if we were responsible for Halle's death, or if I was partially the reason she died, is it possible that we killed her twice? Once here on Earth, leaving her in that house on Cape Cod, and again on Terra Nova, in some alternate sleepy town? Or is it possible that she's still alive up there, some version of her living the life she was always meant to live? Is it possible she's still alive somewhere here, that maybe one day she'll come back?

Just as the sun dipped under the ocean, Bitsy turned to me again. "I wish I had watched more sunsets with her," she said.

Then Bitsy turned and walked away. I never saw her again.

Crisis comes in many forms, and for us, for my entire generation, I think Terra Nova was the beginning of a crisis that might have happened anyway. Maybe we wouldn't have felt it as intensely, and maybe we wouldn't have questioned things quite so deeply, but part of growing up is questioning things, even ourselves. Especially ourselves.

The launch happened in late October, exactly a year after my mother left home. It was hard to believe how much had happened in just a year. Thousands of people flew down to Orlando to see *Copernicus 1* soar into space. You could see them in the crowds, crying, praying, laughing.

"Orlando . . ." My father shook his head at the TV. "They've all forgotten what happened there last year," he said.

And it was true. By now, people had forgotten that only a year back, Orlando was synonymous with mass suicide; they had forgotten Michiko Natori, the woman, the symbol. Most people at school had forgotten about Halle. After a while, everyone wanted to forget those patches of ugliness, that fear.

~

Copernicus 1 will land on Terra Nova in eighty-five years. As of now, it's still on its way. If this mission is successful, we'll turn our energies toward a second mission: transporting people to Terra Nova, communicating with any intelligent life on the planet directly, communicating with our Other selves. By now, we're fairly certain that Terra Nova is our mirror planet, albeit a distorted mirror. Their radio broadcasts continue to come in, but none of us has ever met any of them.

One day, we will. Our children and their children will perhaps meet their counterparts, a strange concept to wrap our minds around, but one day, across great distances, we will meet.

I still think about it all the time—all the other possibilities that didn't occur, all the parallel and unlived lives I'll never know about. Occasionally, I go down to Tod's Point and lie in the grass at Mr. Tod's house. The house that was torn down, the art colony, the plot of land where I was with Nick that one cold Christmas. I look out into the sky and wonder about that Other Tara. About the countless Other Taras, the countless Other Nicks and Halles and Veronicas and Alexas and Megs. I think about the millions of people on this world and on those other worlds whom I'll never meet. And then one day recently, I realized that maybe my only job here on Earth is to focus on those whom I *have* met, those whom I'll meet in the future.

Even though I still think about the Other Tara, it's not in the same way. She's not omnipotent to me anymore, and I don't think she has all the answers. I don't think she's the only person in the universe who will ever understand me. I suspect she has frailties and vulnerabilities of her own. I'm certain that she has fears, things that keep her up late at night too. Even if I were to meet her now, I don't know that I would burden her with my questions. I would say hello. I would ask her about her life, and I would tell her about mine. Perhaps that's where I'll start here too, the next time I make a friend.

ACKNOWLEDGMENTS

ONE of the major themes of this book is finding a place for oneself in the world, and in many ways, *Mirror in the Sky*'s journey from an idea to the book that it eventually became reflects that theme.

Through a serendipitous and almost magical movement of invisible hands, the manuscript for *Mirror in the Sky* landed on the desk of my amazing and brilliant editor, Jessica Almon. For this, I will always be eternally grateful for cosmic forces beyond my understanding. Without Jessica's encouragement, support, friendship, and inspiration, this book would never have become *this* book.

In my wildest dreams, I couldn't have wished for a better home for *Mirror in the Sky* than Razorbill, and I am grateful and indebted to the entire team there, particularly Ben Schrank, Anna Jarzab, and Lauren Donovan.

Thank you to my fabulous agent, the indomitable Jenny Bent, who believed in this book from the very beginning and understood it in ways that a first-time author can only dream of, and the entire team at the Bent Agency, particularly Victoria Lowes, who provided crucial support at various junctures throughout the book's publication.

While working on the manuscript for *Mirror in the Sky*, Katie Robbins, Daniel Berson, Adam Chanzit, Nell Rutledge-Leverenz, and Anna Carey joined me on an unforgettable writing retreat in Palm Springs filled with laughter, long elaborate dinners, and pie-in-the-face, and I will forever be indebted to them for their friendship and excellent notes, but especially for their love and their time in the writing trenches with me.

Here, I must also offer thanks to Matthew Biancaniello for teaching me how to make the cocktails that we drank on that writing retreat.

I am extraordinarily lucky to have found an extended family in my brilliant, kind, and endlessly supportive friends. In no particular order, thanks to Jolene Pinder for always being there and being the most gracious host whenever I visit her in NOLA, Dee Montealvo for some of the most memorable dinners and conversations of my life, Payal Aggarwal-Scott for her steadfast friendship and love, Nathalie Huot, who always encourages me to keep dreaming bigger, Dan Lopez, whose steep aesthetic standards have over the years become my own, and Sam and Jen Sparks for their unyielding kindness.

Thanks to Linda Sivertsen for her excellent notes, but especially for her constant words of wisdom and her belief in me.

For their endless enthusiasm and kindness, thanks also to Veronica Ho, Jenny Rosenbluth, Julie Fulton, Meredith Hight, Kirsten Markson, Jaime Reichner, Julia Ruchman, Susanna Fogel, Stephanie Watanabe, Shelley Marks, Lizzie Prestel, Rahool Pathak, Rebecca Fishman, Krupa Desai, Priya Nambiar, Melissa Brough, and Ernesto Lechner.

Thank you most of all to my parents, Shashi and Satish Khorana, for always encouraging my love of writing and for being the most supportive and loving parents in the world. This book, and for that matter, everything I've ever done in my life, would not be possible without you.

Thank you to the ladies from my Can It! class, who kept me sane and fed me homemade harissa and bread and cheese, among other things: Tabby Nanyonga, Trina Calderon, and Mary Baldwin.

For finding me a room of my own when I most needed it, thank you to Bridget Jurgens, whom I think of almost every day when I sit down to write.

Thanks to Nancy Cannon and Paulette Johnson—two unforgettable teachers who encouraged my love of books at an early age.

Rains Paden first introduced me to Cheryl Strayed's ghost ship column, which eventually became a seed for *Mirror in the Sky*, so thank you for that, Rains. Here, I should also thank Cheryl Strayed for writing the column that inspired this book.

I don't know him personally, but Neil deGrasse Tyson's *Cosmos* allowed me to contemplate a universe that's far more expansive and mysterious than any one of us could ever imagine, and for that I am grateful.

Thanks to Mark Thayer, James Garay, and Isaac Cabrera, who kept me afloat with coffee and great conversation during writing sessions at LAMILL.

Thanks to Percy, who made my life easier with the care she put into her work.

Lastly, this book is already dedicated to my grandparents, but that will never be enough. I've never felt their love and guidance more strongly than when I was working on the manuscript for this book, and wherever they are, I hope they know how grateful I am for every moment we spent together.